A WELCOME COLLISION

No avoiding it, Balfour thought, wishing the bumpy
coach might throw him and Mary together permanently,
in a manner far more intimate than the mere brush of
arms and legs. He was infatuated. No denying it. They
were meant to touch one another. He remembered her
hands in his hair at the optician's. Her hand against his
beneath the table. His hand to hers at Gran's. Her knee
banging his in the coach. He had begun to fabricate reasons why they must spend time together, hoping for another brush of his flesh against hers.

She was a wonder to watch, warming his heart as it had
never been warmed before. Life was something she took
part in to the fullest degree. He did not live life like
that. Might he be happier if he did?

As the coach lurched into motion he refrained from
apologizing for his knee's rocking against hers. And he
was exceptionally pleased to see she did not immediately
withdraw from all contact when the tip of his shoe collided with hers. . . .

On Sale November 15, 1999

A Fine Gentleman by Laura Matthews

Lady Caroline Carruthers was enjoying her visit to the Hartville home. But one thing made life at the estate complicated—Lady Hartville was intent on convincing her son that Caroline would be the perfect wife for him. Who could think of marrying such an obstinate, infuriating man as Richard? But an unexpected surprise arriving on the doorstep turns a far-fetched plan of wedding meddling into startling possibility....

0-451-19872-7/$4.99

The Irish Rogue by Emma Jensen

Ailís O'Neill is not the average Dublin debutante. She spends time teaching English to Gaelic peasants—and painting the local wildlife. But with her brother running for British Parliament on behalf of Ireland, Ailís is expected to socialize with the political set. Her disdain for the English partisans is evident, but no more so than for Lord Clane. And she knows nothing of Lord Clane's notorious past—or that his future includes plans to steal her heart....

0-451-19873-5/$4.99

My Lady Nightingale by Evelyn Richardson

Mademoiselle Isobel de Montargis had a passionate soul, a strong will, and a proud determination to become more than music tutor to the dashing Lord Hatherleigh's niece and nephew. Her dream was to become an *actrice de l'opera*. But how could a lady, respectful of her reputation and social standing, be able to ever fulfill such a daring dream? Leave it to Lord Hatherleigh....

0-451-19858-1/$4.99

To order call: 1-800-788-6262

The Holly and the Ivy

Elisabeth Fairchild

A SIGNET BOOK

SIGNET
Published by New American Library, a division of
Penguin Putnam Inc., 375 Hudson Street,
New York, New York 10014, U.S.A.
Penguin Books Ltd, 27 Wrights Lane,
London W8 5TZ, England
Penguin Books Australia Ltd, Ringwood,
Victoria, Australia
Penguin Books Canada Ltd, 10 Alcorn Avenue,
Toronto, Ontario, Canada M4V 3B2
Penguin Books (N.Z.) Ltd, 182–190 Wairau Road,
Auckland 10, New Zealand

Penguin Books Ltd, Registered Offices:
Harmondsworth, Middlesex, England

First published by Signet, an imprint of New American Library,
a division of Penguin Putnam Inc.

First Printing, October 1999
10 9 8 7 6 5 4 3 2 1

 REGISTERED TRADEMARK—MARCA REGISTRADA

Printed in the United States of America

BOOKS ARE AVAILABLE AT QUANTITY DISCOUNTS WHEN USED TO PROMOTE
PRODUCTS OR SERVICES. FOR INFORMATION PLEASE WRITE TO PREMIUM MAR-
KETING DIVISION, PENGUIN PUTNAM INC., 375 HUDSON STREET, NEW YORK, NEW
YORK 10014.

Chapter One

There was no getting away from it. Not on Regent Street. Not since the new shops had gone in. Well-dressed patrons brushed past, liveried footmen following, parcels stacked high. *Christmas.*

Charles Thornton Baxter, fifth Viscount Balfour, ice blue eyes narrowed against the rush of cold air, refused to bend, either to the season's approach, or to the brunt of the wind as he stepped from the doorway of his London home. It was a grand old Georgian building soon to be torn down to make way for more of Nash's interminably slow improvements along a street Baxter no longer cared for, garbed in the season he disliked above all others.

Baxter did not want to think about Christmas. He did not appreciate the peal of bells from St. Phillip's two doors down. Today was December sixth, St. Nicholas's feast day, only nineteen days until the last ball he would ever hold on Regent Street. Without Temple. Poor old Temple.

A gust of wind flung itself at Baxter from the north, chilly as his thoughts. A lesser man might have stepped back into the shelter of the doorway. Not Viscount Balfour, fair locks swept smoothly from his forehead, every hair pomaded into place, as windproof as his snow white neckcloth tied in the mathematical style, ends tucked neatly away.

His buff-colored coat hung equally unswayed. He had approved each line and seam and stitch, perfectly tailored to fit his straight-backed, perfectly postured form. Like all of his clothes, it bore the prestigious trademark of Mssrs. HJ and D. Nicoll, court tailors. No flapping capes for Baxter, who insisted upon setting his own fashion along lines to make him look tall, clean, neat, orderly, and unobtrusively high quality.

Baxter's only concession to the powers of Nature's blustery breath that morning might be witnessed in the spotless buff glove securely grasping the brim of his sleek black beaver top hat. His head tilted, too, that the wind might the more firmly press hat to head as his high alabaster cheekbones colored faintly pink.

Eyes narrowed to a squint, Baxter examined the blur of oncoming traffic, and addressed his companion without turning.

"You said the carriage was sighted?"

"Yes, my lord." Knob-kneed young Temple, crouched beside him like a half-emergent turtle in a flapping, triple-caped, unevenly dyed black overcoat.

"Downwind, if you please, Mr. Temple," Baxter instructed after the capes twice slapped his arm.

"My lord?" Temple shifted his position uncertainly.

Baxter leaned close to sniff as he sidled past, nose crinkling. "What the devil do you stink of, lad?"

Temple blushed almost as deep a shade as the mulberry muffler wrapped about his neck. "Dye, my lord, to make the coat proper mourning."

"I cannot think your father would have wanted you to reek," Baxter suggested dryly.

Temple's shoulders rounded. "I am told the odor will fade . . ." his voice squeaked uncertainly.

"Before Christmas?" Baxter grumbled.

The tips of Temple's ears flamed red.

"No slouching," Baxter insisted. "If you would reek to high heaven for good reason, do so with pride."

"Yes, my lord," Temple unfolded himself reluctantly, teeth chattering. "It p-p-promises to be a c-c-cold Christmas, think you not, my lord?"

"Is not every Christmas bitter?"

Charles Thornton Baxter's sarcasm was lost on Temple, who had yet to learn his ways, yet to learn exactly why the other servant's slyly referred to their master as Lord Thorn.

*   *   *

Mary Rivers tucked Gran more securely into the Merlin chair, clutched billowing cloak tighter against the wind, and smiled at the two gentlemen standing by the street. She was in the habit of smiling at everyone—and accustomed to most people smiling back.

Lord Balfour stood stiff-backed and proud in front of his enormous town house. He ignored her, frowning into the wind, too great a personage to recognize his neighbor with so much as a good morning, or how do you do. A coldly handsome man—she thought he looked like a young lion. A lion whose eyes passed over her absently, as if there were more interesting prey to hunt.

Beside him, huddled deep in a flapping black greatcoat, expression melancholy, his companion resembled a carrion crow ready to feed on the lion's leavings. These creatures inhabited a world unfamiliar to her. She considered it vaguely disquieting, just standing on the street with them. They were not at all the sort of neighbors she was accustomed to in Glastonbury.

But this was not Glastonbury, she reminded herself as a mud-spattered mail coach rattled by. The post boy, cherry-cheeked, blew a lone-voiced tarantella. Rows of limp black turkeys, feathers fluttering in the wind, dangled from the upper rail, Christmas dinner on the way. Mary wished she might be on her way, too—home for the holidays.

"Well, Mary, how do you like London?" Gran asked from her cocoon of blankets, rheumy blue eyes sparkling, the wind catching tendrils of wispy gray hair from beneath her cap and bonnet, batting them about like thistledown.

Mary forced a smile. Gran would ask just that question in a moment of overwhelming homesickness, a moment when she hesitated to reply lest her voice give way to the ache, the clingy longing in her chest. She was a vine transplanted, without support.

Mary twisted the brake handles wide, kicked the back wheel of the three-wheeled chair into alignment, grabbed up the handle placed inconveniently low on the back of the chair, and set off with a push, wheels clacking. She did not like London, certainly not Christmas in London. She wished she were home.

Gran seemed to require no answer. "It is going to be a wonderful Christmas. I feel it in my bones."

More than a dozen times she had said as much since Mary's arrival a week ago Friday. Gran loved Christmas. She loved it when one of her grandchildren came to stay with her for Christmas. Mary's mother, knowing this, made a point of sending one of her many children to London every year. Mary had been twice before, but not since she was a very little girl, not since Regent Street had been rebuilt, and not since Gran's rheumatism had forced her to depend on the Merlin chair.

Mary stopped the chair at the street corner, clutching closer the billowing folds of her cloak, as chill and uncertain as the wind. Here she was friendless, without the company of so much as one of her seven siblings, who might have helped to push this contrary chair, helped lift it up and down the curb, and steps, and stairs.

Any one of them might have kept her company in the hours when Gran slept. A bit of conversation, a card game or two, was it so much to ask? She voiced none of her feelings. Gran took too much joy in her presence. She could not go two hours without thanking her for coming, her gratitude like a thorn in Mary's side, with which the old lady unknowlingly pricked raw her loneliness.

The carriage cut off any reply, sweeping to a halt just beyond them, a clatter of hooves and a thunder of wheels on pavestone. Sleek matched chestnuts champed their bits, nostrils flaring, heads testing the well-blacked bearing reins that kept all necks contained in the same perfect arch, the animals' breath pluming as if dragons drew the vehicle.

Mary waved to Mr. Twee, the crosswalk sweeper, as she examined the beautiful team. She wished Grant might see them. Her brother loved horses above all else, and these were remarkably well-matched animals of the finest conformation, as sleekly groomed and high-headed as their owner.

A gleam caught her eye as Lord Balfour drew an embossed gold watch from his inner pocket.

"Good morning, my lord," the coachman called with a tip of his hat, neck scarf blowing like a kite tail.

"Is it, Woodrow?" the young lion growled.

"Aye. The lads are feeling their oats this fine, brisk morning." Woodrow nodded cheerfully toward the horses.

"I am quite cognizant of the temperature, thank you. You keep us standing in it."

Was this the way of the London *ton?* Horrible, condescending fellow, she thought. He did not deserve such excellent creatures, nor such doting servants.

Two footmen, as well matched in stature and coloring as the horses, equally matched in the scarlet color of their noses, and wind-watery eyes, leapt from their perch at the back of the coach to open the door, let down the steps, and assist their master's entry into the vehicle.

"Beggin' your pardon, milord," Woodrow called. "Traffic leaving the mews, don't you see. It's a topsy-turvy mess Nash and Burton have made of the street."

"Takes a bit of a mess to change things, for good or evil," Lord Balfour murmured to his black-coated companion.

Gran had been listening as much as she. "I for one do not weep to see the higgelty-piggelty jumble of Swallow Street undone," she said far too loudly, throwing the words over her shoulder like a challenge.

Lord Balfour turned regal head as he mounted the steps to his carriage, enough that Mary knew he heard, not enough to indicate any real interest on his part—the lion, annoyed by midges.

"Take care, Gran," Mary said between her teeth, returning her attention to the chair, that they might make their escape before the viscount settled himself to a clear view through the carriage window. "The curb is always a bit of a jolt."

"Onward, my dear," Gran urged with a cough that ended in a breathless laugh. "I am not made of spun sugar, so brittle that I will break."

*　　*　　*

As buff-colored lap blankets were tucked snugly about their knees and hot bricks placed between their feet, silence stretched uncomfortably between Baxter and his new secretary, but for an occasional watery sniff and the faint clacking of Temple's teeth.

The door slammed shut.

With an elegant turn of the wrist, Baxter whipped a spotless white handkerchief from the pocket of his coat. Temple accepted the offering with garbled thanks and thoroughly blew his nose.

Baxter fastidiously refused to accept its return, saying curtly, "Consider it a gift."

"Bless you, my lord." Temple carefully folded and tucked away the square of lawn as if it were cloth of gold. "Is it true, my lord, as my father once told me, that Christmas is not your favorite season?"

Baxter snorted. "An understatement. But then, your father was always the consummate conservative in expressing himself. I consider the Christmas holidays maudlin, expensive, and a great deal too much trouble."

Temple gaped at him fishlike. "I thought him in jest, my lord," he protested.

"The Temple I knew was no jester," Baxter said flatly, jaw set, no room for tears—no handkerchief.

"But you hold annually the Balfour Christmas Eve Ball, my lord! The most sought after—"

"Yes, yes," Baxter cut him off impatiently. "With one grand gesture I obliterate all obligations to family, friends, and society, and have done with the holidays."

"Have done, my lord?"

The wistful pity in the boy's voice galled, almost as much as the stench from his coat, the foul odor thickening unbearably in the warm, contained air of the carriage.

"Exactly!" Baxter rose abruptly to slide the window down. He longed to toss the boy out on his ear.

Every year he suffered an inadmissible sadness, a deepening loneliness, a despair as unpalatable as the odor of black dye, as unbearable as its purpose. He did not want benumbed emotion brought to fresh life, certainly not by a boy he employed out of pity.

"It is your job"—with gloved fingertip he rubbed a peephole on the frosted windowpane—"as it was your father's, to create the impression I enjoy the festivities—with all haste. The invitations are, already, a week late."

Temple cleared his throat uneasily and consulted the day's schedule. "Your appointment is at ten, my lord. We've plenty of time. And then we've to pick up the invitations."

"I shall miss him," Baxter said as the clear spot his finger had rubbed sent humid tears trickling down the pane.

Temple's head rose abruptly, eyes shining like glass. "Thank you, my lord, for saying so. Christmas won't be the same without him."

"Indeed it won't. The funeral is Friday, did you say? It is penciled in on my schedule?"

Temple nodded, blinking furiously. "Yes, my lord."

Baxter waved at the air above his head. "The trap," he said dryly.

Temple looked up. "You wish me to pull the string, my lord?"

Baxter's brow arched. Was it a hopelessly foolish notion, letting this lad fill his father's shoes? "Pushing it will do no good."

"Of course, my lord."

The trapdoor admitted a gush of cold air, the sounds of passing carriages, and the thin cry of the flower girl on the corner. "Holly. Fresh holly. Straight from the country. Buy a sprig. Buy a bundle. Holly. Fresh holly."

Baxter waggled gloved fingers at the sound. "Another detail to attend to, Temple."

"My lord?"

Did the boy perpetually wear that puzzled look?

"You will write to each of my stewards, asking if I've a fallen tree on any of my land suitable for the Yule log. Ask, too, about greenery for the mantels, picture frames, and stairway banisters. All must be arranged and hung by St. Thomas's Day."

Temple made note.

"All to be taken down the day following the ball."

"You do not wish to leave it up until Twelfth Day, my lord?" Temple's voice shot high.

Baxter sighed. Temple's father had never needed to be told anything twice. Indeed, he had proved at times, a mind reader. "I do not care for the look—the smell of half-dead things—cluttering up the place, shedding berries and leaves."

Half-dead things. The phrase resounded. Had old Temple been a half-dead man and he not keen-eyed enough to notice?

"Woodrow?" he called impatiently.

"Aye, my lord?" Woodrow sounded almost as if he sat beside them in the coach instead of on the box above.

"There is, I trust, good reason why we do not move?" Baxter suggested caustically.

"Indeed, my lord," Woodrow agreed.

"That reason being?"

"I've no desire to run down a pretty woman, my lord."

"You are a man of honor, Woodrow." Sarcasm laced Baxter's voice. "This woman? She blocks our way?"

" 'Deed sir."

Through the trap filtered a voice, calling blithely, "And a good morning to you, Mr. Twee. How kind of you to assist."

A metallic clacking sound accompanied the voice.

"But of course." Baxter sighed heavily, peeved. *"Her!"*

"Her, my lord?" Temple leaned forward to peer out of the window.

"And her grandmother. And Twee, the old doddard. Invariably in my way whenever I am in a hurry."

The "her" in question warned, "Watch the back wheel, Mr. Twee. It has a mind of its own."

"Hold on. Hold on!" Twee shouted. "She's veerin' to starboard."

Baxter flung away his lap blanket. *Confound the woman!* "Why will they venture out?" he demanded of no one, kicking aside the hot bricks at his feet. "None but the chit to propel her." His hand found the door

latch. "Blasted Merlin chair's anything but magical. It's
a wonder how she manages to move the thing at all."

He wrenched at the door handle.

"May I assist, my lord?" Temple offered gamely, too
late. Baxter had already flung himself out. The wind
slammed the door behind him.

Chapter Two

𝒞

"You two!" Baxter gestured the startled footmen down from their perches with a peremptory wave. "Help the ladies cross, if you please. And be quick about it."

"Yes, milord." They swept past him with wish-to-please energy. Temple watched, nose pressed to fogged glass, a young man addle-witted when it came to filling his new position.

Did he do the lad a disservice, Baxter wondered, thrusting undue responsibility upon those narrow shoulders?

He sighed, set off after the footmen, and came lee with the lead horses in time to get a good squint of "her."

She wore the same cloud of billowing crimson-colored cloaking he always saw her in of late, the dark, vinelike mass of her curls dancing about the brim of the same hopelessly out-of-date bonnet, recently refurbished. The crown was bound in fresh crimson ribbon, into which was tucked a festive sprig of holly, country style. The wind had pinched her cheeks a pretty pink. A sparkle lit her deep brown eyes. She looked more fairy sprite than London lady, blown in from the moors or a holly-bestrewn heath. Even through the smeary fog of near-sightedness he could not deny she was an eye-catching Christmas Medusa.

She smiled—always, she smiled—at everyone and everything. A foolishness to do so in London. Too many dangers for ripe young country girls too ready with their dimples, and yet it was a rarity to see her features ar-

ranged in any other configuration. He supposed it a
blessing she possessed a headful of smile-worthy teeth,
unusually straight, even, and of uniformly pearly hue.

Her cheer never ceased to intrigue and irritate him.
What had the woman to smile about so perpetually?
Smiles were fine, in the correct proportion, but this Miss
Merriment smiled to excess. The young woman was in-
decently pleased. With what—her position as caretaker
to an elderly relative? That she found such a position
worthy of unflagging cheer rubbed like a burdock seed
beneath the firmly girthed saddle of his own dissatis-
faction.

Her grandmother loosed a cackle that ended in a
cough, as the footmen, with admonitions to each other—
"Careful now, Will!" "Nice and easy, Ned"—boldly
lifted the three-wheeled Merlin chair and staggered with
it to the walkway.

The street sweeper, old Mr. Twee, tottered after them,
saying, "It is a devil of a time, sirs, trying to get that
chair across the street. The foot support bangs against
the paving stones and that one wee wheel at the back
heads east while the other two are bound and determined to go south, and me no longer strong enough to
insist they should all head north."

The merry Medusa floated in their wake, crying out
with a laugh, "Gran, are you all right? Not feeling
breathless, are you?"

"Fine, fine, Merry." The old lady waved one warmly
gloved hand, clutching her lap blankets with the other,
and called out, "My thanks to you Ned, Will."

Ned asked, "Will you be needing to cross Jermyn
Street as well, madam?"

"Why, yes, if you please." The old woman pointed
her walking stick west. "We are headed that way."

Once again, with a heave and staggering progress, the
chair was borne across the paving stones, touching gently
down in front of Carpenter and Westley's, the local optician's glass-fronted office. Westley himself came out to
wish the ladies a good morning, smiling foolishly at Miss
Merry, as if he were infatuated with the lass, old letch.

Quizzing glass raised, Baxter followed their progress,

declining to cross Jermyn, waiting only to regain his footmen.

"How can we ever thank you enough?" The grinning Gorgon directed expressive and effusively smiling thanks not, as he might have expected, in his direction, but toward his servants. Affronted by such unschooled country manners, Baxter turned on his heel, recrossing the street to his coach. *At last,* he thought, pretending he did not care that the lass ignored him, *I shall be on my way.*

Behind him, Will and Ned's voices drifted in the wind, "It is our master you should thank, miss."

He wanted to turn and shout. Never mind! It does not matter. Few things people say or do really matter.

Temple had managed to slide down the window. The youth's gawky head hung out of the top of it. "Do you require my assistance, sir?" he called.

Baxter shook his head impatiently, irritated with the lad. "Only in sitting yourself back down again, Temple. High time we were on our way."

"My lord." Temple lifted a finger.

"It will have to wait," Baxter snapped.

"But . . ." Temple opened his mouth, finger waggling.

Out of patience, Baxter swept past, rounding the coach that he might enter by way of the door least exposed to wind and traffic.

Ned and Will came swiftly to heel, letting down the step, offering elbows that he might climb safely in. "The lady, my lord . . ." Ned began.

Baxter silenced him. "Yes. Thank you for your assistance."

"No, my lord," Will blurted. "What he means is, she . . ."

She billowed past the waiting horses, who shied and cavorted at the sight of so much undulating velvet, gusting such great clouds of steam it appeared she stepped from a mist. They had tried to warn him of her approach. Baxter felt the perfect fool.

"Stop! Please! Wait!" Breathless, she pressed one hand to the intriguing rise and fall of her crimson-covered breast. "I must thank you!"

Must she?

He carefully schooled his features before stepping down to hear her out. One could not, after all, simply shout fare-thee-well from the window when Medusa came running after one, when she stood flushed and trembling, awaiting his pleasure, *smiling.*

"Had I known you meant to follow, I would have stopped across the street, madam." He bowed, sweeping up her hand, swiftly checking the race of the pulse at her wrist as he politely kissed the air above gloved knuckles.

"The pleasure is mine," he said, and indeed it was so, for the throb of her heartbeat against his gloved thumb, the softness of the glove that brushed his lip, even the faint scent of roses emanating from her wrist pleased him.

He dropped his hold on her with polite alacrity, convinced her heart beat soundly, his own pulse mildly affected by the sweet suggestion of perfumed gratitude.

She dipped a deep old-fashioned curtsy, crimson cloak sweeping the ground. "So nice to know, my lord, that chivalry is not dead."

Brown eyes twinkling, dark curls bobbing, she rose, launching the full power of her smile on him.

She was not unattractive, this Medusa. Her lips, he noticed for the first time, made a perfect Cupid's bow. As if she pinned him with an arrow slung from that gentle weapon, he found himself incapacitated, oddly breathless, smiling stupidly back at her.

"Ahem. My lord? Your appointment."

Reminded of his duties, Baxter tipped his head, momentarily unwary of the wind. It caught his hat, knocked it from his head and sent it bowling into the street.

"Oh, dear," she cried with a startled laugh.

"Excuse me." He leapt after it, not in the least amused.

Will and Ned joined the chase.

The hat bounced and dodged pursuit, rolling between two carriages, narrowly missing a steaming pile of dung before landing neatly in the path of an approaching coach-and-four. Four sets of splashing hooves and four flashing wheels could not avoid trampling the proud black hat into a pulpy squashed thing unfit for any man's head.

Flushed and gasping, pomaded hair blowing limp about his ears, Baxter left his poor hat to the street.

"Oh, dear, oh, dear." Miss Rivers met his disheveled return with a broader smile than usual. She made no attempt to hide her amusement.

Baxter made pointless effort to smooth his locks, gave up and straightened stiffly to his full height of five feet, eight inches, and found himself eye to twinkling eye with his nemesis.

"A pity about your hat." She laughed—an attractive laugh had it not been directed at him. "I have never seen an article of clothing so determined to outrun its owner."

As determined as he had been to outrun her.

"Yes, I fail, while the pluckier hat makes good its escape." Baxter bared his teeth in cool, sarcastic approximation of a smile.

Her laughter faded, then her smile. Her gaze dropped uneasily. "I . . . keep you." she said, and turned on her heel.

He could not agree with her more, and yet it pained him to realize she immediately took his meaning. It pained him more to know he had been unforgivably rude, enough so that he drove her away. It was not at all his custom to turn the bite of his infamous sarcasm on defenseless women.

He opened his mouth to say something, shut it, at a loss, and followed her, as ruffled as his hair. "Miss . . . Miss? I do apologize . . ." He frowned, his contrition genuine.

She stopped, turned, and looked him in the eyes. Hers were big, brown, and wounded. He half expected her to say, "You should be sorry."

He could not meet that gaze for long, his own falling to the muddied hem of her cloak. Customary politenesses seemed fraud, and yet he must make an attempt to set things right. "You know my name, miss, but I have not the pleasure of knowing yours."

She drew a breath. "Everyone in Regent Street knows of Viscount Balfour, my lord."

"Am I, and my wicked tongue, so infamous?" he asked, wondering if she knew him already as Lord "Thorn."

She would not look at him. Her posture, her demeanor, remained stiff and unforgiving, but for the wild softness of her hair. She did not smile.

He frowned. Confound the woman. Why should he care whether she approved of him?

"Small surprise you have never heard of a Miss Rivers from Glastonbury, in Somerset. I am new to London, my lord."

Still she avoided his eyes!

"And so you are a merry Rivers," he said softly, "with holly in your hat, and a smile . . . only I can kill."

That brought her head up with a jerk, dark eyes searching his.

She blinked, the smallest hint of a frown touching her brow, and then she smiled. If not forgiveness in her gaze, in the generous curve of her lip at least humor was restored.

That smile, of all those he had seen touch her mouth, was a special gift. He could not help but smile back, saying, by way of apology, "It is I who keep you, Miss Rivers."

He entertained the fleeting thought that of all the women a man might "keep," it would be prudent to choose one so capable of forgiveness. He echoed her earlier curtsy in bowing low. "A good day to you."

"And you." She stepped back—smiling. What else?

He climbed into the coach, an echo of that smile touching his lips, as if the curve of hers was contagious.

"Well done, sir," Temple ventured to say.

Baxter smoothed his tousled hair, and his features, into their customary unemotional blandness.

Not well done at all, he thought, to play the Samaritan with no other motive than to be on his way, to make a fool of himself chasing after a stupid hat.

Smile fading, Lord "Thorn" turned his face to the

window, his response as frosty as the pane. "I do not think your father would have agreed, Temple."

Temple made uncertain noises. Baxter listened with only half an ear. As the coach got under way, he watched a crimson-clad figure cross the street. One could not but notice such a color—such a smile. The woman was showing off her teeth again.

What would it take to make him equally ready to meet with smiles anything and everyone he encountered?

He wondered.

Chapter Three

Mary watched the smart, crested coach tool away, her pulse racing as if it were she who had gone hat chasing.

The disagreeable Viscount Balfour had taken note of her! She, who had never so much as been given a nod of recognition by anyone of rank higher than the local squire in Glastonbury. If only Ellen were here, so she could share her astonishment at meeting a titled nobleman who rescued them, insulted her, and then cleverly apologized, without ever begging forgiveness.

More challenging than a chess game, the London quality. More warming than hot rum punch, their odd exchange.

Gran coughed, the noise like a dash of cold water on heated spirits. A single cough, not an onslaught, but enough to remind Mary of her greatest fear.

"And what was that, Gran, if not a Christmas miracle come early?" she crooned, tucking Gran more snugly into her chair, surreptitiously studying the old lady's color.

Gran laughed without hint of another cough. "What a to-do!" she crowed. "Rescued by none less than a peer of the realm and his matching footmen. A handsome fellow, the viscount, do you not agree, Mary?"

Twee, who had stayed at Gran's side while Mary ran to thank the viscount, chuckled and winked. "A handsome Christmas package for the fortunate young lady who rapts his interest, Miss Mary. Heir to his uncle's fortune, you know."

Mary did not know from whence his fortune came,

only that he must be in possession of one to dwell alone in the middle of London in such a large and well-kept property. She tipped her bonnet brim in the direction of the handsome, four-storied town house. "Rivals in size Mr. Nash's, does it not?"

"Aye, and that's just 'is London home. 'As another in the country, he does." Twee winked again. "Future heir to 'is father's estate, Thorn is."

"Thorn?" Mary asked.

Twee laughed. " 'Is servants call him Thorn."

"Dear Mr. Twee," Granny said gently from her chair. "Surely you agree, the measure of a man must not be taken solely in the strength of his title or the weight of his purse and properties. I will not have you filling Mary's head with such a nonsensical notion."

"You'll get no argument from me on that score." Twee grinned at her ruefully. "By such a yardstick my measure is shrimpish, at best."

Mary smiled, "Why has this wealthy Thorn not been snagged yet?"

Twee shrugged. "Glossy as a 'olly leaf, 'e is, but prickly, don't you see? Painful to 'old tight. Dozens of young misses and their mamas have set out to cut 'im from 'is bachelorhood, but 'e is a thorny one. Shows favor to few, much less the milk of 'uman kindness. Oh, 'e drops me a copper regular enough, but never a good day to pass 'is lips, or a 'ow do ye do. And scowls! Ruins 'is looks, 'e does, with that lemon look."

"He was kind enough just now—after a fashion," Mary suggested mischievously.

"After a fashion?" Gran protested.

"Aye! 'E were particular polite today," Twee agreed, without questioning her meaning. "Fair took me breath away to see such a show." He grinned, mittened hand raised to hide the gaps in his yellowed teeth. "Cor' what a sight to see him chasing after 'is 'at! I would not have missed it for an earldom, I wouldn't."

"We depend upon your kindness, Mr. Twee," Granny said warmly, opening the clasp of her reticule to offer him halfpence for his assistance.

"Thank ye kindly, my dears." He pocketed the coin.

"It's back to work with me." Away he went to fetch up his abandoned broom, whistling cheerfully.

"Is it true, Gran?" Mary asked as she set the rattling Merlin chair to moving with the shove required to align its third wheel.

"Is what true, child?" Gran rearranged her laprobe.

"That the viscount is a cold man, not given to kindness?"

"Well, Mary, my dear, I cannot say I know any viscount well enough to fairly judge this one. Neither can I say I have ever seen the man step from his coach to offer anyone assistance before. How did Lord Balfour strike you, upon first brief acquaintance?"

Nothing but the squeaking of the wheels broke the silence between them for the length of Capper and Water's storefront before Mary replied. "I found him rude and polite, elegant and disheveled, kind and cruel, unflappable and prickly. Yes, prickly, as if he holds the world at arm's length."

"Haughty, then?"

Mary considered the word. "No. Not haughty. Stiff and proper. Dismissive and distant. He frowns too much."

"Scowls as if he dislikes the world," Gran said flatly.

Mary laughed. "Scowls, yes, but . . . there is . . . a twist to his lips, a narrowed look to his gaze. He hides something. Sadness, or loneliness, or perhaps I deceive myself and it is only contempt."

"I can see you are taken with him."

Mary laughed. "What girl wouldn't be? A handsome, elegant, titled gentleman with such a fine coach-and-four. Surely he turns heads wherever he goes, all of London's titled young women determined to soften him?"

"I would warn you not to lose your heart, child. I have heard a dozen have been thrown at his feet, and not a one to touch his."

"Lose my heart to a viscount! A fellow of particularly contradictory sensibilities? Really, Gran, I am not so foolish. Besides, I am too much the clinging vine to interest the prickly Lord Thorn."

"Now that would be a Christmas miracle, but you would not suit." Gran coughed as she said it.

Mary stopped the chair and twisted on the brake, the coughing painful to hear. She dropped to one knee before the older woman and handed her a fresh handkerchief, waiting until she finished to ask, "Shall we go back?"

"I am fine," Gran insisted. "Don't fuss now, child. You know I do not like to be fussed over."

Mary took her mittened hand, looking her in the eyes with a smile. "Now, tell me, how can you be so sure a wealthy viscount would not suit me?"

Gran's eyes twinkled. She clutched her handkerchief to her mouth with a stifled chuckle. "It is rumored this particular viscount despises Christmas."

"Despises Christmas? What nonsense. No one despises Christmas! He hosts a fancy dress ball on Christmas Eve. Is that the action of a gentleman who hates the holiday?"

Gran chuckled. "And would you care to go to such a ball, my dear Mary?"

"But of course!" She laughed throatily. "As would you." She patted her Gran's shoulder. It seemed too frail beneath the thick shawl. "Indeed, who in London would not like to dance away Christmas Eve at Balfour's ball?"

Baxter doffed his brand new hat and handed it to Mr. Nicoll as he entered the court tailor's pleasant shop.

J. D. Nicoll, short, balding, impeccably dressed but for the measuring tape about his neck, the row of pins stuck in his collar, and the chalk dust on the lip of his pocket, welcomed Baxter graciously, despite his tardiness. "Viscount Balfour! So good to see you. I did began to think my appointment book in error, so punctually is your arrival always to be depended upon."

"My apologies. The wind stole away my hat."

Nicoll stared at the object in his hands, puzzled, before suggesting, "I see you found it again?"

"No. I gave it to the street."

Nicoll's brows rose.

"The street, Mr. Nicoll, does not mind a flattened and muddied hat. I do."

Nicoll deftly turned the hat, examining the interior. "Ah! I see. You stopped at Mr. Barclay's. And a lovely hat it is, my lord."

"Exactly the same sort of hat I have worn for the past seven years, Mr. Nicoll." Baxter was in no mood for niceties.

"And is this young Mr. Temple, my lord?"

"Who else? Resembles his father, think you not?"

Nicoll measured Temple with his eyes. "Cut from the same cloth, my lord. I shall miss your father, young man. A splendid fellow. You would do well to fill his shoes. The coat, my lord, is finished. It should do nicely."

"Excellent!" Baxter yawned, removed his gloves and allowed Nicoll's assistant to take his overcoat. Settling himself in a chair provided him, he said, "I would choose fabric today."

"A suit required by Christmas, my lord?"

"Christmas Eve. Can it be done?"

"For you, my lord? But of course. In black, as usual, or do you care to impress the ladies with the blues and greens that promise to be very popular this year?"

"Black is fine." Baxter sighed, bored already with his errand. Christmas and Christmas clothes were a great deal more bother than they were worth.

"I shall just fetch the coat, my lord."

Temple, who took stance at his elbow, looked anything but bored. Head rotating as if on a swivel, the young man examined everything in Mr. Nicoll's establishment with openmouthed awe. Had he never been to a tailor's before? Certainly not to a London tailor's of the first stare.

Baxter could hear the old man's voice clearly in his mind. "In a country cottage, my wife may look after her mother and feed the children far better than in London."

The lonely boy, Baxter, had been asked, "Do you not miss them, Mr. Temple? And they you?" He had stared at his globe, fingering the pink spot that represented Greece, the spot his parents visited for the season.

"They do. But I shall see my wife and children for the holidays, Master Baxter. And every Sunday your father gives me leave to spend with them."

As a child it had seemed a wealth of time, far more than his own father spent with him, and yet, now, looking back on it, he wondered if young Temple would agree with him.

Baxter's gaze followed that of his new secretary, as the young man scanned with interest the bolts of cloth neatly lining the shelves, floor to ceiling. The place smelled of wool, tanned leather and fresh dyes, chalk dust, and Mr. Nicoll's bay leaf cologne. Everything neat and well stocked. He took out his quizzing glass.

"Nankeen, doeskin, and kid for breeches and gloves," he said, low-voiced, pointing.

Temple started. "My lord?"

"The fabrics you were examining. And here"—he waved the glass—"cashmere, kerseymere, worsted, and merino for coats. Linen, muslin, silk, and bombazine for shirts." He jabbed the glass toward the corner. "Waistcoat whites."

Temple drew hastily from his pocket the calfskin notebook and pencil he carried everywhere.

"And these, my lord?" Temple pointed his pencil stub toward a selection of figured satins, silks, and damasks.

"Nicoll's specialty. Court costume."

Temple gazed longingly at the blue and green fabrics. A young man enamored of fashion, perhaps? Certainly not a conversationalist.

Baxter sighed, interest waning, and tucked away his quizzing glass. Young Temple promised to make this Christmas more unpleasant than usual. Everything must be explained to him. Everything, like a watch unsprung by his father's sudden demise, must be put back into working order, so that life might tick along again without a thousand questions and decisions all written down in cramped notation.

He hadn't said a word about feeling bad, old Temple. Simply clutched his chest with a muffled groan and toppled to the floor in the midst of Baxter's dictation—a letter to his parents, who wintered in . . . was it Spain

this year? They did not care for the cold. Never had.
Owned houses in Italy, France, and Spain. Yes, he was
sure it was Spain.

Temple had mentioned the address—his last words.

A stifled gasp, and he had folded up like an old fan,
the letter fluttering to the floor.

What had become of it? Poor Temple had never seen
to its mailing, that was certain. Unnaturally blue, the old
man's lips had been, unnaturally gray the cast to his skin.

Baxter had fallen to his knees and listened, disbe-
lieving, to his friend and mentor's final exhalation.

Then silence, stillness, his ear bent to Temple's chest.

He shook away the thought—shook away the idea that
Temple had been more father to him than his own flesh
and blood, dismissing the guilty suspicion that in so fa-
thering him, Temple's own son had grown up fatherless.

The Nicolls made ladies riding habits and cloaks as
well as men's formal and court costume. A beautifully
tailored habit in claret-colored velvet clung provoca-
tively to a straw dummy beside his chair, its shoulders
draped with a matching cloak. Velvet softly puddled the
richly carpeted floor beside his well-polished boot.

Baxter fingered the fabric, thinking of the worn and
muddied hem of Miss Rivers's cloak. He imagined her
in the habit, smiling. Of course she would be smiling.

He blinked, dismissing the image. What was there to
smile about with Christmas upon them, and Temple
gone forever?

Chapter Four

🎵

"Here we are, my lord." Nicoll emerged from the backroom. A coat, freshly pressed, hung across his arm, much like the one Baxter had worn into the shop.

"Try it on," Baxter suggested quietly, content for the moment to watch young Temple's reaction.

Temple stared at the coat in dismay. "Me, my lord?"

"All of the staff are provided matching coats, Temple," Baxter explained. "I would not make an exception of you."

"But . . ."

"No buts. Try it on."

"My lord, I do not mean to appear ungrateful, but my family is in mourning. I must wear my blacks."

Baxter fingered the obsidian ring he had donned the day Temple died. Pinch-lipped, he peered at the boy, little realizing how much it looked as if he scowled. "A black arm band, muffler, and gloves will have to suffice. I have not had a black coat made up for you, lad, and I forbid you to wear that one in my presence."

"Yes, my lord," Temple said, much subdued as he held out his arms, awkwardly flailing for armholes.

The attendant slipped the garment onto him and smoothed the sleeves. Temple's expression betrayed an unfamiliarity with being assisted in the donning of his clothes.

Nicoll bent to address Baxter, low-voiced. "My dear viscount, I dare to remind you, it is generally at this time of year that Temple purchases your lordship's annual gift for the parish poorhouse."

"Gift?" Baxter frowned, racking his brain. What gift was this among the scores of gifts and donations Temple had attended to each Christmas?

Nicoll was almost as much the mind reader as old Temple had been. "Handkerchiefs, my lord. Nightshirts. Nightcaps." He wore an anxious expression—fearing the loss of a sale, no doubt.

Vaguely familiar, this list. "Yes, yes." Baxter waved a bored hand. "What did Temple arrange?"

Nicoll smiled. "The same order every year, my lord, for the past seven years. One hundred handkerchiefs. One hundred nightshirts. One hundred matching nightcaps. White linen."

"I see no need to make a change. Inform young Temple of the specifics as soon as he is finished admiring himself . . ."

Temple turned swiftly, one arm in, one arm out of the new coat, as he whipped out his calfskin notebook with unnecessary urgency. "My lord, pray forgive me. You will think me vain indeed to spend so much time before the mirror. One hundred nightshirts, nightcaps, handkerchiefs." He mused aloud as he scribbled. "Anything else, my lord? He hung on Baxter's impending words, Nicoll's dresser stood poised behind him, keeping the new coat from dragging the floor.

"Remove the coat properly, Temple," Baxter suggested wryly. "I do not care for this disheveled look."

Nicoll held up a chalk-marked sample in dark blue. "Can I interest you in the new rolled collar for your evening coat, my lord?"

Baxter sighed as he rose and held out his arms. Why must fashions change? Why could a man not go on wearing the same cut of coat from cradle to grave? Why should the Christmas festivities always require new clothes?

He slipped in his arms, allowing Mr. Nicoll to settle the wadded buckram in place as he examined himself in the mirror.

"I do not care for the shorter cut." He tugged at the abbreviated coat, unaccustomed to seeing so much of his doeskin breeches exposed. "And this puffed and wadded sleeve is not at all to my taste." He turned to frown at his reflection, and found, not only himself in the mirror, but Miss Rivers, smiling merrily, Christmas holly cheerfully nodding from the brim of her bonnet.

He thought for an instant he only imagined her.

"The collar, my lord? Splendid, don't you agree?" Nicoll pinched at the fabric. "We need only nip in the waistline."

Baxter paid him no mind, his attention fixed on the unexpected reflection, watery in his nearsighted perspective, as if a Christmas sprite looked back at him from the bottom of a lake.

"Do not scowl so, my lord. The color looks well on you," Temple ventured to comment.

Scowl? Baxter rearranged his features. *Was he scowling?*

Merry Rivers's smile broadened. Her eyes twinkled with unmasked amusement.

Baxter, unaccustomed to being laughed at, found himself for the second time that morning proving humorous to Miss Rivers. He faced her, voice heavy with sarcasm. "Is it me or the style you find laughable?"

Her eyes widened. Her smile diminished without disappearing entirely. "Neither, my lord. I was amused to think we should end up in the same place this morning. As for the coat"—she cocked her head to one side—"the young man is correct. The color suits you."

"Clarence blue," Nicoll said unctuously, as if everyone knew colors by their Christian names. "The color of your lordship's eyes. I have long thought it would flatter you."

The old lady, chair propped in front of a glassed counter displaying handkerchiefs and neckcloths, drew forth a pair of spectacles and pinched them onto her nose.

Did he scowl so fiercely, he wondered, when he tried to see without the aid of his quizzing glass? He took out the glass, to gaze again at his reflection—at Merry Rivers's.

She stared back, a faint smile upon her lips. Pretty lips he could see by way of the glass. So much of the world passed in a blur, he had not thought to wonder what she looked like in focus. To see her clearly, staring back at him, took his breath away. Eyes, nose, lips—none in themselves remarkable, together created a handsome reflection—a face expressing uneasiness at the moment.

He stared too fixedly, and a glance at his own reflection showed his features arranged in what looked remarkably like a scowl.

Mr. Nicoll asked, "What think you, my lord?"

Baxter turned, quizzing glass still raised, to find everyone present staring at him, their concerted attention bringing him to the blush. He lowered the glass.

"Ladies?" This rare opportunity to gain a woman's perspective intrigued him. Nanny Lumley had first put him in short coats, but since then Temple and Emerson, his valet, had served as his only input.

The old lady said, "I like to see a man in something other than black during the holidays."

Miss Rivers's smiling reflection nodded.

He bowed to the older woman. "In this, then, let me please you, madam. Make the coat blue this year, Mr. Nicoll, if you please."

Nicoll's jaw dropped for no more than an instant. "Very good, my lord. And the collar?"

"What do you think, Mary?" the old woman asked.

Mary's lips curved upward mischievously, eyes twinkling. The same baring of teeth he had in the past found so very irritating, proved not so irritating now.

"Change can be a good thing," she said.

Baxter stepped into the back room, that Walter, Nicoll's dresser, might measure him. He went happily enough, ear cocked, as Walter stretched tape, to hear what went on in the front room.

Miss Rivers asked, "How does your wife, Mr. Nicoll? Is she recovering?"

Nicoll was married? His wife ill? Baxter felt betrayed. He had patronized the man's shop since he was a lad. Never had he heard mention of a wife.

Mr. Nicoll responded, "Thank you for asking, Miss Rivers. Bess does well."

She went on to inquire after his children. She knew their names: Anne, Betty, Tad, and Sophie. "Are they looking forward to the coming holidays?" she asked.

Did not all children look forward to Christmas? Baxter snorted. Even he had looked forward to Christmas as a boy.

"Beg pardon, my lord?" Nicoll's assistant knelt, tape in hand, measuring his inner leg.

Not the best time to be laughing.

"Private thought," Baxter said.

The man rose. "If you will turn then, my lord?"

Baxter obliged.

Merry was saying ". . . written to Glastonbury, asking them to come, if they can."

"Nothing better than a coming together of family for Christmas," Nicoll responded heartily.

Baxter could think of nothing worse. He imagined aunts, uncles, and cousins descending upon the house like a horde of hungry swallows, the way they had for his uncle's funeral—a houseful of strangers, for indeed most of his family were strangers, tied to him in no other way than blood—expecting to be entertained, upsetting his routine.

"My favorite thing about Christmas . . ." The old woman's cough interrupted her remark, a cough that rattled painfully harsh upon the ear.

Had he not just dropped breeches to step into a pair to be altered, Baxter might have burst through the curtain to bang the old woman upon the back while Temple was sent running for a physician.

Baxter closed his eyes, remembering Nanny Lumley. Plain muslin hankies. The hateful smell of the peppermint she sucked to soothe her throat. He could not bear the smell. Always at Christmas came the reminder of his loss.

Gran's coughing stilled.

Mary unobtrusively handed her a fresh handkerchief, smoothed the sleeve of her dress, and resisted the impulse to ask Gran if she was feeling well enough to continue.

Instead, Mary went on with her conversation with Mr. Nicoll as if such an outburst were nothing untoward, though it cost her some part of herself every time she played this part, for Gran's sake. Gran hated fuss. It would mortify her to find Mary hovering and concerned every time she had a little coughing spell, as she referred to her outbursts.

"Gran has come to pick out new handkerchiefs," she said brightly. "We must also have a dozen each, night-caps and handkerchiefs, for the parish poorhouse."

"Yes, indeed." Gran cleared her throat, her voice almost as bright as Mary's. "I wish it might be nankeen breeches I were to have of you, Mr. Nicoll. The parish priest told us Sunday that the poor are in dire need."

"Regrettably, we cannot afford such extravagances." Mary hoped fervently Gran would not insist upon the breeches. Gran's money was running out. She avoided telling the old woman. No need to worry her. "This Christmas we must content ourselves with handkerchiefs and nightcaps," she said firmly.

Chapter Five

ℭ

They bent over the glass case together, Gran examining the array of handkerchiefs and belchers, Mary examining Gran. Her color was good. Mother had cautioned her to pay attention to Gran's color. The cough had been productive, not dry and raspy, which, mother said, was of far more concern than wet and mucousy. And yet, she could not help but worry. Gran did not eat much of late, no matter how Mary tempted her. She would not stay in bed, would not stay comfortable and warm in her new town house.

"Fresh air, Mary. I must have fresh air, my dear. Cooped up in these rooms all day. It is not good for me," Gran insisted.

Dr. Hair had not ordered her bed bound, and so Mary obliged Gran, whose wisdom and clarity of thinking she did not consider in the least impaired.

"What color? White?" Mary forced a smile to her lips, and kept her fears to herself.

"Snuff-colored, my dear. Never white," Gran said decisively. "I don't know how they manage to find money for snuff and tobacco, when they cannot adequately feed themselves or their families, but even the poorest do. The last thing they need for a Christmas gift is a plain white hankie that will be ruined by their first good sneeze."

"And the nightcaps, Gran? Something sturdy and warm?"

"Red flannel. And then home. I am weary, my dear."

Mary agreed, wondering if Gran would fall asleep in

the chair on the way back to her apartments. Fear reared its head again. Was this to be Gran's last Christmas?

He could not allow them to step into the beastly wind without offering his coach as transport, and so Baxter summoned young Temple into the measuring room, and sent him to suggest that Viscount Balfour requested the honor of the ladies' company in his coach for the ride home.

"Surely we take the viscount out of his way?" Miss Rivers suggested.

He heard her low murmur of protest as he emerged, fully clad, the measure of him taken from head to toe.

"Not at all," he said firmly. "I should be happy to set you down. Your apartments are no more than a step or two from my own residence. Indeed"—he knelt before the old woman's chair—"had I known you were on your way here, Mrs. Rivers, I would have saved you the walk."

The old woman chuckled, her wrinkled face as merry as her granddaughter's, despite age and ill health. "It is Merry does all the walking, my lord," she said. "While I enjoy the ride, looking in the windows of the shops we pass."

He glanced up, into Merry Rivers's eyes. She smiled, as was her wont, but he thought a trace of concern darkened her gaze when it fell upon the old woman.

"I would have offered you the use of my carriage, had I but thought to ask your destination," he said.

He convinced them in the end to partake of his largess. The four of them crowded within the coach, Temple proudly wearing his new coat, Will and Ned carefully lifting the old woman from her chair. The wheeled Merlin proved the only delay. It took Will, Ned, and Mr. Woodrow's combined efforts to hoist the chair to the roof of the coach, where it was strapped down securely, windblown wheels whirling.

The return journey might have been accomplished without further complication had not Temple suggested, "We pass Mr. Field's on the way back, my lord."

"Indeed we do," Baxter agreed, hoping the matter might be dropped.

When a small silence ensued, Mrs. Rivers suggested, "You have business at the stationer's, my lord?"

"It can wait," he said.

"So can we," Merry Rivers said cheerfully, as if the matter were hers to decide. "You must not put off your errand on our account. As it is, we shall be home in a fraction of the time it would take to wheel our way back."

Baxter was of the opinion it would require less discussion with this relentlessly genial young woman if he simply complied with her wishes. "Inform Woodrow of your intention to step down briefly," he instructed Temple.

"Yes, my lord," Temple dropped the trap and announced their needs.

Baxter nodded his approval. There was hope the lad might make an adequate secretary yet.

The horses were drawn to a halt in the final curve of the Quadrant, at the corner of Air Street, before the columned and windowed front of number sixty-five, J. Field's Bookseller and Stationer.

Across Air, from beneath the columned overhang that graced all the storefronts along the Quadrant, sculpted headstones glowed whitely at them from the windows of Gaffin's Carrara Marbleworks.

"You do not mean to accompany me, my lord?" Temple asked nervously.

"You must manage on your own, my boy," Baxter replied, "while I stay and entertain the ladies."

"As you will, my lord." Temple jumped down. The wind caught the door, slamming it shut behind him.

"He is new to your employ?" Merry Rivers surmised, a smile upon her lips, as always, and yet the sweet curve of her mouth had a puzzled quality.

"Yes. At present, more trouble than help to me." Baxter sighed and tore his attention away from the windows. No sense fretting. The boy must learn to handle things.

"And yet you keep him?"

"For the present," he said wryly, as if he considered the unthinkable, letting Temple go.

She assumed him in earnest. "I am surprised you

would take on such a young, impressionable lad for a
position of some importance if you mean first to humili-
ate him, and then to dismiss him."

"I've not intention of either, Miss Rivers. His father,
my former secretary, a man of incomparable talents,
died suddenly last week. I had no idea how much I depended upon him, until he was gone. I mean to train his
son to fill his father's shoes."

She glanced quickly at her grandmother, her cheeks
flushed with embarrassment. "I apologize for my pre-
sumption, and I am sorry for your loss," she said. "Especially at this time of year."

"Is death welcome any time of the year, Miss Rivers?"

"No!" That drew a sharp, defensive laugh. "Of course
not. And yet, it is a busy time, is it not? I have heard you
throw a rather spectacular ball every Christmas Eve."

So she had heard of his ball, had she? And angled for
an invitation with her mention of it, by God.

"Temple threw the ball every year," he corrected her,
"allowing me to claim credit." His voice fell as Temple's
son appeared in the shop's window, a tower of brown-
wrapped parcels teetering in his arms.

Surely he did not mean to carry everything out at
once!

"Ben is not the quick study I had hoped he might be,"
he murmured, yanking open the trap above his head.
"Woodrow, send Will and Ned in at once!"

"Aye, sir!" The coach shook as Will and Ned scrambled down. And yet, he could see they would arrive too
late. Temple braced the unwieldy stack with one arm,
steadied it with his chin, and reached for the door.

"Would you cast him off, then, if he proves unsatisfac-
tory?" Miss Rivers asked.

Wind rattled the coach windows ominously. The glass-
fronted door to the stationer's opened. Out staggered
Temple, mulberry scarf fluttering, a flag in the wind, the
door hitting him in the backside. The stack of parcels
swayed. He might have recovered, but another customer
exiting unwittingly added to the problem, plowing into
the boy.

Like a dancer in a clumsy ballet, Temple took a giant

step, arms cradling the parcels. Across the street, Gaffin's marble angels watched, unmoved, as the brown-wrapped packages cascaded onto the pavement, several splitting. Printed vellum, like a flock of pale winged cherubim, rose circling, scattering to the wind.

"Blast the lad for a ninnyhammer!" Baxter muttered, and without excusing himself to either lady, leapt from the coach.

"How very rude!" Mary said as the wind slammed the door in his wake.

"Oh, no!" Gran chuckled, one of her crisp new hankies wiping a clear spot on the misted windowpane. "It would appear today is Viscount Balfour's day for chasing things."

"What?" Mary shifted to the spot where the viscount had been sitting. Mother would have scolded her for such a social faux pas. The cushion, so recently warmed, transferred his heat most improperly to her backside, a vaguely alarming sensation, though not so alarming as the sight witnessed from the window.

"Oh, dear! she exclaimed with a gusty laugh. Will, Ned, Temple, and Lord Balfour, all bent double, chased after a flurry of paper taking wing. A sheet of their wind-tossed quarry plastered itself briefly to the window.

"Can you read it, my dear?"

"You are cordially invited—"

Wind whipped the page away.

Mary laughed. Gran's eyes crinkled as she pressed a hand to smiling lips.

"Oh, Gran. Poor man. Invitations to his ball. Perhaps I had best get out and help."

"Please do, my dear. It looks as if they could use it."

Laughing, Mary fought the door open, then fought to keep it open while attempting to bundle her windswept cloak into submission. Still, it caught in the door as it blew shut in her wake, her skirt with it, so that a drafty great gale of icy air swept under the swollen bell of fabric.

Twice she reopened the door, attempting to extract herself, laughing harder each time, before a buff-gloved hand closed over hers in reopening the door a third time, and his voice in her ear inquired, "What *are* you doing?"

"Trying to help." She waved at the wind-kicked riffle of paper flying about her exposed denim half boots.

"If this is help, I should hate to have you hinder me," he said dryly.

She laughed. Surely he meant her to laugh, or was this Lord Thorn, exhibiting barbs?

He opened the door and helped to free the tail of her skirt, gentle hands brooking no nonsense from wind-skittish fabric. He let the door slam, releasing at once his hold on her dress.

"What a mess," she said, cheeks warmed by her embarrassment, by the sensation of a gentleman's making so free with her clothing.

"Yet another way in which I serve to amuse you, Miss Rivers." One hand pressing hat securely to head, he scrambled to gather up a handful of wind-tossed paper before she could disabuse him of the notion.

She bent to pluck up three invitations plastered to her cloak, letting loose a whoop of surprise when the wind lifted her cloak and skirt for another blustery peek.

The sound garnered the attention of Will and Temple, who exchanged grins to see her swatting down wind-swayed fabric every time she bent to catch up a flutter of paper.

Will elbowed Ned, that he might join in the laugh. Mary chuckled with them. They made a laughable sight, bobbing and dipping, the wind lifting her skirts, their coattails, hats, and hair.

"Leave the rest," Baxter bellowed, the only one among them scowling at their antics, not in the least amused. He waved them back to the coach.

"But, my lord . . ." Ned pointed to a flurry of paper just ahead of Mary across Air Street, flapping against the window front of the marble works.

"Leave it!" Baxter insisted.

"Yes, my lord." They scuttled back to the coach, all but Mary, who calmly cornered an extra sheet or two, and rose to find the viscount staring fixedly at her, the blue of his frowning eyes quite heavenly beneath the well-gripped brim of his wind-pressed hat.

Perhaps, she thought, they focused not *at* her, but beyond her.

She turned. Through the window immediately behind her stood Gaffin's most beautiful marble angel, wings spread.

"I thought for a moment . . ." he said, voice hushed, nothing distant, or disapproving about his ethereal eyes in that moment. "The way you were standing . . . you wore wings."

Not so thorny, this. She laughed, flushing. "I am no angel, my lord, but I take that as a compliment of the highest order. From the way you scowled at me, I thought surely I had done something to displease you."

"Scowling? Was I?"

"Yes." She handed over the muddied pages, but before she let go, asked, "Can you not see the humor in this paper chase, my lord? So grim your expression, it is no wonder your servants—"

"Call me Lord Thorn?" he asked with smooth sarcasm.

She blinked in surprise. "No! At least they have the good grace not to do so in front of me. But they are terrified of you."

"Terrified?" That, of all that had happened, made him laugh. "You think them terrified? You could not be more mistaken. As for the humor of this paper chase . . ." He paused, considering his words. "I am not easily given to laughter."

"Really?" she said ironically, dimples peeping.

He jerked the handful of paper from her and turned toward the coach. When she fell into step beside him, he flapped the wad of ruined invitations. "Needless waste."

"Yes, but accidents happen. Is it not better to laugh when milk is spilled than to be soured over the loss of it?"

"Forgive me." Brusquely, he turned away from her as they came lee with the coach. "I've more milk to order."

Chapter Six

𝒞

Will helped Mary into the coach. "A bit prickly, is he, miss?"

"As the holly in my hat," she said with a smile. "Why do you stay with such an ill-tempered master?"

"Bark's worse than 'is bite, miss. 'E's right gentlemanly most of the time. Funny, if you only listen for it. You've seen him at his worst today."

"I do not know if I believe you, Will, but you are to be commended for defending him."

She let it go at that, wishing they had not to depend on the grouchy viscount to take them the rest of the way home, but unwilling to sacrifice Gran to the elements for no better reason than pride.

She plastered a smile upon her lips and settled herself beside the old lady, saying cheerfully, "Well, that was enough to bring roses to our cheeks, was it not, Mr. Temple?"

Young Temple crouched forlornly in the corner of the coach, his lap loaded with an uneven pile of crushed and muddied invitations, ineffectually straightening bent corners, his gaze skittering fearfully toward the door every few seconds, heartfelt sighs gusting from his throat.

"Are there any to be saved?" Mary asked gently.

Temple blinked, eyes glassy. His chin quivered. "He'll let me go for this, won't he, miss? And without a character. What'll I do?"

"Chin up, lad. No sniveling now." Gran patted his shoulder.

"My mum—the little ones—depend upon the income," he moaned.

"How old are you, Temple?" Mary asked.

"Seventeen, miss. I had hoped to start as an underbutler . . ."

"But you have been given a position of far greater responsibility," she pointed out to him, "at far greater pay."

"And far greater potential for failure, miss. I've no clue what I'm doing. Father never taught me any of this. And the other servants—they seem miffed, marm, that a nobody like me should be given opportunity over and above theirs."

"I cannot believe it is as bad as you suppose."

"You have only to walk into the house while I am there and you will see it is true." The lad had never looked more forlorn.

"As much as I should like the opportunity," Mary said, "I cannot think of an instance where I might be invited to visit a viscount."

"Unless, of course," Gran said, "you were to ask my granddaughter to assist you in addressing what invitations have not flown away, young man. She has a pretty hand, does my Mary."

"I should like that," he said. "The others have no interest in helping me see my way clear, and every interest in watching me fail."

Mary leaned forward. "Then you mustn't fail. And you must rely upon your own good sense. You have been taught to read and write?"

"Yes, but—"

"How many of the other servants are so schooled?"

"Not many, I would suppose, but—"

"No buts. Those are qualifications necessary to the job—a job the viscount wants *you* to do, and no one else."

"What am I to say to him, miss? He must think me the greatest fool!" He shrank deeper into the collar of his new coat. "He will want this back, he will." He smoothed the lapel as if to bid it fond farewell.

"Don't be ridiculous! What should you say to any man in the same circumstances?" she demanded.

He stared at her blankly.

"If they were *my* invitations, what would you say?"

"I would apologize, miss, and offer to pay damages."

"Exactly!" she said with a smile. "Now, you have only to tell him." She gestured toward the coach door, thrown open in that instant for the viscount, who entered the carriage like a cold gust of wind.

"My apologies—"

They said it in unison. Baxter, addressing the ladies, and a solemn-faced Temple, addressing him.

They both stopped. The door slammed behind him, the noise making poor terrified Temple flinch like a gun-shy horse. Was the lad petrified of him, as Miss Rivers suggested? How did one calm groundless fears?

"Apologies for the delay, ladies." Baxter settled himself. "You were saying, lad?"

Words tumbled out of Temple as if a dam had burst. "My apologies, my lord, for the unconscionable destruction of your property. I expect the losses, my lord, to be docked from my first month's pay."

Baxter witnessed Miss Rivers's reaction to the remark before he turned to face Temple. She smiled, not at him, but at the boy. He surmised from the tip of her head, that she approved, perhaps even instigated, his speech.

"A gallant offer, lad," he said, "but unnecessary. Do you think I dock Cook for every dish broken? Or the scullery maid for every cracked glass? I am to blame. I should have ordered Will and Ned to follow you inside."

"No, my lord."

"No?" Baxter did not care for contradiction, especially the contradiction of fools. The lad caught him off guard. "What do you mean, no?"

"I should have asked for their assistance, my lord. It was foolish of me to think I could carry the stack alone."

"It was," Baxter agreed, pleased the lad evidenced accountability for his actions. "And I do not suffer fools gladly. See to it that you take full advantage of my well-paid staff in the execution of any future errands, Temple."

"Yes, my lord."

"You'll catch on, lad," Mrs. Rivers murmured.

Miss Rivers simply smiled, as if she and the lad shared a secret. He wondered if he had her to thank for the boy's sudden show of backbone.

Chapter Seven

𝒞

Later that afternoon, quizzing glass in hand, Baxter sat alone in the carriage, in a section of Regent Street as upside down with construction as his life had become without the stabilizing force old Temple had been. He missed the old man! The gravelly pitch of his voice, the proud tilt of his hat. The carriage had passed an elderly gent with just such a tilt. Baxter had actually turned in the seat to make sure it was not Temple, risen from the dead, haunting him.

Someone else, of course. There was only young Temple now, and a yard-long list of things to do in preparation for a Christmas ball he privately detested—a ball already off to a bad start. Baxter sighed, consulted his watch, consulted his errands list, and thought, inexplicably, of Merry Rivers's smile.

What kept the boy?

The postmaster had set up an office at Newmann's Livery, at number 121 Regent Street, and one must clamber over and around piles of brick and plastering and mortaring materials to get to it this week. There had been no point in both of them mucking through the dust. Temple had asked that he be allowed. Baxter had agreed. He hoped the lad had learned enough from their morning's escapade to manage the mail without losing any of it to the wind.

He had not thought to see Miss Rivers or her smile again that day, but she stepped unexpectedly from the doorway, crimson cape billowing in an eye-catching cloud, mittened hands full of letters.

It was not he who brought a smile to her lips, though he regarded her most particularly through the loop of his quizzing glass, prepared to acknowledge her wave, should she recognize his coach.

She did not see him, did not look up at all as she turned her back to the wind, fingers clutching tight the one letter that appeared to gladden her heart. She tucked the others away in her reticule. Pausing in the windbreak created by a pile of brick, she impatiently tore the seal on that letter.

The wind unfolded it for her.

Through his quizzing glass, he studied her minutely as she scanned the page, her lips absently forming words as she read. Her smile faded, then disappeared.

He thought at first her expression was distorted by an unevenness in the windowpane, but the window was blameless.

Her news was not good news. The light left her face. She stuffed the missive into her pocket, and made agitated search for a handkerchief, which she raised to her mouth to stifle an unhappy cry.

The smile he had long disparaged, he longed for now. Far better to see her eternally happy than to watch her features distort with despair.

What news did this post bring her? Who had the power to so discompose her? Disappointment bowed her shoulders as she took silent communion with her handkerchief, her features troubled by an expression all too familiar, an expression he had seen more than once in looking in the mirror, in studying intently his own blue eyes.

Loneliness. This unwanted letter brought her loneliness. The emotion was unmistakable.

She never looked up—never knew he watched her from the coach. She thought herself alone on the street, her emotions a private thing, until a fellow leading a horse emerged from the livery, and behind him, Temple, carrying a box upon his shoulder.

She no more than glanced their way, their appearance rendering a transformation in her that startled Baxter more than he wanted to admit.

When she realized she was no longer alone with her unhappiness, she squared her shoulders, tucked away her handkerchief, and fixed her lips in the same smile he had until that moment considered completely, and annoyingly, genuine.

He had thought her such a happy creature. He now knew himself mistaken.

Chapter Eight

❦

Mary did not expect to see him again that day, did not expect to see anyone. Her afternoons were for the most part busy but solitary—just she, the ticking of Gran's clocks, and her list of chores and errands. During these quiet afternoons she missed her family most. The noise and exuberant presence of others was a constant in Glastonbury. Housework went swiftly divided between four sisters and three brothers.

Alone, chores were an interminable battle, an unconquerable foe. She waged war with quiet resolve.

Her mother had considered her invitations to stay with Gran a blessing. "What an opportunity, Mary! You shall see a fine part of London from Gran's new apartments. You will have to learn the ordering of her servants. She is bound to have half a dozen. You will have the luxury of a room to yourself. Gran is certain to see you fitted out in London style, as she did Ellen last year, and Evie the year before that. Only think if you could find yourself a husband!"

Mary had refrained from pointing out that neither Ellen or Evie had returned from London with a husband.

"Come now, show me a smile, Mary," Mother had said. "None of my children get along so well with my mother-in-law as you do, my dear. I have every hope she may introduce you to some polite society, and all expectation she has remembered you favorably in her will, leaving at least one of my children well provided for."

Her sisters envied her chance to see the latest fashions. Her brothers insisted she must write to them of horses and vehicles—like Viscount Balfour's coach pulling to a halt even now below her in the street. She paused in her dusting to peep through the lace curtain. An intriguing gentleman, the viscount, Lord Thorn—an interesting morning to write home about.

The door knocker sounded with a brisk bang, the noise out of place, loud enough to wake Gran, mildly alarming.

She flew downstairs to see who it might be, tearing off her unsightly dusting cap and apron. She stuffed them, along with her feather duster, under a cushion in Gran's sitting room. She tidied a stray lock of hair in a mirror over the settee before she flung open the door with every effort to look cool, calm, and collected—a fine young lady who had no need to do housework.

Lord Thorn stood upon the step, one buff-gloved hand anchoring the brim of his new hat, the other raised to knock again.

"What a pleasant surprise, my Lord," she said, smiling at him uneasily, wondering what in heaven's name prompted his call.

"Miss Rivers." He tipped his hat. "How do you and your grandmother do this blustery afternoon? Nothing to trouble you since this morning, I trust?" He peered at her intently as she responded.

"I am well, my lord. And you? What brings you to our door?"

"I know this is going to sound presumptuous," he said, "but may I see your hand?"

She blinked at him, dismayed. Her hand? Out of habit, her unpampered hands were tucked into the folds of her skirt. Hands that regularly scrubbed floors and coal scuttles, wielding duster, broom, and polishing rag were best not seen in the full light of day. She made a point of clipping and cleaning her nails regularly, and yet they always seemed a trifle uneven. The texture of her skin was not as dewy, soft, or pale as she would like.

"I am given to understand it is a fair one," he said.

She smiled uneasily. "How very kind of you to say so,

but could you have mistaken my hand with someone else's?"

"Perhaps I do." He stepped backward, glancing with a frown in the direction of his town house. "I go on Temple's word. He assured me your grandmother said you had a fair hand."

She laughed, feeling stupid beyond measure. "Oh! You mean my handwriting?"

His brow puckered. "What else?"

What she wanted to do was shut out the cold and finish the dusting. What she said was, "Will you step inside—out of the wind?"

He hesitated. "Your grandmother?"

"Asleep. You will not disturb her rest if we go quietly."

He stepped inside, removing his hat. "She will not be distressed to discover you entertain gentlemen callers while she sleeps?"

Mary leaned her head out the door. "There are more of you?" she asked mischievously.

He almost broke a smile, his lips tightening in the restraint of it.

"She will not be disturbed to hear our kind neighbor, Lord Balfour, has called," she whispered. "This way, please."

She showed him past Gran's ground-floor room and up the stairs. To her horror, the door to her bedchamber hung open, bed and washstand in clear sight, dust balls beneath the bed, a damp towel strung up to dry. She hastened to shut it, mortified to discover he followed too close upon her heels, colliding with her as she turned away from the bedchamber door, the stairwell suddenly plunged into greater darkness with its closing.

For an instant she stood pressed to his chest, buttocks banging his hip, hand slipping from the doorknob. Her bedchamber door flew open. Her heel came down on his toe.

"Ow!" He made every effort to stifle the involuntary cry.

His foot a troubling unevenness beneath her heel, she jumped aside immediately without thinking, teetering

heart in mouth upon the edge of the top step of the
stairs, sure she must fall. He grabbed her elbow on one
side, on the other her waist, as if they meant to dance
a jig, then pulled her closer than called for in any dance
she knew, his chest hard against her back, grip firm.

"I do beg your pardon," he said, his breath against
her cheek. "I thought you might fall."

"And so I might have," she said, breathlessly, pulling
away from him to smooth her skirt.

She shut the door again, plunging them into gloom.
"I had hoped you would not see this room," she said.
"It is in sad disarray."

"Difficult to find good help these days," he said.

"Indeed." Cheeks burning, she directed him to the
parlor, where a single tall window looked out over a
columned balcony to the street.

She was pleased to see he did not limp as he examined
the room, quizzing glass raised, his attention fixing lon-
gest on the needleworked fire screen she had made, and
the framed watercolor portraits above the marble fire
surround, also by her hand.

"Pleasant," he said.

She hurried to put away the cross-stitch she meant to
give her mother for Christmas, afraid he must have noticed the dust on the mantel and picture frames. The
grate stood frightfully full of ashes. The window bore a
rash of fingerprints. The upstairs was always last on her
list of things to do. Gran saw less of it than the downstairs. She was less likely to complain that the maid had
not done her job.

"A bit dusty, I'm afraid," she apologized. "Gran does
not often feel fit enough to mount the stairs, and so this
part of the house is always last to be cleaned. Do you
care for tea?" she asked.

"Shall I ring for it?" He reached for the pull beside
the fire screen.

She forced a smile. "You may ring, but no one will
answer. We have recently let go our maid."

"The scullery maid or footman cannot put on the
kettle?"

She smiled harder, cheeks arching. "They could."

He reached again for the pull.

"If we had either."

"Ah!" His hand fell away, the differences in their circumstances sinking in. She could see the beginnings of a frown trouble his features. "Tell me, did you mean to race downstairs and fix the tea yourself?"

"Yes. It would only take a minute. My fair hand, you see, is capable in many ways."

He walked to the window, his lean figure cutting a fine silhouette against the light.

The smudged fingerprints taunted her.

"I would not impose upon your hospitality. It is enough I come to ask a favor of you."

She let down the lid of her blessedly tidy secretary, positioned to catch the best light from the window. From a pigeonhole she pulled a curled sheaf of paper on which she had lately tallied her gran's sadly dwindling accounts.

"A sample of my hand." She held it out to him.

He caught up the pages, peered at them briefly, handed them back to her, and turned the quizzing glass instead on the view of the street. "I see. An excellent hand it is! I wonder if you would mind terribly—"

"You wish me to assist in addressing the invitations to your ball?" she interrupted to suggest.

He cocked his head to look at her through the silver-rimmed quizzer, one thin brow arched high. "Are you a mind reader?"

She flushed. "N-no."

He waved the quizzer like a baton. "I was convinced my nanny was a mind reader when I was a boy. Temple came very near to it in the years before he died. Perhaps I am too predictable. Yes, I wondered if I might induce you to help me. Young Temple assures me his hand is not fit for the task, and I do not relish the idea of doing it alone."

"How many invitations, my lord?"

"No more than two hundred."

"So many!" She gasped.

"You will be richly compensated, of course." He jingled the silver in his pocket.

She cleared her throat, considering how best to refuse him.

He dropped, quite unexpectedly, to one knee at her feet. "Please, Miss Rivers, I beg your hand." Mischief marked the pale cerulean of his eyes, the lazy tilt of his head.

She smiled nervously, uncomfortable with his pose, tempted to grab him by the shoulders and force him to rise. "I beg you will stand, my lord. The floor is dirty. The knees on your breeches will be soiled, and this looks and sounds too much like another kind of proposal to please me."

He smiled, lowering his eyelids to half mast. "Your answer?"

"I cannot, my lord."

He rose.

She longed to brush off his knees, to run in with a mop to tidy the floor, to chase him out of the house with it.

Unconcerned with the state of his breeches, he focused his quizzing glass instead on her. "You will not give me your hand?"

"No. I am very attached to it."

He let loose a harsh bark of laughter and melodramatically pressed his hand to his chest. "You break my heart."

It was sarcastically said.

She wished him gone, wished she had four more hands for all the tasks she must accomplish today. And yet, she was reluctant to offend him. He was the only titled gentleman to number among her acquaintances. "Will it please you to make temporary use of me?"

He sighed heavily, pocketing the quizzing glass. "You do not love me, will not give me your hand, and yet I may make temporary use of you? Not marriage, but an affair we discuss, Miss Rivers."

Her mouth fell open, but only briefly. She had smart-mouthed brothers. They had tested her with better taunts than this.

She responded straight-faced. "You may depend upon my willing participation in this affair for the next two hours. No more than that. Gran usually naps that long, and then I must prepare her supper."

His tone changed, no longer in jest. "I am grateful."

"Grateful enough to invite Gran to your Christmas Eve ball?" Her turn to taunt.

He laughed. "Wants to come, does she?"

"It is her favorite holiday. And this one may be her last." She wondered why she told him. She had not intended to reveal so much.

He regarded her quietly. "But of course I intended to ask the two of you."

"Really? Because I chased after your invitations and will now address them?"

"Because . . ." He stared at her a moment, his expression inscrutable. "Because I would like you to come."

Chapter Nine

℃

He sent Temple in first, carrying a small lacquered portable secretary into which had been packed a list of whom he meant to invite to his ball, a blotter, a ponce box, pens, nibs, ink, a box of dark red wax, his family seal, and a metal rule.

Will followed with two great silver candelabra and set to work filling them with fresh candles pulled from one of the hampers Ned carried.

These wafted aromatically of the gingerbread Cook had made fresh that afternoon. The hamper's primary burden was a great assortment of food. Baxter had not been sure what Miss Rivers and her Gran liked. He brought up the rear of their invasion with the broken parcels of invitations that had survived the street.

"We shall require a larger working surface, and chairs for all," he said to Miss Rivers as he walked in.

"Yes," she agreed. "Will and Ned have only to bring the rector's table down from the attic, and Temple, two more chairs from downstairs."

"Yes, miss," they responded at once.

"Quietly, if you will, so as not to wake Mrs. Rivers," Baxter reminded them.

"Yes, my lord."

"What smells so good?" Merry asked when they were alone.

"Supper." Baxter hoped she would not refuse it.

"How thoughtful."

He tried not to stare too openly at the tempting curve of her backside as she bent to light one of the candles at the hearth, using it to light the others. She had bumped against him with that generally untouchable part of her anatomy in their collision in the hallway. His hip still tingled with the memory. His body did, in fact, remember every inch of her that had banged against him, a throbbing sort of memory that had nothing to do with bruises.

He distracted himself from such untoward thought by rearranging the room in preparation for extra furniture.

In doing these simple tasks, in the intrusion of familiar objects from home, the room in some way became his, as comfortable and welcoming as the smile she turned on his servants when they returned.

"Put that there!" Baxter said.

"That goes here!" she said. In unison they directed the table to two different spots at exactly the same moment.

Will went one way, Ned the other. The table jerked them to a stop in the middle. They glared at one another.

"My lord," Will said.

"Miss?" Ned inquired.

"To catch the light," she suggested, pointing.

"That we may not be observed so readily from the street." He directed them to another spot.

"We have only to draw the curtain." She put words into action.

"And then there will be no light from the window," he pointed out.

"As he says," she said.

"As she says," he contradicted her in the same breath.

Will and Ned and the table danced a confused jig. Temple stood waiting in the doorway, hugging the back of a heavy chair, his face getting pinker by the minute.

Merry Rivers laughed, a loud, unfettered laugh, her hands flying up to stifle the sound.

Will snickered. Ned guffawed. Temple set down the chair with a sigh.

Baxter cut a bow and said, "I beg your pardon, Miss Rivers. It is your home, and I act as if I were master

of it. You will do as Miss Rivers wishes," he directed
his servants.

Merry stopped laughing, wiping her eyes, and pointed
to a spot both close to the window, and yet out of the
direct line of sight from the street.

Baxter threw open the drapery saying wryly, "Very
diplomatic, Miss Rivers."

"Merry," she said.

"In what way merry?" he asked.

"My name. You may call me Merry." She blushed,
suddenly awkward, uncertain in directing his servants in
the placement of things on the table and in the arrangement of chairs.

"Is this to your liking?" she asked at last.

"Excellent!" He tore the list of names down the middle, placing each half on the table before two facing
chairs. "You and I at this end, Merry. Will blotting, Ned
folding, and Temple at the foot of the table, affixing wax
and seal."

"Splendid!" Taking the chair he indicated, she picked
up her half of the list.

They set to work, pens scratching, nibs clinking against
ink wells, the ponce box thumping as Will blotted, paper
crackling in protest as Ned folded, and an occasional
muffled yip as Temple singed himself along with the wax.

There was a mind-numbing rhythm to the process as
the gold-edged paper formed a beautiful creamy pile of
finished invitations. Nothing distracted Mary from the
careful forming of her letters, until Lord Balfour
bumped his boot tip against her slipper.

She looked up to acknowledge his "Beg pardon" with
a blush, and found herself looking straight into the
wrong side of the viscount's quizzing glass lens, which
he raised with squinting scowl to regard her response.

In seeing his nose greatly diminished by the glass, at
last it penetrated her brain that Lord Thorn used the
quizzer not that he might peer scornfully down his nose
at the world. He truly did not see well!

"My lord, forgive me if this sounds forward . . ."

Such a beginning could only serve to prick up the ears

of Will, Ned, and Temple, who all three bent closer to their work, as if they were deaf and mute to such exchanges.

"No, no. It is I who must apologize for rudely bumping your—"

"Not that." She stopped him, then stopped herself from blurting out the words, wondering if she was not the greatest fool to think she might instruct a viscount.

"What then?" His brow furrowed as he narrowed eyes again to peruse her expression.

Out with it, she instructed herself. The worst he can do is never speak to you again. "If you cannot see," she blurted, "why not wear spectacles, instead of squinting ferociously at everyone through that dreadful quizzing glass?"

He reacted as if she had struck him. All movement at the table stilled for an instant before renewing with added vigor.

"Is it dreadful?" He regarded the quizzing glass, a pretty silver-rimmed thing with an exquisitely etched handle. "I always thought it far less obtrusive than spectacles, which must be pushed about on one's nose, or swabbed off because the cold fogs them over."

She smiled, regretting the harshness of her remark immediately. "Perhaps you are right. I do apologize for saying anything."

She went back to writing the next address.

His pen did not similarly resume its scratching. "Do you know I began this morning believing you incapable of either frowns or rudeness? I find myself mistaken on both points."

She squeezed her eyes shut, wishing she might squeeze back in time to undo her words.

"Come now"—he tapped her fingers with the silver rim of the quizzing glass—"defend yourself."

She sighed, put down her pen, and held out her hand. "May I demonstrate?"

He handed over the glass.

"It is not the quizzer that is unpleasant so much as what it does to you, my lord." She lifted the glass to her eye and scowled at him.

Magnified, his brows rose. His eyes widened in alarm. Clarence blue, she thought, and a very pretty color it was.

He sat back, smoothing his expression. "That bad, is it?"

"Perhaps I exaggerate," she suggested, thrusting the quizzing glass toward him.

He waved a hand dismissively. "No backing down now, Miss Forthright." He reached for the glass, misjudged the distance, and grabbed her hand instead.

Her breath caught, hand flinched, and fingers let go. The quizzing glass hit the table with an ominous clink, then bounced to floor in an unpromising explosion of glass.

"Oh, no!" she cried, thrusting her head beneath the table.

He bent down as well, reaching simultaneously.

Their hands and heads bumped.

"Ow!" she cried.

"Damn!" Baxter flinched, glass slicing his thumb as she jerked one way and he the other. A hiss of pained surprise whistled through his teeth.

Temple bent to peer at them from the far end of the table.

"Oh, dear," Mary said. "You bleed."

Will and Ned now bent heads to look upon them as well.

"It is customary when one's thumb has been rudely sliced open." More prickly than ever, Baxter held the dripping digit away from the rug.

"Oh, I do beg your pardon." Without thinking, she dragged the plain white fichu from her neck, that she might press it to his wound.

He tried to refuse the piece of cloth. "No, really! It is only a scratch, and but one more way in which I suffer for this stupid ball."

"I am such a fool." She laughed, kneeling that she might pick up the silver handle of the shattered quizzer. "You must allow me to replace this."

They were staring at her, round-eyed—Ned, Will, and Temple. Baxter, too, blue eyes at a squint.

"No, no. Get up, Miss Rivers." He dove under the table and grabbed her elbow abruptly, hauling her to her feet. "Temple will get that, won't you, Temple?"

"Of course, my lord."

"As for replacing the glass . . ." He stood in such a way that his body blocked her view of the others. "It has recently been suggested to me that a set of spectacles might better suit." He jerked the handle of the broken quizzer twice in the direction of her neckline, gaze dropping swiftly to her bosom and swiftly rising again, his brows angled suggestively. "There is so much I feel I am missing a good look at, don't you see?"

She glanced down.

"Oh!" She did see.

They had been staring, Will, Ned, and Temple, not at her, but at the cleavage she carelessly revealed in handing over her fichu.

Her hand rose to her throat that she might cover herself.

"Are you chilled, Miss Rivers?" Baxter suggested.

There was an undeniable draft.

"Perhaps a shawl is in order," he suggested.

She nodded. "You will excuse me?"

He bowed.

She made herself walk rather than run to her room for a fresh fichu and shawl.

Closing the door behind her, she leaned against it, mortified, thus hearing every order Lord Thorn barked at his servants.

"Temple, this glass must be picked up before anyone else cuts themselves."

"Yes, my lord," came Temple's low-voiced reply.

"Will, Ned, thrust your eyes back into their sockets and return the room to order."

"Yes, my lord."

"And Temple . . ."

"Yes, my lord."

"We shall visit Mr. Carpenter first thing in the morning."

"Yes, my lord. I shall make a notation."

Chapter Ten

ℭ

Baxter hovered in the downstairs doorway, propped against the jamb, listening to the low murmur of voices, his servants in the sitting room, the Riverses in the old lady's bedroom on the backside of the stairwell. The darkness of the stairs led to greater darkness above, a ghostly darkness. He could almost feel Temple hovering a few steps above him, watching. Such an evening would have never happened had Temple not died—a strange idea.

Merry had brought all the lamps and candles downstairs.

"We practice economies," she explained.

He was unaccustomed to such measures. His town house blazed with light, top to bottom, from dusk until such time as he cared to go to bed, no matter how many candles it took. There had always been money to buy more, always would be now that he had come into his uncle's inheritance.

His view of the world was limited to its customary blur, without so much as the occasional moment of clarity his quizzing glass afforded. He felt more isolated and alone than ever, as if he sat at the bottom of a well, the stir of life around him distant, separate. He did not belong to this world, this house, to the sweetness of her voice, to her imagined smiles as she roused the old woman.

With a pang he realized he would like to.

"How are you feeling, Gran? Peckish?" she asked, her voice so gentle and loving it brought a lump to his throat. "I have the most wonderful surprise! Guests for supper."

He and his food constituted the surprise, and yet he did not feel wonderful, only lonely, unloved, no one to ask him how he did, no one to surprise him. He had just addressed hundreds of invitations to people who knew no more than the surface of him, all that he allowed. The affection he heard expressed mutedly from the bedroom was as foreign to him as if they spoke Chinese.

He did not know what to do with the restlessness and discomfort roused within him, other than long to be done with this evening's business, to be home in comfortable seclusion, locked in routine, alone but for the servants, no conversation to be made, no niceties to observe, no expectation of politeness and sociability to fulfill. At home he need struggle for no thought other than those generated by a good book and an excellent snifter of brandy. He liked it that way.

"Who is it, child? Have your sisters come for Christmas as you hoped they would?"

"No, Gran, not family—Lord Balfour. I do not think we should count on family for Christmas. I have had a letter." Her voice thinned. "They do not mean to come."

The letter.

So it was her family who disappointed her. He knew too well the feeling. Had old Temple really been there, he would have placed a hand on his shoulder, saying, "Never mind, young man. You will make a family of your own one day." As he had said on more than one Christmas when Baxter had heard the same news about parents not coming.

"Here you are, Gran. A bit of water to splash your face, a fresh cap to cover your head. I shall braid your hair the way you like it, shall I?"

She reopened wounds with her sugared tone, their pain as distant as the activities of Will and Ned and Temple in preparing the table. Their shadows loomed upon the far wall as they shook out linen and napery, clattering china and silver.

He remembered shadows on the wall as a child—his parents returning from their evening's entertainments;

his mother, hair piled high, feathers bobbing, pearls glinting in the darkness. She slipped in, quiet as a wraith, smelling of tuberose, drop earrings jingling faintly as she bent to kiss his forehead.

On rare occasions, the reek of cigar drifted in the door to his room, Lord Balfour's shadow never detaching itself from the doorjamb, his voice hushed in saying, "We leave first thing in the morning for France, Nanny. Home sometime after Christmas."

It had seemed an eternity to the child.

Nanny proved his only constant, stoutly pinafored, hair in a tight knot, a whiff of peppermint as she bent to check that he was safely tucked in.

"Did the girl come to clean this afternoon?" the old woman called.

"No, Gran."

And never will again, he thought. Had Merry Rivers not just told him they had let the maid go?

"We shall have to let her go." The old woman echoed his thoughts

"Yes, Gran."

Nanny Lumley had always insisted upon strict cleanliness and competent performance in the servants. She had loved him. He knew that now, but she had never hugged him, never kissed his cheek.

Her cough had been given a name. Consumption, he was told as Temple packed up his bags to send him away to school.

"That they might make a man of you." His father peered at him through a haze of cigar smoke. "You've been tied to the old woman's apron strings too long, my boy."

School. The very thought made his knees weak. He abandoned the prop of the doorway for the nearest chair, a Queen Anne that had seen better days, lumpy cushion askew.

He straightened it, found it not so much lumpy as endowed with a bundle of rags. Not rags—an apron, a mobcap, a feather duster.

He squinted at the things, confused. The maid's? No. Miss Rivers had apologized for the dust upstairs. He lifted the cap to his nose. It smelled of vanilla, cloves, and roses, as she did. He carefully folded the cap back into the apron, considering its significance, its placement under the cushion.

Figures rose in his mind, a row of figures. He closed his eyes, trying to recall. What was it he had seen in the sample of her handwriting? A dwindling tally.

He looked about. The chair had seen better days. The settee, too. A dwindling fortune?

They approached from the hallway, Miss Rivers whispering, "Are you sure you've no need for the chair, Gran?"

"Lend me your arm, my dear. I shall do just fine," the old lady assured her.

Hastily, he tucked the apron bundle back under the cushion and went to lend the old woman his arm, surprised to discover it was not a permanent disability she suffered. Rheumatism he surmised from the careful way she took her steps.

Chapter Eleven

℃

Mary saw them from the window of the upstairs sitting room the following morning as she dusted—Lord Baxter and his secretary. She abandoned the duster at once, pulled the mobcap from her curls, and checked the riotous arrangement of her hair in the mirror before she took the stairs at a run, caught up her cape by the door and called out over her shoulder, "I am just stepping across the street, Gran. Back in a minute."

"All right, love," Gran called cheerily from the kitchen, where she sat cracking nuts for their Christmas cooking. Mince pies this afternoon, and the Christmas pudding, to be wrapped away in oiled cloth to age.

A bright, cold day; the wind had died. Mary waited for three carriages to pass before she darted across the street to the corner of Regent and Jermyn, the heavy coin purse in her pocket bumping her thigh with every step. They needed the money, and yet she could not keep it. Would not. It hurt her pride.

Carpenter and Westley's had a faux columned front and a sign stating that they were not just lens makers and spectacle salesmen, but opticians. Another sign in the window proclaimed that bifocals might be made up upon special request.

Mary paused, considering what she must say, blankly staring at the display of folding lorgnettes, single lens spyglasses in fans, on walking sticks, and on watch fobs. There were also quizzers, prospect glasses, perspective glasses, green-tinted "weak eye" glasses, opera glasses, and lorgnettes with mirrored arms for watching what went on behind one. She watched what went on before her, gaze drawn to the scene inside the shop, where Baxter and Temple bent over a glass case with Mr. Carpenter, friendly, graying, a pair of steel and tortoiseshell spectacles perched on his pudgy nose.

She had enjoyed Lord Thorn's none-too-prickly company the night before, enjoyed addressing invitations to the Christmas Eve ball. How satisfying to send off the promise of fun and good food, entertainment and good company to so many people.

They had chatted like old friends over the feast Baxter had brought with him, the servants at the foot of the table, everyone relaxed and convivial.

The evening might have been labeled a perfect joy had she not found the bag of silver left upon the mantelpiece. *Payment.* He meant to pay her. They were not friends as she had begun to believe, but employed and employer—nothing more.

The bell over the door jingled when she gathered courage and pushed her way in. Carpenter raised his head to call, "Good morning, Miss Rivers. How's your Gran? Be with you in just a minute."

Baxter looked up, squinting. "Miss Rivers? What a happy coincidence. You must assist me."

Mr. Carpenter evidenced a trace of surprise at such a peremptory demand.

"Must I, my lord?" She smiled as she asked, but was not at all amused by his manner.

"It is only fitting you should choose a replacement for my quizzer," Baxter suggested dryly.

"Why? Because I broke it?"

The faintest hint of a smile touched his lips.

Their exchange threw the shopkeeper's features into even more interesting disorder.

"Not at all," Baxter said languidly. "Because Temple gives me no opinion, and I know you to be decidedly free with yours."

Mary grew serious as she drew the jingling leather pouch from her pocket and placed it upon the counter. "Actually, I came to return this to you, my lord."

He squinted at the pouch with a sigh. "But you did

me a great service, Miss Rivers, and at short notice. You deserve adequate compensation. I shall not feel free to cal upon your services in this affair in future if you do not allow me to compensate you for your time and energies."

An attentive stillness seized Carpenter.

"I cannot accept payment, my lord," Mary insisted. "I offered you my assistance freely."

Carpenter blinked several times in quick succession, as though her words shocked him. Temple hovered silently, eyes downcast.

Baxter slid a quick glance in Carpenter's direction. The hint of a smile touched the corners of his mouth.

It occurred to Mary that the word affair coupled with the idea of payment lay open to gross misinterpretation.

"I mean . . ." she said.

"I know perfectly well what you mean, Mary," Baxter said wryly. "You mean to give up one evening to me, and then refuse my offer of payment so that you no longer feel obliged, and I shall feel I take advantage of you."

"Not at all. It is I who take advantage of you," Mary protested. "Unless . . . you will allow me to pay for the replacement of your smashed glass, as we discussed."

Baxter's eyes narrowed. "I do not remember approving such a nonsensical notion."

"We were under the table," she reminded him.

Carpenter's head jerked.

"Ah, yes," Baxter said. "Forgive me, my mind was at that moment preoccupied."

Heat rushed to Mary's cheeks as she remembered what had preoccupied all present.

Baxter picked up one of the sets of spectacles. "I thoroughly enjoyed the generous favor of our evening together, Miss Rivers," he said.

A fresh spate of coughing seized Carpenter.

"Are you ill, sir?" Baxter asked, all concern, leaning over the counter to pound him on the back. "Temple, fetch Mr. Carpenter some water."

"Back of the shop," Carpenter wheezed, waving his hand.

"Take him, please, Temple," Baxter said quietly.

"Yes, my lord." Temple led Carpenter away through a curtained doorway to the back room.

As the sound of Carpenter's discomfort receded, Miss Rivers, with a worried look through the window said, "I should be getting back."

Baxter lifted a pair of heavy dark tortoiseshell glasses to his nose. "What do you think?"

"Those are made to be tied on." Miss Rivers reached out to assist, as he had hoped she might.

From behind him, she took hold of the strings, fingers skimming his temples.

Baxter closed his eyes, shocked by the power of her touch. She straightened the string, the movement pulling the tortoiseshell frames taut against the bridge of his nose, as if she touched him there as well.

He was unused to contact with anyone other than his valet. Certainly he had not been touched by a woman since Nanny Lumley had cared for him as a child. Not that he did not like women, not that he had not fantasized about intimacies. However, he was slow to trust, had never cared for the idea of going to a prostitute for satisfaction of his fantasies, and had, with his sarcastic tongue, frightened away most of the women of his own class thrust upon him by hopeful mamas in search of a monied match for their daughters.

To be touched now, the tips of his ears grazed, set every cell, every iota of his being afire with the languid brush of suppressed desire. The string moved in his hair. Her fingers straightened it, separating the strands—her touch vibrating along his temples—stirring feeling in so many parts of him at once, all words, thought, and feeling tied themselves in an inarticulate knot.

"There." She smoothed a lock of hair from beneath the strings and stepped back to face him. He felt the wisp of her breath, savored the odor of toast and tea, and opened his eyes.

The world was a greater blur than usual. "I cannot see at all well," he said.

"The lenses must be very wrong." She laughed. "In

keeping with the frames. They do not suit you at all. Would you try something else?"

"I would," he agreed, "as soon as I can untangle myself." He slipped the knot she had made, only to find his hair caught in the string.

"Ah." She reached out to help, fingers touching his, not lingering seductively, but helpful, as a sister's hands might be, had he any sisters. Efficient and gentle, her touch, far more arousing to him than seduction ever might have been. A few gentle tugs and she freed him.

Miss Rivers bent over the trays of spectacles as he smoothed his hair, recovering himself. "Do you like tortoiseshell, or would you be willing to try something else?"

"What are my choices?" He squinted at the blurred line of her profile.

"Gold, silver, iron. I believe these are ivory." She held up a very pale pair. "Then there is tortoiseshell, bone, or horn."

"What do you think suits me? I trust your opinion." She seemed surprised.

"Well . . ." She held the folded ivory spectacles before his face. "These are too pale for your complexion." The world swam clearer for a moment, clear enough that he could see the spectacles did not impress her.

"Yes. Ivory is out. Shall we try the gold?"

He slid them obligingly onto his nose.

The world went briefly in and then out of focus as the spectacles did their best to ride slowly down his nose. He thought for an instant he saw Temple standing beside her, an impossibility so alarming he said *no* with untoward violence, and when she looked at him quizzically, no ghost beside her, he wrenched them from his nose to look about the shop, saying, "Too heavy."

"Ah," she said. "Perhaps silver. Do you want them collapsible?"

"Not really." He squinted at the empty space beside her, wondering what trick of light and shadow had betrayed him so completely. The hair on the back of his neck prickled uncomfortably. He ran a finger along the edge of his collar without much relief.

"Perhaps these with the extendable arms? I think the ones with the hinged nose bridge look odd."

He put on the pair she held out for him. Lightweight, the lenses small and round, they perched upon his nose comfortably enough. The world fell into focus. No Temple.

Better than that, he saw her, really saw her for the first time—a face unblurred, mouth, nose, and eyes crisply delineated, every curling strand of her hair discernible, every lash distinct, brown eyes revealed not brown at all, but hazel, specks of gold in them. Her complexion, clear and pale, had a marvelous delicacy. Her mouth, more than anything else, drew his attention and held it. Hers was an unnaturally wide mouth, her lips the perfect Cupid's bow he remembered, her teeth straight and white and even. He wondered if that mouth had ever been kissed.

"How's that?" she asked, staring at him intently.

"Amazing!" He breathed the word with awe, which made her blink. He did not stop to explain, his eyes hungry to see more. He examined the shop, Mr. Carpenter and Temple as they emerged from the backroom, the window, and through it, Regent Street. He could read quite clearly on the far side the sign for Hill and Co., Tailor and Military Warehouse.

"Absolutely amazing," he breathed. "I can count every brick on the face of my house."

He did not want to blink, did not want to close his eyes on this new world, for risk of losing it again, this world he had been missing. "Good God!" he said, hushed, stunned. "Is this what everyone else sees?"

Miss Rivers made a sympathetic noise, dark eyes shining, mouth upturned, dimples playing. Her beauty struck him anew.

Her smile faded. "You stare, my lord."

"Pray forgive me, Merry." He stepped closer, unable to wrench his gaze from her face. "I would memorize your every feature."

"Would you?"

"Absolutely. You are responsible for this miracle of vision I experience."

"I must make a habit of breaking gentlemen's quizzing glasses it would seem." A mischievous gleam lit her eyes. The curve of her mouth was exquisite.

"I had no idea you were so pretty, Miss Rivers."

Carpenter chuckled. "You should have come to me sooner, my lord."

Rendered temporarily speechless, she tempered their compliments, saying, "I wonder what you will say when you encounter the true beauties of London."

"I have no idea," he said. "But I've a great desire to see many things with these fresh eyes of mine. Tell me, do I look ridiculous?"

She regarded him, head cocked. So lovely were her features that he hoped, above all things, she did not find him repulsive. She smiled, a smile to make his pulse race. "See for yourself." She pointed to the mirror Mr. Carpenter held out to him.

He regarded himself with interest. The silver-framed spectacles were not terribly attractive. They got in the way of his face. The thought generated a frown.

"Come now," she said at his elbow, her face framed in the mirror beside his. "No frowning, my lord. It was in an effort to do away with frowns that I suggested spectacles."

"You do not think me a spectacle in them?"

He startled her with the question. She did not know what to say in reply to his uneasy vanity. He read every nuance of her expression as never before. And then she smiled and, he could see, used the pleasant turn of her lips like a shield.

"Be plain with me," he insisted.

She slid an uneasy glance toward Mr. Carpenter.

"I think, my lord, a gentleman is never so handsome as when he can see clearly," she said.

Carpenter bowed from behind his counter. "I think, Miss Rivers, that you see clearest of all."

Chapter Twelve

C

Mary did not expect a pair of spectacles to make such a difference. And yet, they did. A wall she had not known existed between them fell. It was not just that Baxter no longer squinted, no longer frowned. He looked at her—saw her—as no man ever had before. Not her father, certainly not her brothers, and while there had been men in Glastonbury who admired her with their glances, none crept, as Charles Thornton Baxter did, into the heart of her, examining her with an awareness too delving to ignore.

A thief, his gaze stole her breath, robbed her of secrets. Lord Balfour had given an impression of remoteness before. No more.

She had, in past encounters, found it easy to remember him a viscount, far above her in rank, status, and financial situation. The distance of his gaze had distanced him. Now she forgot class distinction, forgot to remain guarded in her feelings. He stared at her with unmitigated fascination, and she felt inclined to return that stare.

"If you will not accept my money, Merry Rivers, how can I repay you?" he asked as they stepped from the shop, his spectacles paid for with the money she had refused of him.

He offered his arm, eyes twinkling. She felt compelled to accept it.

"I am happy to help," she said, afraid he would hear the pounding of her heart.

"Not good enough." Gaze sweeping the street, he

fixed his attention on the business opposite and struck out across the road. "Come! I've an idea."

She exchanged a confused look with Temple, who trotted ahead to hold the door for them.

"Very good, Temple." Baxter nodded his approval.

Mr. Hill, himself, whiskers thicker than ever, paunch growing ever more pronounced, greeted Mary as she stepped into the smell of wool, boot blacking, and brass polish, into a world of nothing but military accouterment.

What did he think to give her here?

"Miss Mary! How's your Gran?"

"Does everyone on the street know you?" Baxter murmured under his breath, no bite to the words other than that of envy.

She flushed, more than a little pleased a viscount should find anything to envy in her.

"Mr. Hill, my lord, proprietor of this noble establishment," she introduced them. "Do you know Lord Balfour, Mr. Hill?"

"We've never met, though we are neighbors." Baxter extended his hand in greeting.

Mr. Hill waggled the stub end of his right arm, causing Mary a moment's concern. She had not thought to warn Baxter of Hill's infirmity.

Hill had no qualms about explaining his loss. "Beg pardon, my lord, I've no longer a right to shake. You must settle for the left that is left. Lost the other in Salamanca, you see. I miss it greatly when it comes to shaking a man's hand."

"Indeed, I understand." Baxter clasped Hill's hale hand between his two, the enthusiasm of both grasp and reply a relief to Mary.

Her composure was short-lived.

Mr. Hill's chin whiskers bristled as he asked brusquely, "How can you understand, young man? Too young to serve against Boney, unless I miss my mark."

"Correct, sir. I was fifteen in fifteen. I did not have opportunity to serve, and perhaps best I did not."

"Why so, my lord? Have you not the stomach for fighting?"

"Is it not stomach we Baxters lack, sir, but vision"—
he pointed to his new spectacles—"and survival instincts.
I lost an uncle to the fighting, and I miss him at least as
much as you miss your hand."

"How sad!" Mary shivered, chilled.

"Yes," Baxter said briskly. "Sadder still to think it is
in his passing that my fortune was made, some of which
I hope to spend with you today, Mr. Hill."

With no more than a few words he managed to turn
the conversation from maudlin to mercenary.

They passed by tables piled high with scarlet, chalk
white, and blue breeches, gleaming canary-topped jackboots, a wall thick with ready-made jackets piped and
laced in white or gold, brass and gold buttons gleaming.
Above the racks rose tightly packed shelves of shakos
and two-cornered hats, perched like brightly plumed
birds so thick were the feathers, cockades, and glittering bullion.

"How can I help you, my lord?"

"Have you any secondhand breeches and coats, of a
design or style no longer used by any regiment?"

"I do, my lord, I do. Whatever would you be wanting
with them, if you don't mind my asking?"

Mary wondered as well.

"They are made of the best English wool, are they
not? Sturdy clothes. Warm in the worst weather?"

"On that you may depend. Well-mended, too, else I
would not have them in my shop."

"Perfect for my purpose, then. I have in mind, Mr.
Hill, they might make a desirable Christmas gift for
my neighbor."

"Miss Rivers?" Hill turned to Mary, brows raised.

"Not Miss Rivers," Lord Balfour corrected him.

"Thank God for that, sir! I could not imagine the
young lady strutting about in jackboots and a shako."

"What a picture you paint, sir." Baxter's lips twitched.
His gaze met Mary's with an unexpected blend of heat
and amusement. "It is her grandmother, Mrs. Rivers, for
whom I must have them."

Chapter Thirteen

𝒞

Mary opened her eyes at the first hint of light, Lord Balfour's elegantly munificent and completely irresistible gift on her mind. Clothes for the poor, in Gran's name. She had not said no to his generosity, had no desire to say no. He had risen in her estimation considerably by way of his gesture.

A passing comment of Gran's, and he had remembered and acted upon it. *Impressive!* She had never met a more gentlemanly gentleman. His thoughtfulness both warmed her heart and served to remind her of his wealth, of all that might be had with a snap of his moneyed fingers.

Gran would be pleased. She felt pleased, herself, and yet, at the same time . . . inadequate. Lord Thorn she had felt herself equal to, Lord Balfour, she did not.

She rose, clothed herself, and arranged her hair. Not the pale graying of the dawn and the noises of a rousing household to stir her here, as at home, but the sounds of wheels on cobblestone as traffic swelled, and the cries of vendors walking the streets—this, the music of London.

They came early, the costermongers, before the Regent Street shops opened their doors. Maids, footmen, and cooks hailed them from doorways and windows, darting out into the chilly street to fill their baskets.

"New oysters, new!" came the cry. "Hot pippin pies, hot!" "Ripe walnuts, ripe." "White turnips, white."

A buxom young woman with a fine voice and a basket across each arm had "Rosemary and bay, quick and gentle." An old man with a pot like a hat upon his head voiced in melodic singsong, "Ha' you work for a tinker?"

Gran's house, by contrast, held its breath, but for the somnolent ticking of her clocks. They were never so obvious as in the morning, counting the minutes until Gran woke. Mary suffered the hushed quiet, the uneasy, waiting stillness, alone.

She did not know what to do with quiet other than to stay busy. She missed the voices of her sisters chattering and bickering as they dressed for the morning milking. She missed the thunder of her brother's boot heels on the stairs as they went down to bring in the cows, calling cheery "Good mornings" and "Did you dream last night?"

She had dreamt last night, of Balfour's ball. They were dancing in the dream, she and Baxter, only the dance was interrupted as others cut in—her grandfather looking exactly as he did in the portrait above the fireplace, her father and brothers, even Temple, who worried that he would be let go without a character for daring to do so. She did not realize the floor beneath their feet was a great quizzing glass until it shattered, the fall waking her.

The upstairs case clock counted the steps as she crept lightly down them. The downstairs mantel clock picked up the tune, gently chiming in on the quarter hour as she quietly swept the grate and brought in fresh coal to start the fire in Gran's sitting room to take the chill off.

Her grandfather, not dancing now, held silent court from the wall, captured in uniform. The mantel clock, his long-ago gift, counted away years' worth of lonely holidays.

Gran had long outlived her husband. How difficult was it, to spend so many minutes alone, skin, hair, and teeth losing their dewy bloom of youth while one's husband smiled down on one, forever young?

Mary went to the kitchen to wash the coal black from her hands. She put the kettle on and a pot of hot water to soft boil eggs. She poked a long-handled toasting fork in the fire, armed with slices of day-old bread. She missed the smell of fresh hay in the morning, the sound of the cows contentedly munching, the warm curve of the cow's belly against her head as she milked, kittens winding about her ankles begging cream.

At home the kitchen would be abuzz with laughter and talk. There, heaping platters of ham from their own pigs and plates of stewed mushrooms and tomatoes from their own garden made their way to a table already armed with toast, eggs, and crocks of freshly churned butter.

Gran's needs were simpler. A light eater, she was easy to please and consistent in her desires. Her egg must be served in one of the yellow Limoge egg cups mother had given her for Christmas the year she and father took their honeymoon in France. Lightly browned toast went in the rack Mary's brother had sent Gran from Brighton when he joined the Guard, a dollop of oat porridge, with raisins, in the crock Mary's sister had made for Gran's fiftieth birthday, a wedge of yellow Cheddar from home, all brought in on the wood inlay bed tray Mary's father had fashioned as Gran's rheumatism worsened.

The same every morning, and yet these small tokens of affection always brought a smile to the old woman's lips, a gleam to her eyes. She remembered exactly which Christmas or birthday had brought each gift, which family member had so honored her.

While Gran ate, Mary wound the clock, dusted the mantle and swept the sitting room, with a quick swipe of a cloth over the bric-a-brac and porcelain figurines that clustered in a glass fronted cabinet. She thought of home, of her parent's pride in their dairy, in their cheeses. She thought of Lord Balfour. What did he take pride in?

"Oranges! Seville oranges!" At last came the thin cry.

From the doorway she beckoned, shivering, wondering what it was like to wander the city streets, as this young girl did, complexion tanned like leather by the elements, fingerless mits foul with dirt and falling to string, her thin cloak deeply muddied at the hem.

"Oranges and lemons today, Kitty." She jingled coins in her hand. "A large bagful, please. I mean to candy peel."

The girl licked wind-chapped lips. "Your Gran will like that, now, won't she? 'Ow's 'er 'ealth, Miss Mary?"

"She does not complain, and is very happy to think she may be going to Lord Balfour's Christmas Eve ball."

"Bless me! Will she, indeed! It is true, then, as Mr. Carpenter says, that you and 'is Nibs"—she jerked her thumb toward the Balfour mansion—" 'ave become familiar?"

Mary smiled. "We have become acquainted. Lord Balfour is a rather interesting neighbor as it turns out, and far kinder than I expected. Gran sends you these." With a broad smile she drew a brown paper–wrapped parcel from beneath her apron.

"Whot's this?" Kitty grinned uncertainly, bad teeth revealed.

"From St. Nick, Gran said to tell you." Mary smiled, wondering if the child would receive any other presents on this special day for children. "Go ahead. Open it."

Eyes glowing, Kitty set down her heavy baskets to tear into the paper. "New mitts!" She held them up, delighted, before slipping them on over the top of her old ones. "And a scarf!" She wound it instantly about her scrawny neck. "That's warm, now, innit? And such a pretty color!"

"Gran knit them for you, my dear. She thought you looked cold last time she saw you from the window."

"How kind!" The girl held forth her hands, wiggling her fingers that she might admire their new covering. "Shall I just nip in to tell your Gran thank you?" She winked. "Or is it Father Christmas I should call her this morning?"

With Kitty on her way again, Mary took away the tray, helped Gran to rise, and opened the lid to the fine French commode at the foot of the bed, another gift from the captain. As close as they were, there was always a moment's awkwardness in Mary's helping Gran take advantage of her husband's all too earthly remembrance. Gran would, she knew, like to sit herself down for this the most private of acts, but the maid had always helped her in the past. "Old bones are too brittle," she

reminded the older woman. "I will not have you breaking a hip while I'm here."

She took the tray away and washed up the dishes and
set water on to heat for Gran's ablutions before she
returned to help her to her feet, took out the slops, made
the bed, and set out Gran's dress, underthings, stockings,
and shoes. Gran liked to do most of her morning's toilet
herself, insisted upon it, in fact. No matter that it took
a great deal of time and effort. She rang the bell when
she needed Mary to do up buttons, or tie tapes her
twisted hands could no longer manage, and to dress
her hair.

Mary set a kettle of sugared water to boil upon the hob.
Sitting alone in the kitchen's silent warmth, she peeled the
first of the bag of oranges and lemons, the smell of citrus
permeating the room, her mind equally fragrant with
memories of home, the kitchen a teeming flurry of activity for days on end as she and her sisters made ready
the feast she now tackled with none but Gran to help.
What a blessing it would be to have an extra pair of
hands.

A knock sounded upon the kitchen door, a door
Gran's servants had once frequented, which now went
largely unopened.

Mary wiped orange-stickied hands upon her apron,
unsure by way of the befogged kitchen window whether
this announced the expected coal delivery or the local
milkmaid with her cow.

She opened the door to find neither. A girl stood upon
the doorstep, not plump and rosy-cheeked like the milkmaid, but willowy and wan, dressed all in black, the color
accentuating her pale complexion and narrowness of
stature. A stiff breeze would blow the poor creature
away.

"Yes?" Mary wondered who she was.

"Are you the cook?" the girl asked. "I'm the maid."

"The maid? Well, my dear, you have been misdi-
rected. We haven't a maid here. What address are you
looking for?"

The girl huddled deeper in her cloak, a fledgling crow
unused to winter. "Number seventeen Regent Street,

marm. The Rivers household. Miss Mary Rivers? My brother, Ben, told me I would find work here."

Mary fell back a step. "I am Miss Mary Rivers, but I am not expecting a maid. Who is this Ben you speak of?"

"Ben Temple, miss, secretary to his lordship, the Viscount of Balfour."

"Temple?"

Gran rang the bell. Mary turned her head, opening the door wider. "There is some mistake here, but I must answer that. Do come in. I will not keep you standing in the cold, Miss Temple."

The girl stepped inside as if she would just as soon run out again.

"I shall just ask my Gran to give me a minute to straighten this out."

The girl nodded meekly.

"What is it?" Gran asked. "Did I hear someone knocking? Has the coal delivery come? I need you to do my hair."

"A bit of confusion, Gran," Mary said, unwilling to go into it further. If she mentioned the girl was a maid, Gran would want to keep her. If she turned the girl away, Gran would want to know why. That meant explaining the reduced state of her finances. Mary hoped to avoid the subject until after Christmas.

"It is Temple's sister."

"Lord Balfour's Temple? She has got the wrong address."

"Yes, I mean to straighten it out. I shall just be a minute."

"Go on, then." Gran waved her away. "Never mind me. I can see to myself."

It was at times like this, Mary thought, returning to the kitchen, that she missed her sisters most. In Glastonbury there was always someone with whom to share responsibilities, someone to help carry every burden.

Miss Temple stood exactly where Mary had left her. The girl looked as if she were afraid she had done something wrong.

Mary smiled. *Poor child.* She had not been met with

the welcome she had expected. "Do take off your coat and bonnet. You look as if you could use something warm to drink. A bit of hot cider, perhaps?"

"I don't want to be any trouble, miss."

"No trouble. It heats on the hob. I have only to pour you a cup, and then I shall just run next door and see if we can straighten out this muddle."

The girl shed her bonnet, muffler, and mittens, unbuttoning her cloak with stiff fingers.

As Mary took down a cup and poured the cider she said, "We could use a maid, but I'm sorry to say, cannot afford one."

"I am already paid through the month, miss."

Mary paused in handing the girl the cup. "I do not understand."

The girl blew on the cider, looking up through the steam to say, "He said you would teach me how to be a maid, miss. Housecleaning and such. I shall have no luck finding a permanent position else, and he was thinking you would not be needing me above a couple of months, at most a year."

"He? Do you mean your brother?"

"No, miss." The girl sipped, careful not to burn herself. "Lord Balfour made the arrangements."

Chapter Fourteen

𝕮

Mary strode out of the kitchen, red velvet cloak thrown on over her apron, and hastened next door to bang upon the servants' entrance.

Temple opened it, asking eagerly, "You have met my sister?"

"Where is your master?" Mary asked.

"In the cellar, miss, choosing wines for the ball."

She noticed as he led the way, that the clock at the base of the stairs was stopped, the mirrors covered, all draperies drawn— evidence of a house in mourning, evidence of how much Temple Senior had meant to Lord Balfour.

Young Temple asked with puzzled expression, "Did you not like her, miss? She is small, our Beth, I know, but quick-witted and eager to please. Will she not suit?"

"When did his lordship decide to make her mine? Do you know?"

"While he arranged Father's funeral, miss. The minute Mother said she was interested in placing Bethany in service somewhere, he thought of you. Said he was quite sure you were in need of a maid, and that he could not think of any two kinder ladies with whom Beth might learn how things are to be done."

"He said that, did he?" She slowed, rubbing the knot between her brows, feeling guilty and ungrateful.

"Yes, miss. Down here if you please." He opened the door on a set of steps leading into a space cool and dank, the walls of stone, whitewashed, the light dim and flickering, fat candles under glass globes strategically placed to light the way.

A tall, thin gentleman with an emotionless demeanor and a black crepe band about his sleeve turned from a large basket, in which he stacked dusty wine bottles with French labels. "You know better than to come down here," he remarked coolly to Temple.

"Yes, Mr. Holloway, I do, but Miss Rivers insisted upon seeing Lord Balfour."

"His lordship is busy, Temple. You must declare him not at home to visitors until you are informed otherwise."

"Yes, but . . ."

"I barged in," Mary admitted. "Rude, I know, but I have myself received an unexpected visitor this morning, courtesy of your master."

Temple looked worried. "You do not like her then, miss? Do you not want her?"

Holloway regarded Temple with irritated condescension.

"I do not know her well enough to determine any feeling, Temple," Mary said.

Baxter stepped from the stacks, bearing more bottles of wine, black armband stark against the white of his sleeve.

"Good morning!" His tone was warmly welcoming. She had never seen him smile so broadly. "To what do I owe the pleasure of a visit, Miss Rivers?"

"To whom, my lord, rather than what," she said.

Worry faintly darkened his features. "Little Beth arrived, did she?"

"She has, and seems a sweet, biddable girl. I cannot help but wonder why you did not see fit to mention you meant to send her to me."

Baxter handed the bottles to his waiting butler, brushing dust from his hands. He looked her straight in the eyes, the blue of his magnified by the new spectacles. "I was afraid you might refuse her, just as you refused my money."

"You begin to know me well, my lord. I would have."

Temple's mouth and eyes fell open in shocked surprise, but he refrained from saying anything before Baxter responded, "And now that you have met her? Can you turn her away?"

Mary forced a smile, unwilling to say anything that might hurt the feelings of either Temple or his sister.

"I cannot afford her, sir," she stated bluntly.

"She is paid through the month."

She glanced uneasily at Temple, then at the butler. "I cannot afford to be obligated to you, my lord."

He shook his head, expression troubled. "You dispel any obligation in addressing my invitations."

"An uneven exchange, my lord."

"I disagree, but perhaps this is better discussed in private."

"I—" She shook her head and rubbed at the tightness between her brows again. Her hand smelled of oranges, reminding her of her morning's task. "Oh dear. The sugar!"

She turned, clattered up the stairs, rattled and displeased with the outcome of their confrontation.

She did not count on him following her. He called out when she reached Gran's front door, which she might have slammed unwittingly in his face.

"Wait, Miss Rivers!"

A trace of desperation in the cry made her pause on the steps, hand on the door.

"I would have this resolved." Coatless, shoulders hunched against the wind, his breath clouded white between them. "If you mean to toss the girl out, *I* must know."

"Come in! Come in!" She gestured impatiently. "I am no more in the habit of tossing people out than I am of keeping them standing in the cold. But I must see to the syrup first. Will you wait here?" She indicated the ground-floor sitting room.

"As you wish." He crossed the room to warm his hands by the fire.

No smell of burned sugar in the kitchen, only a pleasant citrus tang, and the sight of a row of fresh strips of peel on the cutting board. In the syrup, more peel.

Mary's pulse galloped all out of tempo for such a

scene. The girl had washed up the cider cup. Juice from the skinless fruit had been squeezed into the pitcher set out for that very purpose.

No sight of Beth. Had the girl run off with the silver, like the last of Gran's cooks?

At a noise behind her, Mary turned. Beth stood in the doorway, as meek, colorless, and nonthreatening as a dust mouse, tray in hand.

"Your Gran, miss," she said hesitantly, as if caught in a misdeed, "called for tea."

"Of course," Mary said. "How kind of you to take it to her. And what a lovely job you have done with the peel."

Beth bobbed her head, the tips of her ears turning red in just the manner her brothers' did. "I hoped it would please you, Miss." She set down the tray and hesitantly took from the cupboard a pair of matching cups and saucers. "She has asked for another cup, miss, for Lord Balfour, who has come to call. I suppose it was you who let him in. We were all in a dither, for having heard the door open and close, we found him alone in the front sitting room, and foolishly supposed he had invited himself in."

Mary chuckled. "I would not put it past him."

"Really, miss? He seemed too much the gentleman to do such a thing. Temple has nothing but praise for his manners."

"You must trust Temple's opinion above mine. Your brother is far better acquainted with the viscount than I."

"Will you take tea with them?"

"Yes, please." Mary felt she had no control over anything that happened this morning. "Gran's hair!" she cried, turning for the door.

"I took the liberty," Beth said meekly, ducking her head as if afraid she overstepped her bounds.

Mary felt more heartless than ever in questioning her place in their household. The girl fit in so seamlessly.

There was nothing to do but say, "Thank you. You've done very well. If you will carry on with candying the peel, I shall be happy to take in the cups."

Beth bobbed a little curtsy, and with a pleased expression poured boiling water into and then out of each of the cups before she placed them on the tray, that they might not be ice cold.

Wondering if there was any way she could rearrange Gran's finances enough that they might manage to afford the girl, Mary returned to the sitting room to find Gran and Lord Balfour sitting together, Gran's hair prettily arranged, a lace cap atop the neat coil.

Gran said, "How very kind you are, my lord, how thoughtful, to solve our dilemma as well as the girl's. She seems a sweet, taking little thing."

"I hope she is not quite so taking as your last maid," Mary murmured to herself on entering the room.

Balfour looked up.

"Mary!" Gran turned to greet her with a smile. "See who has come to call."

"Yes, Gran." Mary arranged her features in what passed for a smile. "Very kind of Lord Balfour, I'm sure."

He met her expression with a lift of his brows and the faint twitch of his lips she grew accustomed to. She set out the cups and poured steaming, fragrant Darjeeling.

Gran sipped at hers and asked Lord Balfour about his new glasses, about Beth, whom she accepted already as part of the household, and about the latest plans for his Christmas ball. He answered without hesitation, his gaze drifting in Mary's direction only rarely, his look keen when it did.

Mary let Gran talk. Indeed, she was pleased to hear her chatter on so contentedly. After a quarter of an hour had passed by way of the mantel clock, she rose to excuse herself, pleading kitchen duties.

"But it is you Lord Balfour came to talk to, Mary." Gran stopped her. "I'm sure of it, and I must go and show Beth how we make our plum pudding now that the peel is ready. I promised her I would." She smiled at Baxter. "Do you mind terribly, my lord, wheeling me back to the kitchen? I used to have a footman to do such things, but Mary has often told me I do not require so many servants now that she is here to see to things."

"I would be happy to." He stood, setting the Merlin chair in motion with polite speed.

When he returned, Baxter paused in the doorway a moment to stare at Merry, who sat, head bowed, her expression one of deep contemplation.

Sensing his presence, she raised her head, eyes luminous, her face a fresh delight. He stepped into the room, asking half in earnest, "Shall I search out a footman?"

She politely refused the offer, exactly the reaction he had expected.

"How bad is it?" he asked, triggering a puckered brow.

"Whatever do you mean?"

"Your grandmother's financial circumstances," he pressed bluntly. "She does not know they are in a bad way, does she?"

"And how would you know otherwise?" she asked, equally blunt, the false smile she had worn the past half hour fading.

"You showed me," he said softly. When she opened her mouth to deny it, he said, "The first day we met, you showed me your hand—a list of sums. It took no more than an instant to recognize that the numbers got smaller rather than the reverse."

She sighed heavily. "How foolish of me." Her blunder quieted her, lips pinched.

"Can you not confide in me?" he asked. It was not his intent to add to her concerns.

She frowned.

"No footman. I promise," he cajoled.

A pained smile formed, her armor for all situations. "There is little more to say. You see clearly, of course, why we cannot afford Bethany?"

"Will you not help her, then, as a favor to me? She and her family are in dire need since the death of her father, who was their sole support. She requires training to be fit for any kind of position, and I have neither the time nor the inclination to take in another Temple. She looks too much like . . ." He stopped, eyes stinging, thought better of what he had been about to say, and went on, lacing his voice with the bitter sting of sarcasm that had so often soothed his pains. "It is job enough to train her brother to my ways."

"But—"

He touched her hand, no gloves between them, his flesh to hers, stilling words, stilling movement for the moment.

She glanced down at their hands, lips parted, cheeks coloring a pretty pink.

"I owe it to her father."

She slid her hand away from his. No more than an instant his touch, and yet it was too long for propriety's sake, too short for satisfaction.

He closed his eyes, shutting out the pull of her gaze, the flesh of his fingertips tingling. "I must see his family safe from want."

She rose to freshen his cup, the teapot stoneware, not china, a blue-and-white pattern, the matching cup heavier to his hand, cruder of design than he was accustomed to.

He frowned at the portrait over the fireplace—a captain. A relative, perhaps? He knew so little about her, only that he wanted her approval, her understanding, her companionship, the flesh of her hand beneath his fingertips.

"This in no way obligates you or your grandmother to me. To the contrary," he suggested, regarding her intently, the taste of Darjeeling aromatic in his mouth. Her eyes, dark as the tea, were like those in the painting. "I would be indebted to you."

No smile for him, no sign at all what she was thinking, head bent over her cup, lashes thick upon her cheek.

"He was with you long?" she said at last, looking him in the eyes, the topaz depths of hers compelling.

"Temple?" A pang every time he said the name. "Yes. Since I was a boy, he spent more time with me than anyone else in the world."

*   *   *

Except your mother and father, she almost blurted, but something in the faintly bitter twist to his lips, stopped her.

"I see," she said, not seeing at all, unable to fathom a childhood in which a servant meant more to one than family. She imagined the man as boy, left to the care of hired help—unloved—a pitiable picture.

"You will keep her then? I may tell Mrs. Temple not to worry?" There was in the way he asked a hint of the boy to his tone, as if everything connected to this elder Temple affected him deeply, as if at heart the lion, thorn in his paw, was far more vulnerable than she had initially supposed.

"I will keep her."

Relief swelled his chest, as if he had been holding his breath. He sat forward, smiling, the blue of his eyes warm and cloudless as a sunny day's—the eyes of a child well pleased. And then, no child at all, he touched her with his gaze as palpably as he had touched her hand earlier, vaguely improper, more than a little disturbing, a look that lingered too long.

He rose.

She did not want him to go. Her hand flew of its own accord in his direction. "When is the funeral?"

"The day after tomorrow. If you've no objection, I shall come by for Beth?"

"Yes, of course. That would be very kind."

She followed him to the door, conscious of his every move, of his black-banded shirtsleeves, bare head, bare hands. His presence filled the space of Gran's house, filled a space in her heart she had not known to be empty. He was improperly attired for the cold he was about to step into, improperly attired for a house call. She did not want him to go, did not want to return to the ordinary and appropriate activities of the day.

He stopped, hand on the latch, a contemplative expression puckering his brow. "I wonder. Have you half an hour I might impose upon, Miss Rivers?"

She frowned. "Right now?"

He nodded.

"Whatever for?"

Chapter Fifteen

𝕮

He wanted her to go with him to a mourner's warehouse at the far end of Regent Street, to replace Temple's cloak, he said. "Which has the misfortune to be imbued with a most malodorous dye."

"Ah!" She chuckled. "That explains it."

"What?"

"Bethany."

His lips lifted briefly. "Smells as well, does she?"

She smiled.

He came briskly to the point. "All the more reason you ought to accompany me."

The intensity with which he voiced his request disturbed her a little. She laughed to dispel her uneasiness. "Why not take Bethany? Or are you prepared to convince me I do you greater favor in coming myself?"

"But of course, it is true."

She smiled. The lift of his brow and the cant of his head warned her he was in a mood for banter. "How so?"

"A majority of Temples? Surely you jest."

Brows raised, she asked, "That would place you at a disadvantage?"

"Indeed!"

She smiled, waiting for more. There must be more.

"Imagine if an argument arose over my paying for the replacement of these smelly cloaks. I would be outnumbered."

"I see." She bit her lip, determined not to laugh, a failure in the attempt. She did see more clearly than

ever what a deviously generous man the much misunderstood Lord Thorn was. "I'll go with you," she agreed.

Arm in arm therefore, they stepped through the double doors at Mr. Jay Chickall Pugh's. She would never
have realized, had he not gripped her elbow tighter, how
much the place affected him. No change of expression
gave Baxter away. He made no sound, just tightened his
clutch, arm stiffening beneath her fingers.

He paused, as if to get his bearings, his chest ex-
panding with a breath so deep she was tempted to consider it a sigh.

Black met their gaze—an abundance of black, floor-
to-ceiling black. Black crepe for armbands, black bombazine and netting for hats and weeping veils, black serge
suits. Silk tabby for dresses. Black plumes, rosettes, and
trappings for horses.

The weight of death and funerals hung heavy here.

Mary thought of Gran, and her eyes misted over.

Still, Lord Balfour stood motionless. Puzzled, she
blinked her tears away, concerned by his immobility.

"There's no escaping it here, is there?" he said under
his breath.

Behind them, Temple sighed. "I had no idea there
were such places."

A whey-faced clerk in head-to-toe black rustled forward to help them. "My dear sirs, madam," he said unctuously, voice laced with professionally cultivated
sympathy. "How may I help you in this most difficult
of times?"

Baxter looked at the fellow blankly. Temple's chin
quivered.

"Armbands," Mary said. "And we require cockades."

Baxter recovered himself. "Plumes for the horses."
Voice ragged, he cleared his throat. "Rosettes, as well,
and black velvet caparisons."

"My lord!" young Temple protested quietly. "We can
never affor—"

"I will entertain no discussion on the matter," Baxter
said firmly. "My own team must take your father to his
final resting place."

"But, my lord—"

"I insist."

No fight to him, Temple wiped away a tear.

Baxter patted him awkwardly on the shoulder. "You will see to choosing something appropriate?"

"Of course, my lord." Temple was led away.

Baxter removed his new spectacles, pocketing them abruptly, as if there were much he did not want to see.

"And now, cloaks, Miss Rivers. You will help me?"

"Of course," she said, beckoning the ready assistance of another hovering clerk.

Blindly he followed, blindly agreed to whatever she picked out, deaf to what she said, oblivious to the quiet clerk who offered low-voiced suggestions and went away again, chosen cloak in hand.

"And now gloves," Miss Merry instructed, as if from a great distance, her smiles warm and concerned, more comforting than usual. "And scarves. Something simple and durable, in a sturdy wool."

"Make sure it is of the finest quality." His lips moved in some way disconnected from his mind.

"Yes, my lord, Very good, my lord." The clerk fluttered about like a cabbage moth, blending so perfectly with his surroundings at times he seemed to disappear. Baxter paid him little mind, as gloves and mufflers were modeled.

Dear Temple had helped him many times donning gloves, winding woolen mufflers about his neck—buff, not black.

"A subtle color would be preferable, Master Balfour," Temple had admonished when he begged for scarlet. "Understatement rather than overstatement is best suited to a gentleman of means."

When he evidenced his displeasure by dragging his scarf and mittens in the mud, Temple had taken them from him, saying, "Articles of clothing are not to be abused, young man. They are evidence of your position. Do not let me see you abusing that privilege, or your mittens, again, else I shall give them to another lad."

Had he meant his son? Baxter eyed young Temple, imagining him in buff scarf and gloves.

Merry Rivers spoke, her words and tone so gentle they made no impression other than that of kindness.

"What's that, you said?" he asked.

"How thoughtful you are, my lord. How generous."

Her admiration too profuse, he looked not at her, but at Temple, his head bent over a tray full of braided rosettes. "Why then do I feel only guilt, Miss Rivers?"

"Why, indeed, my lord?"

Silence weighed heavy between them.

He blurted, "I loved him too much."

She remained silent, waiting for more, without pressing for more. He felt he might tell her anything.

"I owned him, you see. Held him too close. He was not his son's at all." He closed his eyes and inhaled shakily, determined not to let his emotions best him.

Shamed afresh, he opened his eyes to the sight of Merry's concerned face. He knew every line, every curve, even without his glasses. He took his spectacles from his pocket and concentrated on carefully wiping them with his handkerchief. Best not to look at her. "I am ashamed to admit it did not really suit me to remember his family existed."

"Until now," she said with the tenderest of smiles, disarming him with the unexpected pressure of her hand upon his sleeve. "When they need you the most."

He thrust on his spectacles and stalked away.

She feared she offended him with her remark. She wondered what regrets she might suffer in losing Gran. What words went unsaid? What deeds undone? She had been away from Gran's side too long this afternoon. She wished their errands done in the same instant she wished she might spend time unending in the stimulating company of this tenderhearted young man.

As if he read her mind across the room, Baxter lifted his attention from black velvet, braid, and tassels. The sky blue gaze carried unexpected heat. She must remember he was Charles Thornton Baxter, Lord Balfour, and stop blurting out whatever came to mind when he was near, stop meeting his gaze with a hunger for more.

He made everything right with the cant of his head,

the rise of his brows, and a rueful lift of his lips—an odd sort of thank you in this language of his body.

Magic hung in the moment, in his gaze, inappropriate as it might be. Why now, she wondered, with *this* man, of all unattainable men?

The interior of the viscount's coach no longer intimidated Mary. Indeed, she felt more comfortable with the coach than its owner. He sat beside her in such a position and upon such a road that his noble leg on more than one occasion bumped into hers, each touch shooting like flaming brandy along her leg. Her foot, ankle, calf, and thigh tensed, burning, backing away from contact with him, the very rigidness of her stance increasing the difficulty of avoiding rolling into him.

The stretch between the Quadrant and the warehouse still being in a great degree of upheaval, the coach threw him into her and she into him again and again, until she was sick of his apologies.

She did not want him to be "sorry, so sorry" that he bumped into her. She was, herself, intrigued more than filled with regret at such contact.

"Please stop," she said at last with a forced smile.

Brows raised, he leaned forward, hand reaching for the string above his head. "Are you ill?" he asked with deepest concern as the trap dropped open and the driver called, "Yes, my lord."

"Stop the coach!"

"No, no!" she cried. "I did not mean for you to stop the carriage."

"Drive on," he called as the coach slowed. "My mistake." His gaze dropped from the closing trap to stare at her, bemused. "What then?"

The coach lurched in resuming its former speed, throwing him into her again, so that he said it again. "So sorry. I do beg your pardon."

"That!" she said. "Please, stop begging my pardon."

His head tilted. His brow furrowed. Temple's brow mimicked that of his master.

"You see, I understand you do not mean to bang against me, that it is not your intent to familiarize me so intimately with your elbow, thigh and knee, and that there is no avoiding it."

Baxter's eyes locked on hers for a moment as they were thrown together once again. "You are perfectly correct, of course," he agreed. "Simply no avoiding it."

No avoiding it, he thought, wishing the coach might throw them together permanently, in a manner far more intimate than the mere brush of arms and legs.

He was infatuated. No denying it. They were meant to touch one another. Her hands in his hair at the optician's. Her hand against his beneath the table. His hand to hers at her Gran's. Her knee banging his in the coach. He had begun to fabricate reasons why they must spend time together, hoping for another brush of his flesh to hers.

A funeral warehouse! He took her to a funeral warehouse! *Surely you can do better,* Temple would have scolded.

And then again, perhaps not. He wanted her, needed her, as buffer between himself and the moment.

They had purchased all that was necessary, and more, and still it was not enough to honor Temple. Baxter wanted to tell Temple's son that his father's death marked his every moment, that the hole left in his household affected him more deeply than that of his own parents' absence.

They were always gone. Temple never.

To lose him now, in a season when all around him seemed bent on being gay and carefree, was hardest of all. But young Temple needed no more reasons to grieve. He had ample excuse already, and so Baxter held silent, no part of his sorrow voiced to any but Miss Rivers.

She was a wonder to watch, setting about even minor tasks with an energy and enthusiasm, a good-natured cheer, that warmed him as he had never been warmed before.

Life, her every action demonstrated, was something she appreciated, and took part in to the fullest degree. She assumed everyone her friend, everything of interest.

He did not live life like that. Might he be happier if he did?

They stopped again at the stationer's, Temple disembarking, no request for Baxter's assistance. He merely stepped down, beckoning to Will and Ned.

Baxter was pleased.

Merry Rivers broke the intimate silence left them within the coach. "I would not have you think me hardhearted," she said, her look so troubled he could not imagine what on earth she referred to.

"I assure you that is not what I think of you at all."

"Gran had servants when I arrived." She went on confusing him. He did not try to stop her. He liked to watched her mouth as she spoke, her lips entirely captivating.

"Two maids, a cook, a footman."

Her cheeks took on a most delightful color.

"I had to let them all go."

Unsure how what she said applied to him, he suggested, "That must have been a difficult task."

"Not as difficult as you may suppose."

The light caught and amplified the gold in her eyes as her gaze darted uneasily toward the window.

"I am sure Bethany Temple is unimpeachable, but . . . you see . . . Gran's servants robbed her."

He concentrated less on her lips and more on what they were saying.

"Her silver, her best china and linens, even a vast quantity of candles which I cannot otherwise account for, were stolen. On top of which, she was overcharged for everything from meat to marmalade."

"Ah!" She left him speechless with such a revelation.

"Gran was well fixed. She had more than enough to last the rest of her days. It would break her heart to know otherwise. My family thinks"—she frowned— "well, no matter what they think—I did not want *you* to think I would refuse Bethany a job lightly."

"I see." He nodded.

Temple opened the stationer's shop door, ushering out a sensibly laden Will and Ned.

"Your secret is safe with me. I thank you for taking me into your confidence and for taking Bethany in."

All out of breath, Temple joined them, the footmen assisting.

"Are we still welcome tomorrow evening?"

"This evening, if you care to come," she said.

"We do," Baxter said. "We shall."

As the coach lurched into motion, he refrained from apologizing for his knee, which rocked against hers, exceptionally pleased to see she did not immediately withdraw from all contact when the tip of his shoe collided with hers.

Chapter Sixteen

𝒞

Temple stamped the Balfour signet into the wax seal on the last of the invitations to the tune of a little cheer and applause. With Bethany there to swell their numbers, and Baxter's own performance enhanced by improved eyesight, they were done swifter than before. He was freshly amazed at what old Temple had quietly and efficiently done for him every Christmas, for how many Christmases?

He rose reluctantly from his place at the table opposite Merry saying, "We will trouble you no more, Miss Rivers. I do thank you for all of your assistance."

"We are not yet done." She stayed him with a glance, placing on the table a square stack of white paper. "There is something very important I was to have accomplished in the evenings when you occupied me otherwise."

"I do beg your pardon," he said earnestly, sinking into his chair. "What have we kept you from? How may we help to make it right?"

She smiled mischievously, handing them each several sheets of white paper. "I had hoped you would ask. Indeed, it pleases me immensely to hear your offer to make amends. It is simply done and in no more than a quarter of an hour all shall be set to rights with so many here to help."

She handed them each a pair of small, sharp scissors. "What are we to do?" Temple asked.

"Create a white Christmas for Gran. She speaks of nothing so much as how pretty snow would be, and

weather obliging, or not, she shall have it." She folded
a piece of the paper in half, in half again, and then fan-
folded it from one corner.

"Ah!" Will nodded. "I see." He folded his paper in
half and half again.

"See what?" Baxter asked, bewildered, as Miss Rivers
snipped away at the fan, bits of paper cascading to the
table in a flurry.

Ned folded his page. "I'm with you."

"We do these every Christmas at home," Temple said.

Irritated to be left in the dark, Baxter refused to admit
his ignorance, mimicking, as best he could, Temple's
movements as he folded his page. Who had taught the
boy? Had dear old Temple cut paper thus with his son?
He could not picture it.

Miss Merry unfolded her finished cutting, the paper
clinging to itself with a peculiar noise, so lacy had the
riddled page become. Carefully separating the layers, she
held the page to the light. A snowflake.

Baxter frowned at the thing. He had seen cut snowflakes before, of course, but how on earth had she
managed to produce something so pretty so quickly?
Will unfolded his page, Temple, too, black armbands
forgotten. They, too, had produced lacy white
snowflakes.

"You do not approve, my lord?" Miss Rivers flushed,
her coloring very pretty in the candlelight. "I hope you
don't find my request too foolish, but it occurred to me
that if each of us did five or six we would soon have
enough for all of Gran's windows."

Temple rose to hold his snowflake to the window with
a smile of pure delight. "How do you mean to affix
them?"

"Flour paste," she said.

How easily she managed to bring them good cheer.
How completely he had forgotten this evening how
much he hated Christmas. He picked up his folded bit
of paper. "I must warn you," he said, "I am not very
artistic."

She smiled, and plucked up another page.

He watched intently, finishing the folding of his own page to match hers.

She caught him watching, stopped what she was doing, opened her mouth as if to say something, and thinking better of it, continued her folding and cutting, slower now, holding the page and the scissors in just such a way that he might see what she was doing.

It humbled him to think she understood his dilemma and quietly meant to make his situation easier. It pleased him deeply that she responded with such sensitivity for his feelings, refraining from revealing to the room at large this minor deficiency in his knowledge of the world.

How satisfying to unfold that first snowflake. What a heartwarming look of mutual pleasure they shared. He wanted very much to reach across the table to touch her hand. He refrained, of course.

Now that he saw how the business was done, he did his best to outdo that first snowflake in the care and complexity of his cutting. Child's play, and yet it kept them all royally amused for the next quarter of an hour, until Ned asked if Miss Rivers had any colored paper, then showed them how to plait paper hearts, as his Norwegian granny did. And so they spent another half hour cutting and plaiting paper hearts until Temple suggested they should make some as decorations for the Christmas Eve ball.

Temple Senior would never have approved, but all of his servants were nodding, expressions merry, and so Baxter agreed.

Merry's gran woke then, with a muffled bout of coughing. Pacified with horehound drops and a cup of honeyed tea, she came to lend a hand, while Temple ran to the Balfour mansion to fetch more paper and paste. Gran suggested that as long as they were cutting and pasting they ought to cut stars and cornucopias. Baxter had not the slightest inclination to refuse the old woman; he wondered how serious her condition was.

He ended the evening, not long thereafter. No sense taxing the old woman's nerves.

The table was sufficiently covered in paper cuttings of

every size and description. "A lovely evening," he said as Will, Ned, and Temple packed up paperwork, his seal, and pens. "I cannot think when I have enjoyed myself more."

He handed each of the women one of the invitations from the pile Temple carried out in a box. "May I entertain you as grandly on Christmas Eve," he said.

Merry Rivers smiled in taking her invitation, and looking down at it, frowned before she smiled again, saying, "Did you mean to make a pun of my name?"

His brows rose, her words a surprise.

"Have I spelled it wrong?"

She laughed. "Merry. You have spelled it as if I were named for happiness rather than the Virgin."

"Oh!" Her name was Mary? His lips parted. How awful, to get it wrong. "I do beg pardon. I thought you aptly named. I mean . . ." He flushed, stammering, "N-n-not to say you are not aptly named."

She laughed. "My sister, Ellen, would disagree with you. She is forever reminding me I am named after our aunt and not the mother of Christ."

He did not know what to say to that, did not know what to make of sibling banter. "Shall I leave an extra invitation, that she might come to the ball?"

She shook her head, smile forced, as she turned the invitation in her hands, expression pained. "Very kind of you to offer, but I do not count on her coming."

He left them, said good night and thank you, then herded his helpers and all they had brought out the door.

She wished him a good evening, a smile plastered on her lips, mouth aching, heart aching, suddenly weary.

He did not know her name!

She closed the door on him, on his entourage, on the noise and joy of an evening strangely distant, all her pretensions of friendship with a viscount unfounded. Gran had warned her not to lose her heart, and yet she had, to a gentleman far above her in station, a man who counted noblemen and noblewomen among his friends and acquaintances.

She flushed with embarrassment. What a fool she had been! She had dared talk him into cutting snowflakes! She—a nobody from Glastonbury! He needed her to address invitations, nothing more.

Chapter Seventeen

𝒞

The funeral went well—as well as a funeral in December might go. The day was cloudy, cold, and still, no wind to trouble them graveside, no rain to wilt the black plumes. As if Temple himself had ordered it, Baxter thought.

Miss Mary Rivers, nothing Merry about her today, and yet she seemed to bring light and cheer into the darkness of the moment, put in a brief appearance at the wake.

"I came for Bethany's sake," she said, "but cannot stay long. Gran is not feeling well."

He did not speak to her above a sentence or two, and that not enough. Distance welled between them from the beginning of their brief exchange. A distance born of the day, he thought, and their grim purpose in meeting.

On Saturday, the funeral behind him, if not his sadness, he hungered to see her, but could think of no reason, no legitimate excuse to place himself in her company. He had much to do in preparation for the upcoming ball, and yet it meant nothing to him. The sight of bobbing black plumes, black gloves, and arm-bands remained too fresh. The house still spoke blackly of the void Temple left in his wake, mirrors still draped, clocks stopped. The days dawned disorganized and uneasy.

Sunday was cold and wet. He did not want to stir from his bed, did not want to dress himself to a nicety, to thank the Lord for blessings blurred by loss. Temple would have scolded had he known, but to turn in the direction of St. Phillip's was contrary to his inclination.

He would rather have stepped down the street to the Rivers's address.

It would seem all roads led to Mary, for who should be the first person his eyes fixed on in the dim light of the chapel but she.

Miss Rivers had the look of another Mary, head bent, her smile peaceful and sweet, Advent candles casting a golden glow along her cheekbones, as if painted there. Beyond her, an empty manger awaited the Christ child near the altar no less expectantly than he waited for her head to rise, hazel eyes kindling with recognition.

Above them, a kitelike papier-mâché lantern, in the shape of a tailed, gold star, hung as high as his hopes rose at sight of her.

No doubt she had sat in the same pew every Sunday since her arrival in London. How many weeks had he let slip without realizing her presence? How many times had he walked blindly past?

Their eyes met. She smiled. How could he have disliked such a smile? The nod with which he met that smile stirred whispers. He knew to the eyes of those who cared about such small matters of prestige the inclination of his head would not go unnoticed. He wanted to exalt her in society's estimation, to shower her with favors large and small, to change her life for the better, as she had changed his.

It was, after all, a season of change. No forgetting it. Personal change, in his loss of Temple, spiritual change to be witnessed in the three flat, painted, two-dimensional, dummy-board kings making their slow journey with each Sunday's passing, up the main aisle toward the manger, the light of a paper star to guide them toward a Child who had changed the world.

He felt a kinship with the kings as he made equally slow moves with Miss Rivers, his expectations . . . What did he expect? Something wonderful. He trusted in it, as he trusted in God. And yet he remained full of doubt, as doubtful as Temple's death made him in the ways of the Lord.

Was there some pattern he missed in the timing of the old gent's demise? What purpose did death serve?

Would Mary Rivers understand such a question, or find it blasphemous?

Theirs were separate worlds. He could not ignore that fact. Even here, before God, the placement of their pews spoke of the distinctions that separated them—money, title, influence. He liked to forget all three when she was near.

Not their differences, but their similarities he concentrated on, the likenesses of mind and heart.

Was it a sister he longed for—a female friend and confidant? His kindred spirit in a dairyman's daughter? He was sure only that his loneliness diminished in her company. He felt as if he might say anything to her. She brought to him new awareness, new sensibilities of hope and a positive nature. He would not, could not, abandon her light, now that he had basked in it.

He watched her, the spectacles she had pressed to his nose, the clarity of vision they brought, a constant reminder of how dramatically she had already changed his life. How appropriate they should lift their voices together in song, their eyes meeting four times in singing "The Holly and the Ivy." It occurred to him that he was the holly, stiff and prickly—she the ivy, winding herself about his heart, clinging to the best in him.

Her throat, her mouth, he found beautiful to behold. An honest mouth, he thought—fearless, outspoken.

As though the carved angels stepped down from the walls to carol, the choir sang "O Come, O Come Emmanuel," voices high and sweet, a sound so beautiful Mary Rivers closed her eyes to listen, lashes like soot upon her roses-in-snow cheek, her Gran beside her, hands clasped, eyes shining.

She smiled as she listened. Life pleased her, sight unseen. The faint upward curve of her mouth, once so distasteful, proved his greatest pleasure now that Temple's death brought him melancholy and despair. A dairymaid's life was not easy—he knew that. And yet, she smiled.

The music stirred an idea, a means to do just that. He could not wait to speak to her after the service was finished, to share his idea.

The vicar forced him to wait his turn.

"Thank you so much, Mrs. Rivers." His voice echoed in the emptying chapel. "For your generous donation to the poor. The breeches and coats will be well received."

The old woman looked confused. She wrung gnarled hands in agitation. "Coats? But you thank me for someone else's charity," she said.

Baxter smiled as Miss Mary bent to her grandmother's ear, confiding something that made the old woman tear up, face crumpling. The vicar handed her a handkerchief. She dabbed wrinkled cheeks, eyes bright with joy.

"My lord!" she called, catching sight of him, querulous voice echoing from the high ceiling. "What a dear man you are."

The spirit of St. Nicholas himself reached out to him as she held out her hand, blue-veined, knuckles distorted, skin soft and paper thin. Hands like Nanny Lumley's, he thought. He half expected to smell peppermint.

She squeezed his hand firmly, her gratitude unexpected balm to his spirit, the tearful gleam in her eyes a gift.

"My pleasure, Mrs. Rivers," he said. "I was happy to have it brought to my attention what was truly needed by the poorhouse. Tell me, did you enjoy the choir this morning? They seemed in better than average voice."

"There is nothing I like better than beautiful music," Mrs. Rivers confided, still clinging to his hand as if she had not squeezed enough thanks from her fingers to his. She nodded and let go when he offered to push her chair. "Brought tears to our eyes, did it not, my dear?" Her bonnet swiveled. "Almost as many, my lord, as your kind gift."

Mary nodded and smiled. "Indeed. Most moving."

He wondered if she meant the music or his gift. Her smile warmed him, and yet he felt a gulf still yawned between them.

"I dare ask you," Baxter addressed her grandmother, "would you ladies care to join me on Wednesday evening for a Christmas performance sponsored by the Philharmonic Society?"

"The concert at the Argyll Rooms?" Mrs. Rivers

asked, dark eyes sparkling, smile dimming her wrinkles, transforming the old face. She must have been stunning when she was young, like her granddaughter.

"Christmas music, unless I miss my mark—strings and trumpets, handbells, I believe. I reserved a box I intended to share with a party of friends, but they mean to go to the country, and I hate to sit alone."

Mrs. Rivers gasped and clapped her hands, gleeful as a child. "How lovely! Would that not be lovely, Mary?"

"Indeed. Splendid." Mary's response was far more reserved. "How kind of you to ask, my lord."

He walked them home, pushing Gran's chair, his conversation directed largely to Gran, blue eyes quietly observant of Mary through the lenses of his new spectacles. He sought the connection of her gaze again and again over Gran's bonnet and against the backdrop of busy Regent Street, everything moving, everything hurrying—except the heaven of his eyes.

And still Mary could not read him, could not decide if his searching glances were anything more than charitable.

"Oh dear, Gran! Ought we go?" she fretted as soon as the door shut on him.

"Why ever do you ask such a question?" Gran attempted to loosen the ribbon to her bonnet, her fingers too stiff to do a good job.

"Let me." Mary gently took over. "He did not really mean to take us, did he? We are but secondhand seat fillers, are we not?"

"I never thought to hear you so ungrateful, Mary," Gran scolded. "He would not have asked us if he did not want us to join him. A gentleman of the viscount's means simply leaves his box empty for months on end if he prefers not to go. Can you not see he likes you?"

Mary bit her lip as she lifted the freed bonnet away from Gran's head. "Whatever makes you think so?"

Gran's gnarled fingers smoothed her crushed hair. "I saw the way he nodded to you in church."

"Set everyone whispering," Mary complained. "Will

it set even more to whispering to be seen in a box with the viscount? Arriving in his coach!"

"And what would they say other than that he does his neighbors great honor?"

Mary could think of a great many things. "You do not think they will wonder why a gentleman of means and standing should so favor a couple of nobodies?"

"And how should they know we are nobodies?"

Mary laughed. "They have only to look at my clothes, Gran. We do not keep fine company in Glastonbury."

"What? Have you nothing decent to wear? Well then, we must simply hire a modiste to put something splendid together."

"On short notice? Only think of the exorbitant fees during the Christmas season."

"Never mind that. I should very much like to treat you to a gown. You've two grand occasions to wear it, for you must have something lovely for the ball as well."

Mary sighed, perplexed by this new financial challenge to Gran's lean purse.

"Have you fabric about the place?" she asked. "An old gown I might refurbish? We are forever updating our gowns at home. No fabric to go to waste. A stitch here, a ribbon there, a fresh hem, and I shall feel as if I am quite splendid."

Gran's face lit up at the thought. "In the attic," she said. "There is a trunk or two of my favorite old ball gowns—dresses I could not bear to throw out."

There were in the attic five trunks in all, each a dusty, cobwebbed window to the past, gowns ten to fifty years old, the oldest made for panniers. Everything smelled richly of lavender and vertivert—beautiful garments of the finest fabrics, even the mourning blacks.

The dresses had a storybook quality, Gran's life pressed between their folds. She spoke of the ports her husband had visited, of the bolts of fabric, the lace collars and cuffs he had brought back with him. She painted a picture of her youth, of the love she and her husband had shared so briefly.

"I hate to cut into them, Gran," Mary said, dresses

piled about them like colorful flotsam. "I will feel as though I cut up your history."

Gran smiled and shook her head. "Nonsense," she said. "Grandfather would be very pleased to think his gifts made both wife and granddaughter beautiful. He cared for waste no more than you do. It will be good to see my old dresses reborn. Where are those fashion plates, my dear?"

He had asked them to accompany him, and then Baxter worried if it was the right thing to do. Had old Temple still lived, he would have consulted him for wisdom in the matter.

He made the mistake, instead, of confiding in his cousin, Gilbert, from his mother's side of the family, whom he saw no more than a half dozen times a year, who had originally agreed to go with him to the concert. Gil voiced his amazement over a glass of fine French brandy when they sat together in the bay window of Boodle's elegant saloon two days later.

"How could you be so foolish, Baxter, old man!" he barked sarcastically in a voice just loud enough to be overheard. "You mean to be seen in public places with a dairymaid! Is she pretty?"

"One might go so far as to call her beautiful." Baxter, absently studied the Greek fresco above the elaborate Adam fireplace. It depicted a well-shaped, diaphonously draped woman, reclining, a cherub at her feet.

He held a picture of greater beauty in his mind.

Gilbert leaned back, fingers laced across the plump swell of his waistcoat. "A beauty of no birth or connections. Sounds like the makings of a mistress."

"Never that," Baxter snapped, turning the heads of two who spoke quietly by the door.

Brows raised, Gilbert chuckled suggestively. "Do you begrudge this beauty a plump purse or two? I know it is not your habit to keep a female, but this country lass is after your money. Trust me. I have had some experience with such females."

Lips pursed, brows furrowed, Baxter looked out on

the traffic in St. James's and said nothing. *Was she after his money? Mary?*

He thought of the touch of her hand in his hair, the brush of her hand under the table. He had never kept a mistress, though there had been ample opportunity. The notion had simply never appealed, and Temple had always said he was too much of a gentleman for such behavior. He would have a family of his own one day. Did not his future wife deserve better?

Was Miss Mary Rivers wily and wanton, the consummate trickster with her ready touch and incessant smiling? Could he err so completely in reading her?

The moment in his carriage when their knees had bumped replayed itself in his mind. She had insisted he stop apologizing. She had brought up the matter of money. Did she hope for the offer of his protection, and he too blinded by schoolboyish admiration and Temple's rigid code of honor to see it?

"You are wrong," he told Gilbert, the mellow burn of brandy a stinging comfort on his tongue. "She is not like that."

Gilbert shrugged, swirling the bronzed liquid, plump, pink lips still wet from the latest suckling of his snifter. "If you say so, cousin." He sounded skeptical.

"I do," Baxter said with conviction.

"I hate to be the one to burst your bubble, cuz, but I have heard the young lady in question entertains a gentleman of some standing. That she refuses to allow him to pay her for her charms."

Baxter frowned, but said nothing, gaze rising to the ceiling.

Gilbert sighed, chair creaking beneath the shift of his ample girth. "There will always, of course, be talk!"

Baxter eyed the bas-relief medallions above, a row of Greco-Roman figures who heard much and said nothing. "Gossip means little to me. It is so very rarely accurate."

"Ah, but once talk is flying, mark my words, the old woman will do her best to place the two of you in a compromising position. She can then insist you must marry the girl to save her reputation. Or at the very least, support her. Tell me, has she thrust the chit beneath your nose at every opportunity?"

Baxter frowned, his eyes drawn to Gilbert's smug expression. "No. We have no more than bumped into one another on occasion in Regent Street."

"I see." The answers to all life's questions would seem to be found in the bottom of a brandy snifter. "Are you confident these meetings were not contrived?"

Baxter's mind flitted back over their recent encounters. If anyone had contrived their meetings, it had been he. The girl had not placed herself in front of his carriage on purpose, had she? Had not broken his quizzing glass by design? Surely not!

"You are a cynical creature, cousin." He set aside his glass, rising to take his leave. "The girl has no such designs in mind."

Chapter Eighteen

Satisfied with her recent sewing efforts, Mary certainly believed there was nothing to embarrass the viscount in the dress she and Bethany and Gran cobbled together in a mad frenzy of stitchery. She had never seen, certainly never worn, anything so fine. Six of Gran's old dresses lent themselves to the creation of the new one.

Layers of old skirting, all shades of plum, freshly hemmed with lace, in silk, tulle, and velvet re-created the staggered flouncing shown in the most current fashion plates. The body of the dress was deepest plum, her Gran's favorite color. A Christmas color, sugarplums and plum pudding, Mary thought. Rich and tempting.

She took pains to square a rounded neckline, the resultant plunge of décolletage lower than she was accustomed to. She doubled sleeves, plum velvet on ecru and plum figured silk in the slashed Spanish look currently popular. She even fashioned herself a new black cloak from the skirting of two of Gran's mourning dresses.

The results pleased her. No need for the viscount to know she had bitten off the last stitched thread in the instant before she opened the door to him.

"You look splendid!" he said with gratifying enthusiasm, eyes sparkling. "New dress?"

"Yes." She meant to be put out with him, for he had invited them secondhand. She meant to be wary. He was the gentleman who had not known her name, but she found she could not be anything but excited wearing her beautiful new dress. After all, a viscount clad in elegant black swallow-tailed coat and high white neckcloth stood ready to take her into the cold, black velvet of the London night, his gleaming, crested coach waiting.

"Mary's cloak is new as well," Gran informed him as her chair was fixed atop the coach. "My niece is a dab hand with a needle."

He assisted Gran into the coach as she said it, returning to help Mary into her "new" cloak, hands lingering on her shoulders a fraction of an instant too long, the weight, the heat of his hands setting her pulse racing.

"Cashmere," he murmured, voice soft as the cloth. "French?"

"Yes." She was surprised he would know, pleased to accept his arm, relieved and disappointed that fabric made his hands linger on her shoulders, not an excess of feeling.

French cashmere.

He did not want to believe it, had to ask, felt betrayed when she said yes. As if it were of no consequence that her cloak was made of yards and yards of a cloth so dear when she had so recently claimed penury.

Odd that something so soft cut him to the quick.

He dismissed the enticing sensation of Mary Rivers's shoulders, bones straight and firm beneath the most touchable of wools.

A sickening feeling mounted in his gut as he cataloged the equally expensive fabrics of the dress that had momentarily left him breathless: heavy velvet, glacé silk, Italian Gros de Naples, yards and yards of lace.

She looked good enough to eat. A plum tart, he thought cynically, who lied to him about her reduced circumstances. He did not want to believe her capable of deceit, nor to hear Gilbert's warning resound in his head, but such fabrics did not come cheap. Had she assumed he would not notice?

Dab hand with a needle, indeed! He had never heard such a Banbury tale fall so easily from an old woman's lips. Were both of them liars as Gilbert had warned? Two spiders ready to gobble him up, in public, and he, the stupid fly, helping them into his coach?

Baxter sank against the cushions, stiff-backed and

wary, every nerve on edge. What to say to such a pair?
How to behave?

The old lady wanted to talk: the weather, the approaching ball, her professed love of music.

All he could think of was what a fool he was, how
completely taken in, how pained he was to discover the
unpleasant truth of their lies. The eight blocks to the
Argyll Rooms seemed to take forever. The evening
stretched before him, a torturous eternity of forced
politeness.

Something had changed between them. Mary felt it
keenly within the confines of the coach. Despite Gran's
rattling monologue, conversation flowed awkwardly.
Lord Balfour's expression, his few words, were always
polite, never annoyed, but distant and reserved.

Had Lord Thorn returned? Was it a trick of the light?
Did the curve of his lip speak on occasion of contempt?
Taking off his glasses, he stared for long moments out
of the window, without seeing, as if murky darkness
pleased him more than they did.

The truth never occurred to her. The idea that she
overwhelmed him with her finery would have set her to
laughing. She fretted over every stitch, worried she
would be spotted as a dowd in secondhand clothes from
the moment she took off the cloak.

She gazed at him often, longing for warm, speaking
glances in return, something to calm her growing terror
at appearing in public in a dress she had thrown together
from six. Not once did he look at her while the coach
was under way. Not once. To so avoid her eyes, in such
a confined space, took effort.

She wondered why. Was her appearance an embarrassment? Had she said or done something gauche? Did
he regret their company?

She came to no sound conclusion before their destination was reached. Easy to spot, there were no other
buildings along Regent Street so brilliantly lit. Carriages
stopped on both sides of the street to let down passen-
gers. Pedestrians crowded the walkways. The dome that
served as landmark by day, obscured now by darkness,

gave hint of its presence by way of columns silhouetted against three enormous golden rectangles of flickering light. More windows wrapped the building beneath the shadowy Italianate suggestion of porticoes, a glitter of movement within. Those opening onto the first-floor balcony spilled gentlemen who wished to smoke into the night, sleek black top hats blooming pale aromatic clouds.

The rooms, inside and out, had been built with an eye to impress. Mary, who had seen the Philharmonic Society's showplace only in passing, poised now on its glittering threshold, clinging to Lord Balfour's arm, overwhelmed.

Behind them, in a great stir, Will and Ned attended to Gran and her chair. Together their little entourage passed through double doors into an opulence unlike anything Mary had ever seen.

"Oh!" she gasped. "How lovely."

Her grip on his arm far too possessive, Baxter shifted his elbow uncomfortably, Gilbert's admonishment resounding in his ears. He helped her to remove her cloak, unveiling the new dress, struck again by its richness, struck afresh by the number of heads Miss Rivers turned.

The men who eyed her let their gazes linger. The women who noticed pretended not to. The color of her dress was more forward than that favored by any of the other ladies present. Pastels of a similar cut and style, but in sarcenet, poplins, and lutestring, paled meekly before the full-bodied richness of plum velvets and silks.

His jaw tightened. She meant to make a spectacle of herself. He could think of no other likely explanation.

She watched the crowd, and they watched her. He and his guests had become part of the evening's entertainment. Usually he took little note of the audience. Tonight, in the light from glittering chandeliers, through the polished lenses of his new glasses, he saw with fresh eyes.

The beau monde had turned out in customary style— Regent Street's finest. However, Miss Rivers, with the flash of a smile, her fresh, clear, country complexion, and dark silken hair, outshone them all in plum-colored elegance.

Exquisitely coiffed heads turned to observe their progress, encumbered by the Merlin chair, which must be carried up the stairs to the private boxes, the old lady carried as well, Will and Ned bearing her between them in a short poled sedan chair. Mary Rivers followed sedately on his arm, her beauty a siren's call in danger of smashing his thus far unsullied reputation against the rocks of speculation.

Lord Balfour, it was whispered, made waves. He wondered if Temple turned in his grave.

Mrs. Rivers insisted on walking the last bit of the way to her seat, her becalmed pace commanding further attention. The pit studied his box with fascination, a sea of opera glasses winking.

Acquaintances and business connections circled, hungry-eyed, complimenting Baxter on his new glasses, dropping by to tell him they looked forward with great anticipation to his Christmas Eve ball. He was not fooled—all attention drifted swiftly, fixing on Miss Rivers's eye-catching beauty.

"The young lady's name?" the gentlemen asked. The women eyed her surreptitiously over their fans.

Pinkney Wilburforce, an old schoolmate who was free with his wealth, and a favorite of the ladies about town thanks to a handsome face, a headful of Cupid curls, and winsomely winning ways, beckoned to him outside the box before the music started. "Is this the beauty reputed to have refused your purse?" he murmured.

Baxter frowned, wondering how *that* story got into circulation. "Miss Rivers is my neighbor," he said stiffly.

"Sly dog." Pinkney waggled his brows suggestively. "Dashed high flyer, and favors for free. I should have such a neighbor. The old lady has no idea, has she?"

Baxter frowned. "As to what?"

"Why, that you receive such attentions."

Baxter blinked, taken aback. He eyed the crowded rooms, wondering with some astonishment how many here mistook Mary Rivers for his mistress.

"They are . . ." His voice betrayed none of his uneasiness. ". . . women of good character."

Were they, indeed? He wondered.

Pinkney winked and gave him a nudge. "Will she be at the ball, this obliging neighbor of yours?"

"She will."

The man could not take his eyes off Mary. "Introduce me, won't you? At the very least, tell her I admire her from afar. Gorgeous girl. I could eat her with a spoon in that confection she wears. Something quite out of the ordinary, isn't she?"

"In many ways," Baxter agreed, adding on impulse, "Join us."

"What? Really?" Pinkney's handsome face lit up.

"Yes. Yes. Come in. You may fawn over her in person."

Pinkney grinned. "I must warn you, I shall do my best to winkle her away from you."

"That I should very much like to see," Baxter said dryly, curious to know if Mary Rivers might so easily be diverted.

Chapter Nineteen

ℭ

Mary knew it was ill-bred to stare, to crane her neck and look about her like some awestruck country loobie, but she could not cage her curiosity. She had never seen such a crowd, such a room, so many beautiful people. Miss Turney's elegant dresses paraded here. Pierre Chantaume's French boots and shoes. Status, wealth, and title draped the shoulders of those who came to hear the music like the exquisite barege silk shawls that were all the rage.

Mary felt like a little girl playing dress up, like a stray vine among hothouse flowers. She did not belong among the *haute ton,* painted in an outmoded color that marked her for the uninformed outsider she was. She did not appreciate the stares turned in her direction, so much direct, unguarded attention from complete strangers, at least a dozen of them gentlemen regarding her intently through opera glasses as though she were a curiosity.

She fingered the slashing on her sleeve. *That* much she had gotten right, but all around her Mr. Ackermann's fashion plates came to life, examples of what she had gotten wrong.

Ostrich-feathered satin toques were popular, and hair dressed à la Gabrielle. A few of the braver beauties drew stares with high Turkish headdresses crowned in drooping bandeaus of pearls and bobbing marabou feathers.

Gallo-Greco bodices were much the fashion and cut much lower than her own, brazenly dangerous, without tuckers or lace. Wide sashes cinched in many a waistline, not ribbons as bound her ribs, and they tied in front, not to the back in love knots as she had supposed.

Formerly so pleased with her stitchery, Mary considered herself an oddity in passé plum. Her gloves bore no puffed ribbon edging. Her velvet reticule was quite outré. Red Morocco leather, finely beaded, proclaimed the current taste. The viscount had said she looked pretty, and yet, the longer they sat beneath blazing chandeliers, everyone eyeing everyone, the more uncomfortable she became.

Despite her fashion failure, she held her head high. Good posture became any outfit, Gran always said. The old lady looked very stiff-backed herself at the moment.

"Isn't this wonderful?" she asked when Mary bent to see how she did.

"I am not so sure," Mary said uneasily. "That gentleman below and to our right will not stop staring. And when you are not looking in their direction, those two there make a point of lowering their glasses to wink and nod. I am unaccustomed to such forward behavior from strangers. Is it common in London?"

Gran pinched on her spectacles and peered at the gentlemen in question. "Perhaps they are friends of Lord Balfour's," she suggested. "Here, we shall ask him. Do you know the gentleman who stares, my lord? And those two who wink and nod at Mary? Oh, but I do beg your pardon. Who is your friend?" she asked.

Balfour had returned to the box in the company of a handsome, smiling fellow in bottle green.

"A good question, marm. Are you my friend, Pinkney?"

The stranger laughed heartily, the sound so pleasant Mary had to smile.

"The best of friends," Pinkney said playfully. "You may depend upon it, Baxter, old boy."

"I depend upon nothing and no one but myself," Baxter said, voice firm. "But I will allow Pinkney Wilburforce, a force to be reckoned with, let me warn you."

"Call me Pinkney." The newcomer briskly bent to salute Gran's hand. "Everyone does. Wilburforce is my

father, the earl. I always turn to look for him when anyone addresses me as such."

He took Mary's hand in his then, the gesture as prac-
ticed and fluid as the elegant leg he made, saying, "As
to those other fellows"—he nodded in the direction of
the gentlemen who eyed the box—"beautiful women
must grow accustomed to being stared at by rogues,
Miss Rivers."

"What a lovely compliment," Gran said.

Mary could not agree, for Pinkney Wilburforce stared
at her roguishly as he said it, his hand grasping hers a
trifle too tight, a trifle too long, as he bent to salute her
gloved fingers.

With a frown, Mary withdrew her hand from his grasp.
"Must I grow accustomed to gentlemen who take all
kinds of liberties?" she asked by way of reprimand.

Wilburforce smiled. "One can only hope," he said
playfully, dark brows arching.

Blood rushed to her cheeks. She looked to Lord Balfour for assistance. Surely he could curb his friend's im-
pertinence better than she, but he was staring over their
heads at the stage, the light from the chandeliers re-
flecting off the lenses of his glasses. "The music starts,"
he said smoothly. "Sit, Pinkney. I cannot see through
your head."

Thus Mary found herself captive of the force called
Pinkney, who sat promptly between her and Gran, a
chair she had hoped the viscount would fill. Not that his
schoolmate was not charming, perhaps too charming.
The power of his smile, his manner, overwhelmed. Pinkney Wilburforce was too lavish with his praise, too ador-
ing in his glances, as if he knew the strength of his
charms and would weaken her with frequent use of
them. She could not look at this handsome fellow without him flashing a cheeky grin, could not speak without
him listening so attentively she felt inadequate to the
task of filling his ears.

She smiled back, of course. Smiles came easily, and
they chatted freely. He was gifted in small talk. But she
felt like a lamb beside a wolf, comforted only by the

thought that he could not eat her with Gran and Lord Balfour in the box.

Lord Balfour increased her sense of uneasiness in taking the chair directly behind them.

He leaned forward, hand warm against her shoulder breath warm in her ear, to say softly as Pinkney rose to greet someone in the neighboring box, "A conquest, Miss Rivers. Pinkney did most particularly wish to make your acquaintance."

He did not laugh as he said it and was not smiling when she turned to gaze at him. He did not look her way at all, eyes fixed upon the musicians below.

Conquest? What did one do with a conquest, she wondered.

"My first," she said. "How kind of you to tell me."

"A faradiddle," he snapped gruffly. "It does not become you to lie."

"What?" Passion fired his voice, she knew not why.

"Not your first at all," he contradicted her, as unpleasantly prickly as when she had first met him.

"No?" He confused her thoroughly this evening.

"No," he said, gaze settling on her briefly, heat in the word, in his eyes. "I can think of at least one other you have vanquished with your smile."

He left her speechless. Could he mean himself?

He moved, as if to sit back. She stopped him, turning more completely in her chair, unable to dismiss the notion she in some way offended him. "Are you angry with me, my lord? Is something wrong between us?"

"Not at all," he said crisply, the edge to his voice in direct contradiction to the words. Heat still smoldered in his gaze. "What could possibly be wrong?"

The music began, a muted peeling of handbells fading into a stately string overture punctuated occasionally by horns. *Christmas music!* How he hated the gay sound of these same predictable songs, leading each year with gay abandon into the New Year. Always the same—inevitable and orderly.

Not at all like his life.

He studied the back of her head, tendril curls drawn

into a simple knot at the crown, candlelight bronzing
them, her profile gilded like his mother's had been when
he was a child and she turned to smile, to laugh, to
speak—to another, more important than he.

Damn Pinkney! Damn the past.

She ought to be whispering in his ear, his words bringing a sparkle to her eyes. But no, past and present became one. He must view his tainted, conniving beauty
from afar—as had his father before him.

Was she tainted? Was she conniving, like his mother?
He did not really want to believe he had fallen for the
same sort of female, did not want to admit himself lonely
again, betrayed by yet another loved one.

Her hair smelled of roses. The nape of her neck beckoned. He wanted her, conniving or not. Could have
her—if his suspicions were true—as his mistress. Was it
not enough? The idea of making love to such a creature
was stimulating, to be sure. To share kisses, to share his
bed with her, the very thought aroused, but the idea that
they were not friends, as he had begun to suppose, that
he might one day tire of her, leaving her to the arms of
another—a Pinkney—revolted him.

The music soured in his ears. He closed his eyes, then
opened them to see Pinkney leaning close enough that
his shoulder pressed hers.

She moved circumspectly away, light from the stage
shimmering on figured silk. *Odd,* what relief he took in
the glow that grew between them.

Pinkney said something, gesturing as he spoke, his
arm sweeping wide, hand crashing into hers. No accident, that. No accident, either, his swiftly taking up
her hand in apology, tone sympathetic, manner solici-
tous and grasping.

She thanked him and slid away. Again Baxter drew
breath.

She sat unhindered for the length of a piece of music,
but then her back stiffened, a gasp slipped her throat,
and she turned, lips thinned, to say curtly, "Your foot,
sir."

Pinkney leaned close, as if he could not hear. An opportunity to brush sleeves again.

"What?"

"Please be so good as to keep your limbs to yourself!" she hissed.

"Something amiss?" Gran asked.

"Oh!" Pinkney pretended surprise. "I do beg your pardon." He leaned into Mary's arm as he bent to examine their feet. "Was that you? I thought I twined leg about the chair, my dear. Please forgive me for such unforgivable familiarity. It would seem I am drawn to you as a vine is drawn to a trellis."

Baxter could bear it no longer. He leaned forward, pressed a hand firmly against Pinkney's shoulder, and said very quietly, "Beware, old chum! I've a pair of snips with which I will not hesitate to pink the Pinkney back to root stock if you persist in vexing the lady."

A moment of silence, broken only by the music, before Pinkney rose, saying, "Best put me out of temptation's way, Baxter. Shall we switch seats?"

Chapter Twenty

He settled beside her, all stiff and prickly comfort in formal black and starched white neckcloth. *Glossy as a holly leaf,* she remembered Mr. Twee's words. A difficult man to hold fast, and yet, with him her sense of safety and well-being were restored. Between them lingered the same tension she had felt from the moment they had met—edgy as standing beneath a kissing ball for the first time.

The music was wonderful. It allowed her to relax and diverted attention away from her. She allowed herself to enjoy, despite Lord Balfour's earlier frostiness, despite the stares and her dress.

A full handbell choir took the stage, fifty-two bellmen in green and gold.

"They played for the king," Gran said, "and met with royal approval." They played now for the king's most noble subjects, white gloves flashing, bells chiming, the music charming in its familiarity: "The Holly and the Ivy," "The Praise of Christmas," "Silent Night," "The First Nowell."

"Do you like it?" Lord Balfour asked Gran at one point, his shoulder brushing Mary's as he turned to ask. She jumped a little that he should touch her, but minded not the contact of their sleeves—a different feeling entirely than when his forward friend had forced similar contact.

Gran beamed at him, no words necessary.

He was beautiful when he smiled, Mary thought—far more attractive than his friend, both gentlemen completely at home in this glittering world of finery and musical magic.

Despite the brush of sleeve to sleeve, how beyond her touch he was. He would marry one of these perfectly fashionable and regally bejeweled young misses, who had never sullied their fingers on a cow's teet, who eyed their box and her host with genteel hunger, and wondered, gossiping, behind fluttering silk fans, who the devil she might be.

As the final tune began, she leaned toward him to say a quiet, "Thank you."

He turned, his breath fanning her face, a faint whiff of coffee and cinnamon. His shoulder met hers with the gentlest of bumps. "Whatever for, merry Miss Mary?"

"Tomorrow Shall Be my Dancing Day" was the song, and though the bells provided none of the lyrics, so familiar were the words they ran through her head. "Singing all my love, my love, my love, my love—Singing all my love to my true love."

It brought a blush to her cheeks to lock eyes with him as it played. Transfixed, the room forgotten, nothing penetrated her thoughts but the firm resistance of his shoulder supporting hers, and his eyes, blue as a robin's egg, warm, searching, as if she knew answers to questions he forgot, as if she were a puzzle he would solve.

How did the pieces fit? What did he want of her? Was there any possibility he loved her? True love, like the song? Or was this heated look no more than the same lustful desire she had witnessed in the eyes of complete strangers, men who knew her not, and yet wanted her, as his eyes revealed he wanted her now.

Pulse pounding in her ears, breath coming fast, she admitted herself drawn to that look in *this* man's eyes.

"Why do you thank me?" he asked, the brush of his breath against her lips tantalizing.

"For the night, my lord. For the music. For saving me from your friend's unwelcome advances."

She told herself she must distance her arm from his, must still the tantalizing brush of fabric to flesh. And yet, she could not. Her arm remained where it was, wantonly delighted, while the rest of her body wished to wind about him like a vine and a heat built within her unlike any she had ever experienced.

"My pleasure," he said as the refrain ended. He turned coolly to applaud, the movement separating them, Lord Thorn again.

It took her a moment to recover, to look about at the gathered beauties in all their trappings, to remember him a viscount, as removed from her as the man in the moon. And yet not so removed that he might not stir her heart, stir desire, and in so doing, jeopardize her reputation. Their interaction had been observed.

A dozen or so sets of opera glasses turned in their direction. The same gentleman who had watched her so brazenly before deliberately lowered his glass to wink.

The music ended, applause swelling, rising around her like a dawning awareness.

They thought her his mistress!

These men who stared so blatantly, these women with noses hitched too high—they already considered her good name forfeit! Why else would a viscount keep such company as she and Gran?

They thought her his mistress!

Applause thundered in her ears, as if the *ton* applauded her realization, delinquent though it might be.

The idea dizzied her, sickened her, battered her already beleaguered self-esteem. She wanted nothing more than to creep from the Argyll Rooms without looking back.

No chance of that. They must exit as slowly as they had entered, Gran's chair their ball and chain, precluding haste.

Mary held her head high, her back straight. She need not look as beaten as she felt.

Lord Balfour was further accosted as they went, acquaintances politely nodding, their gazes searing like flames. She felt shamed, though she had done nothing to be ashamed of.

"Looking forward to your Christmas Eve festivities," Baxter was told over and over, the words changed, but not their meaning.

"Yes, yes." He nodded and waved, in no hurry to

leave, oblivious to her discomfort. He introduced his guests with perfunctory politeness. "My neighbors," he kept referring to them. "In town for the holidays. Yes. They will attend the ball."

The carriage sighted at last, relief flooded Mary's heart as Gran was loaded into that dark oasis of calm. They would escape now, her brush with society at an end.

But no . . .

"Lord Balfour, how good to see you!" A pair of young ladies delayed their departure, both dressed in the highest kick of fashion, glossy close-cropped curls topped by striking sultan-style turbans, gold feathers waving as enthusiastically as did their mama from the doorway of a waiting carriage.

"Mama wanted us to let you know we have just received invitation to your ball, my lord," the younger girl, green-eyed like a cat, with a heart-shaped face and a coy tilt to her head, said. "You must count upon us coming. Mother was in high gig, thinking you had forgotten us."

"The invitations went out later than usual this year." Baxter directed a bow and a tip of the hat to the woman in the carriage. "I do apologize."

"I hear anyone who is anyone and still in London for the holidays will be there."

The elder of the two, a fair-haired creature of perfect complexion, even features, and a breathy laugh, looked Mary up and down as she spoke, as if to question whether she numbered among the "anyone" to whom she referred.

Baxter smiled politely. "Miss Kemp, I don't believe you know Miss Rivers. Mary, may I introduce you to the Honorable Miss Bernice Kemp, and her sister, Armona."

"Rivers." The Honorable Miss Kemp flicked her gold-edged fan Mary's way with an elegant turn of the wrist. "One of the Boxhill Rivers?"

"No. We are largely settled in Glastonbury," Mary said, reading her assumed inferiority in Miss Kemp's every gesture, in the proud tone of her voice.

"I did not know there was any society to be had in Glastonbury." The younger sister chuckled as she said it.

"Perhaps none so honorable as that to be found in London," Mary retorted, smile forced, teeth on edge.

She had meant to take the veiled insult quietly, she really had, but the words leapt to her tongue and were out before she could curb them.

The Misses Kemp blinked at her as if they knew not what to make of such a remark.

Gran's face appeared, frowning, framed in the window of the coach.

Baxter cleared his throat, mild reproof in his tone, though whether it was meant for her or the Misses Kemp, she could not tell. "I look forward to sharing such polite and honorable company again on Christmas Eve." He bowed over each of their hands, turning to help Mary into the coach with a face devoid of emotion.

A spoiled evening—she could think of it in no other terms. From beginning to end, a fiasco. Drained, empty, Mary had no more words, no more quips, no more smiles. She could not look Lord Balfour in the eye.

Nor did it seem he had any desire she should. Silence sat between them like a pregnant woman, pensive and waiting.

Gran tried to ease the tension with talk, her voice all rattle and hum. She praised the music and weather, the springs on the carriage, the shape of the moon. She talked until she went dry, her cough stilled with a horehound drop. The carriage pulled up to her step in an awful silence.

Mary made some attempt to thank Balfour.

He waved them away with a silencing gesture.

"My pleasure, ladies. It will give me even greater pleasure to see you safely inside without further ado."

And so they parted, uneasily, Mary humbled, convinced they would never receive another such invitation from this gentleman whose respect she had lost just as she came to treasure it.

Chapter Twenty-one

With the unruffled facade he had long ago perfected, Baxter stepped from the contained bubble of his coach into the quiet sanctuary of the town house he had inherited. Outwardly calm, he mounted the stairs to the seclusion of his perfectly comfortable room, turmoil roiling, images boiling to the surface of his discontent—her smiles, her posture, the dress.

It was all he could do to ring for his valet as he loosened his neckcloth with unreservedly frantic hands and drank in ragged gulps of air.

Emerson entered to find him already divested of his coat and waistcoat, no easy task, so tight were they tailored. He had fought them off, discarding them inside out on the floor in his wake, shedding as much of the evening as he could, impatient to be done with it, with her, with lies and looks and gossip.

"I trust the evening went well, my lord," the old man said as he always said, as he had said for years and years of evenings out.

"It gave me the headache," Baxter replied faintly, smoothing his hair, wishing he might as easily smooth his thoughts.

"So sorry you are not feeling well, my lord." The old man made his slow way to the bellpull. "Shall I send for hartshorn and water?"

"And a brandy, if you please."

"But of course, my lord."

The valet's familiar, unobtrusive routine soothed Baxter. He was helped, without further question, from his shirt and shoes, breeches and stockings. His coat and waistcoat were picked up, righted, smoothed, and hung away.

Emerson had always organized his disordered wardrobe, Temple his mind. There was no one else in the house he could speak to so candidly. Did the old man ghost about the place, Baxter wondered, ready to listen, trying vainly to advise?

A knock sounded upon the door—the maid. Emerson greeted her with quiet orders.

She went away to turn the gossip mill in his own house. He could almost hear the whispers. A night of unpleasant tale-telling, and he must hold himself together—evidence no displeasure, no anger, no regret for the space of time it took for Emerson to assist him into his nightshirt and set out his hairbrushes, his toothpowder, and the case for his glasses. Then the household descended upon him, expressions vaguely anxious. He was not prone to headaches, to ill health of any kind. Will came first with hot water for his evening toilet.

He filled the washbasin. Emerson set out fresh linen. The door was opened for Holloway, brandy decanter and a snifter on a tray, at his heels the underbutler with a second tray bearing a pitcher of water, a glass, the vial of hartshorn, a spoon. The two of them poured and splashed and stirred with a minimum of clinking. The maid, Millie, entered last with the glowing bed warmer, her cheeks pink with the heat. Emerson neatly folded back the bedcovers that she might rub hot brass between the linens.

Baxter forced himself to smile during the invasion. He nodded throbbing head. He took the clouded liquid, threw back the foul taste in a single gulp, chased the bitterness away with a sip of brandy, and bade them go.

They bobbed their way out, wishing him good night, trying not to appear to be observing him more than was proper. Emerson shut the door ever so quietly.

Baxter breathed a sigh of relief, removed his glasses, pinched the bridge of his nose, and stood at the window, nightshirt flapping against bare legs, brandy in hand, staring at the blurred white crescent of the moon. It shed thin light on the city, on his problem.

The windows level with his on the opposite side of the street glowed like unfocused starbursts of gold. Nash's new gas lighting. Mr. Nash entertained again. Anyone who might invest in his dreams was invited to dine and to examine his exquisitely decorated apartments lined with books, Roman statuary, and models of his proposed projects, Regent Street among them.

Baxter had been one of those to walk the gallery. He had seen the plans, the dollhouse-size models, the proposed remaking of his world, before the area had been turned inside out, before the sound of hammering took over and the street was torn up for repaving, his future upended, all that was familiar about his childhood lost. He had wondered, at the time, as he had never dared to wonder before, why he stayed in a house filled with unpleasant memories. He ought to have sold the place as soon as it was signed over to him.

A lone horse clopped by in the street below. He warmed his tongue with the mellow burn of brandy, and leaned into the cool of the pane, hoping the pounding in his head would stop, please stop, that he might think what to do, what to say and to whom, to stop the gossip, the whispers, the sly innuendo and quirking lips. He would not follow the path his parents had taken.

He remembered the contemptuous looks his father had received when he was a lad, the whispers that had followed his mother. Too painful the memories, too lasting their effect on his life. He had risen above it—built himself the best of reputations. All gone in an instant, all due to one completely innocent moment of weakness and one conniving woman.

The world was ready to believe her his mistress, just as Gilbert had warned him, just as Pinkney had proven. What other reason had a gentleman of his standing, of his family history, favoring the company of a country nobody?

"Clever of him to bring along the Granny," he had overheard someone say. *"Discreet, like his father."*

A sly laugh. A wink. *"Some semblance of propriety that way. A clever facade."*

"A beauty he has captured. Will she be at the ball?"

The hot-blooded among them wanted a closer look. The judgmental wished to condemn.

He paced from the window to the bed and back again, the moon disinterested, the watch calling out the hour and all was well. But it was not well. His loneliness had never pierced so completely.

The world judged him far cleverer than he was, far more fortunate. Moonlight pooled silver on the empty bed. He remembered how she had looked that day outside of Gaffin's Marbleworks, all angel's wings and smiles—in church on Sunday, head piously bowed, Mary, not Merry. What would she look like, he wondered, hair fanned like wings upon his pillow?

Was she a gift from God or the devil? Virgin or vixen? He had not the answers.

He paced until his feet grew chilled, then slid into the unsatisfying embrace of bedcovers gone cold. Heart and head throbbed. His body ached with need, with yearning, with an urgency that kept him tossing and turning in search of release, in search of answers.

Sleep eluded him, and comfort. The feather mattress seemed too big and filled with bricks. He longed to pillow his head elsewhere.

Had he misread her from the beginning?

He recalled the exact tone of her voice as she rebuked Pinkney for daring to touch her. How to explain why she then allowed him similar familiarity without objection? What was he to think? To do?

He made every effort to sleep, without success. Dreams woke him. Her hands in his hair. Her knees bumping his. Her shoulder leaning, lips within kissing distance. She wrapped around his mind like a trailing vine. What was her every touch but an attempt to similarly enwrap him with her arms, her body?

Could so much physical contact, so many speaking glances, such an eye-catching dress be perfectly innocent? He thought not.

Temple would have said gentlemen and ladies do not

call attention to themselves. Temple would have reminded him to behave in a discreet and gentlemanly
manner. He would have a family of his own someday,
and he must conduct himself in a manner worthy of their
respect. But Temple could not tell him how to handle a
situation in which his name was already tied to a tempting plum tart of a girl he longed to lavish with kisses,
as he pummeled his pillow into submission and stared
at the ceiling, bedclothes tented about his need, his hand
discreet but decidedly ungentlemanly beneath the
covers.

What to do? What to say? The sun rose on questions
unanswered, with but one logical course of action. He
must remove himself from temptation, avoid Miss Mary,
do his best to still gossip of his assumed misconduct with
the girl, and get on with this dreadful season.

The Christmas Eve ball hung over him like a sword
of Damocles. He would see her again then, and only
then. He would demonstrate to others his disregard, his
self-control. She was his neighbor, due to disappear into
the hinterlands of Glastonbury with the coming of the
New Year—nothing more, nothing less. Hang the gossip!
Hang speculation and whispers and sideways looks.
Hang the loneliness that had driven him to acts of
indiscretion.

He rose exhausted, face haggard, blue smudges dark
beneath his eyes, determined to return order to his life,
determined to plunge himself in arrangements for the
ball. Food and wine must be ordered, rooms aired and
decorated, gifts purchased. He made a long list. Temple
had left him with much to do.

She stood at the window, heavy-eyed as the overcast
sky, listening to the chill whistle of the wind at the pane,
no sun to be seen, no brightness or warmth but the cup
of tea in her hand and the sound of coals shifting in
the grate.

Outside, up the street, a flurry of buff-colored coattails
caught her eye, the top of his hat revealed itself, the tips
of buff-gloved fingers evident as he held the hat against
the wind, the brim hiding his eyes. Straight-backed, jaw

set, he stepped swiftly from door to carriage, Temple at his heels. No glance in her direction. A brisk snap of the door and Will and Ned scrambled aboard. A familiar picture, an echo of the day they had met.

Woodrow called to the horses, "Walk on."

The words resonated. Life walked on, and she, crippled, crawling, spirit bruised, failed to keep pace.

The clock ticked loudly from the sitting room, Gran's spoon clinked against her cup, the cup against the saucer, horse's hooves clopped in the street. She stared at her reflection as the coach pulled away.

What had she expected? A wave? A smile? Would he ever look favorably again at the unconnected Glastonbury girl who stared back at her from the glass?

"Splendid music last night, was it not, my dear?" Gran's voice jerked her from her reverie. "And you so lovely in your dress."

Mary closed her eyes on the chill view. She took a sip of tea, turned once more into the warm closeness of the room, and considered wearily all that she had yet to do.

"The music was nice," she agreed.

"And your stitchery such a success. Lord Balfour's eyes on stalks, all of the gentlemen staring. I must write to your mother."

"No, Gran. Please don't," she said, too strident.

"Why ever not?"

A knock at the door. She knew it was not he, had just watched him drive away, and yet her heart leapt with hope and her hand, suddenly clumsy, tipped the cup, staining the front of her bodice.

Mary dabbed at the tea stain with her apron, the sound of voices at the door distracting. She could not tell whose.

"I would prefer Mother heard nothing," she said.

Gran shoved aside her tray, china rattling. "Why ever would you want to keep your success from your family, my dear? I do not understand."

A tap at the door and Bethany pushed it wide, a whoosh of cold air accompanying the enormous nosegay in her hands—hothouse tulips, red and yellow, heads already droopy with the cold, a sprig of Crown Imperial, a spray of bold red carnations. "These came," she said. "For you, miss. Aren't they lovely?"

"What an extravagance!" Gran crowed. "Lord Balfour shouldn't have."

Mary read the card. "He didn't. Pinkney Wilburforce sends his regards."

"Did I not tell you the evening was a success? I daresay he will call on us before long."

"And you will refuse him entry," Mary directed Bethany.

"To my house? You will do no such thing!" Gran contradicted her.

"Will you be so good as to put these in water?" Mary shoved the flowers in Bethany's direction.

"Yes, miss." She carried them away.

"No letter to your mum, no entry to Mr. Wilburforce. Whatever has soured your mood this morning, Mary? I have never known you to be rude."

"It is Pinkney Wilburforce who is rude."

"Rude? To send you flowers? Why ever should you think so? Next you will claim every man who set eyes on you last night rude for staring at you."

"You did not find anything exceptional in it?"

"You were breathtaking, my dear. Gentlemen cannot help but stare at a pretty young woman."

"I was overdressed, Gran. Could you not see it? Men stared because I did not fit in."

"Don't be silly!"

"I am not being silly." Cross, she took up the tray, heading for the door.

"Well, don't think that I shall not write to your mother of it, for I shall." Gran threw aside her covers, and with a pained expression swung her legs out of the bed. "I have never heard of anything more absurd than this reticence on your part to admit the evening a success."

Mary stopped at the door, the tray gripped so tightly her knuckles hurt. She felt like crying or shouting, but could not quite decide which reaction might prove more gratifying. She restrained both emotions, saying, "I beg you will not."

"You will take me to the desk, if you please." Gran imperiously grabbed up her walking stick from beside the bed. "I have correspondence to catch up on." She planted the stick on the floor with a thump and leaned into it, rising slowly. "I mean to write your mother and nothing you can say will stop me."

Mary licked her lips and stared down at egg-stained Limoge. "Not even if I tell you they think me his mistress?"

Chapter Twenty-two

Baxter stood in J&J Holmes's Shawl Manufacturers, trying to decide between two barage silk shawls for his niece. The odor of fresh dye stung his eyes. The faint whir of the looms intruded from the backroom. Memory of Mary Rivers's shoulders, of the softest of cashmere, disabled him.

Activity, and plenty of it, he had thought, would help him to forget her, push her from the forefront of his mind, calm his desires, still the voice within that harked back to the tawdry notion Gilbert had planted—that he should take Mary Rivers as his mistress.

His plan proved flawed.

Twice he convinced himself he saw the young lady, only to find himself mistaken, his eyes drawn to a similar set of the head, to the drift of a red cloak caught on the wind. She was everywhere and nowhere, a memory that clung. He expected at every moment to catch sight of her reflection in the windows they passed.

And in those windows, the perfect gift, not for the names on his list, but for her. She had so little.

In examining china teapots for his aunt, he considered replacing the chipped one from which she had served him. In searching out his mother's favorite French soaps, his senses homed in on exactly the rose scent that Mary Rivers used. He looked at pearls and diamonds in Lancaster's and imagined them around her neck. He walked past Lucas's furrier and longed to clothe her. He stopped beneath the sign for Lipscomb's corsets and longed to unclothe her.

He fixated on what she needed, no matter how hard he tried not to.

"And what do you want for Christmas?" Temple asked him at one point.

He was thinking of her in that very instant. What did he want that he did not already have?

The answer was so easy, so obvious. He wanted her—however he might have her. He wanted Mary Rivers. He would not spend another Christmas, another night, alone. Why should he not have her? Everyone in London thought he already did. Was he the only one to hold himself to a higher standard—the only lord in London without a mistress for Christmas?

When he failed to answer, Temple pressed, "In case anyone should ask."

His response was deliberately enigmatic. "What every man wants, Temple."

Notebook ready, Temple guessed. "Brandy, my lord?"

Baxter laughed. "Something spirited, yes. To warm a cold night." *You are closer than you realize, my boy,* he thought. *Your father would have known in an instant.*

Temple bit the end of the pencil stub, puzzling the matter.

A bell rang—St. Phillip's. A Christmas sound. Lonely, he thought, until the solitary ringing was joined by an echoing peel from All Soul's at the other end of the street.

"What is there missing in my life at the moment?"

"A Yule log, my lord?"

Baxter enjoyed this game. "A good guess, lad," he said. "What I want does involve heat—one that threatens to consume me."

Temple frowned. The pencil stub wavered uncertainly. "Hothouse fruits, my lord? I know you are fond of pineapples."

Baxter threw back his head and laughed, the laughter liberating. His mind was made up. A great weight had been lifted from his shoulders, a great burden of good behavior. He was hungry, no denying it, for fruits young Temple did not yet fathom. "Sweetness, yes, and tart," he said, mouth watering with anticipation, pulse quickening. "Something to quench the emptiness within. That is exactly what I want."

It smelled like snow as he returned home, brisk purpose quickening his errands, most of his purchases made with businesslike efficiency. He was met by Holloway, dour-faced and worried.

"I could not turn her away, my lord," were the first words from his mouth. "She insisted she must see you. Insisted upon waiting. Said she meant to stand on the doorstep if I did not let her in. I thought it best not to turn her away."

Baxter smiled, heart lifting. *Mary!* She had come to him.

"How long has Miss Rivers waited?" he asked, already on his way to the drawing room.

"The last quarter of an hour, my lord, but it is Mrs. Rivers, not Miss."

Baxter frowned. "She comes alone?"

"Yes, my lord."

Curious.

"In her chair?"

"No, my lord. No chair."

Even more curious.

"Thank you, Holloway. Well done."

She turned her head when he entered, the down of her gray hair windblown as gosling feathers, her expression agitated. She planted her cane and tried to rise.

"Please don't get up," he said. "I am very sorry to keep you waiting. I had no idea you intended to call. I have been shopping."

"I thought you would never come," she said quietly, her hands atremble on the cane.

He wondered, as he drew a chair closer to the sofa she had chosen, where she fit into his new course of action. Would she make noise? Or was Gilbert right, and Mary's Gran but part of the deception?

"Is anything wrong, Mrs. Rivers? I was startled to hear that you had walked in this cold. I think we shall have snow before the day is out."

"Mary thinks me napping." She frowned, as if her

deceit pained her. "I did not want her to know I came to you."

"This sounds rather nefarious. How may I help?"

"Well, I hope you may do something. Mary tells me it is too late. But I would not hear it. Some effort must be made. If anyone can make this right, it is you."

His brows rose. "Make what right?"

"This stupid notion Mary has taken into her head. I am not even sure she has the right of it. I hope, for her sake, she does not."

"Notion?"

Mrs. Rivers kneaded the top of her cane with twisted fingers. "That she must refuse Mr. Wilburforce's flowers—that people are saying dreadful things about her. I never heard such nonsense."

And so it began, he thought, just as Gilbert had warned him. *Once talk is flying, mark my words, the old woman will do her best to place the two of you in a compromising position. She can then insist you must marry the girl to save her reputation.*

"What nonsense?" he asked, dreading what came next, dreading confirmation that Gilbert's jaundiced view of the world was accurate, no matter that it might get him what he wanted. Bittersweet, this Christmas gift.

She sighed and wrung the neck of her cane, as if it needed strangling. "It is too dreadful," she said. "I cannot even voice it."

He took a deep breath. Her act was convincing, if act it was.

"Shall I coax it out of Mary, then?" he asked, convinced it would not take much to coax all that he wanted out of Miss Mary Rivers.

She was his for the taking.

Chapter Twenty-three

Mary pulled her shawl a little closer and adjusted her chair by the window, that the milky light might better illuminate the pale fabric stretched tight upon her embroidery hoop. The needle pierced the picture, dark green silk floss following, another stitch taken in the table runner she made her mother for Christmas, bordered in holly and ivy—holly for Christ's crown of thorns, evergreen as was his memory.

As was her memory of the previous evening. She could feel the stares, hear the buzz of whispering. Her skin burned.

She sighed and sank the needle home again.

Her sister, Evie, said if you put a sprig of ivy under your pillow on Christmas Eve, you dreamt of your true love.

She did not need ivy. He had troubled her all night long, his shoulder to hers, his breath in her ear, his hands . . . ah, nothing prickly about Lord Thorn in her dreams. All softness, and warmth, he had cradled her in his arms. She had lifted her lips to be kissed. There was mistletoe and music, violins playing Christmas dances, the Christmas Eve ball come early.

She had twirled and cavorted, skirts whirling, heart racing, waking to find it was not Christmas at all, no reason for dancing, the house still and lonely, bedclothes tangled about her feet.

A stitch, another stitch, and here was a holly leaf, as spiny as her thoughts. Trivial, these dreams of true love when her chances of such with a viscount were as unlikely as the idea that she would ever agree to be his mistress. Why did she spend her morning preparing gifts for a holiday that could bring her no joy now that her name, character, and formerly spotless reputation stood in question?

She sighed and rethreaded her needle, her thoughts like the ivy, ever winding.

People—strangers—spoke ill of her, suspecting behavior of her completely contrary to her nature. *Repugnant!* And yet, her dream had not been in the least repugnant. She jabbed the needle unwarily, pricking her finger, a drop of crimson staining the cloth. She sucked her fingertip. The season had never seemed so bleak.

Below, a knock upon the door. She missed a stitch. Strange how her heart persisted in hoping it might be he, even as her brain told her not to be foolish.

She could hear Bethany open the door, a masculine voice, not deep enough for Lord Balfour, and then the door closed, shutting out the noise of the street, and Beth's footsteps clattered on the stairs.

She had the error repaired on the holly and looked up, completely calm, when the girl stepped in to say, "My brother, miss, is at the door."

Her heart missed a stitch. Balfour's secretary came knocking?

"Not bad news from your mother, I hope?" she said.

"No, nothing like that, miss. His lordship sends him. Your Gran is taking tea with him, and he wonders would you care to join them?"

"Gran? But she's downstairs asleep."

"No, miss." Bethany hung her head. "Her room is empty. Crept out, she did. I never heard the door open or close."

Mary set aside her embroidery hoop as she rose, stunned. "She walked? By herself? When it is so cold? Whatever does she think she's doing?"

He knew she was coming by the length of time it took Temple to return. It seemed an eternity of chitchat, he and the old woman exhausting any number of topics, chief among them his Christmas Eve ball.

Would there be singing and dancing? Mummers? Kissing balls? What sort of food did he plan to serve? And his family? Would they be there as well? His parents were touring the Continent, were they not?

He was saved from this last uncomfortable direction in the conversation by their tread on the stair, her voice in the hallway. The painted porcelain doorknob turned.

Her Gran's face lit with expectation, questions forgotten. His blood raced with anticipation.

She dressed plainly, the green dress outmoded, the lace collar a poor attempt to distract the eye from its faded color. She looked not at him when she entered, as he had hoped, but at her grandmother.

"Did you mean to frighten me witless, Gran?" She crossed the room in a hurry, expression troubled.

"Not at all." The old lady stamped her cane. "Sit down, Mary, towering over me like that. I am fine. My rheumatism troubles me less than our situation."

She looked at him—a glance, no more. No delight in her expression, only concern, and a hint of embarrassment.

Temple's gaze zigzagged back and forth between them.

"I fear you will begin to feel we monopolize your time, my lord," she said. "And take undue advantage of your kindness, burdening you with our troubles."

Her manner was reserved—her tone, distant. He found it vaguely amusing, even admirable, that she dared to suggest she would not push herself on him. Was it not her design all along? She kept him wondering. It added to her allure.

"Bother all." Mrs. Rivers wrung the neck of her cane. "He is directly affected by our 'troubles.' "

He was unused to such a stir in his sitting room, to voices raised and passions roused. He was unused to airing his concerns so freely in front of the servants. He longed to shout, Be still! I will take care of everything.

"I am always happy to spend time with you," he said instead, his voice calm, manner unruffled.

He had almost forgotten the pull of her gold-flecked eyes, the power of her mouth, not smiling today, but thinned into a worried line. Beguiling nonetheless, a vine that bound him to her.

"Even though it causes talk?" she asked.

She leapt to the point without preamble. The question hung uneasily between them.

Temple and the old woman faced him expectantly. He had no desire to further their discussion in the presence of others.

He rose, saying, "I wonder if you would care to see my uncle's collection of rubbings, Miss Rivers?"

She seemed for the moment nonplused. Chin up, she asked, voice thin, a trace of fear in her eyes, "And just what did your uncle rub, my lord?"

He smiled, might even have laughed had she shown the slightest trace of humor. "Brasses," he managed to say in all seriousness as he held out his arm to her. When she evidenced no sign of comprehension, he added, "grave markers."

The light of understanding glowed in her eyes.

Temple stepped forward. The old lady held out her hand that he might help her to her feet.

Baxter hastened to say, "Temple will entertain Mrs. Rivers with his plans for the ball, won't you, Temple?"

Temple bowed and sank into the chair across from the old woman. "A pleasure, my lord."

"It seems a morbid preoccupation—rubbing at graves," Mary said quietly as she placed the warm weight of her hand in the crook of his arm.

"Perhaps you will change your mind when you see them."

The display room was conveniently connected to the sitting room. His uncle had enjoyed exhibiting his collection to guests. Baxter opened the door and stood back that he might watch her face as she crossed the threshold.

"Oh, but they are beautiful!" she exclaimed, eyes widening.

Her voice, awestruck, echoed. The room was sparsely furnished, peopled only by the enormous gilt-framed charcoal images, men and women, not quite life-size, in the costuming of the past.

A black knight and his lady stared down at them as they first walked in the door. He in full armor, dark shield raised, black sword on one hip, black dagger on the other, a black heraldic dog beneath chain mail–covered feet. His wife stood beside him, wimpled and veiled, black cote-hardie caught up in an elegant fold in the bend of an elbow, embroidered black kirtle peeping from beneath.

"It is the only room in the house I have done nothing to change," Baxter said, eyes on her, not the rubbings. She seemed always new to him, a mystery to unravel, her figure tempting despite the poor cut of her clothes, her stance one of a woman completely fascinated.

"It is as though we have stepped into the presence of the past, the dead." Her voice was suitably hushed. Her gaze drifted past him along the row of dark figures, her steps drifting as well. "And yet they do not seem dead."

"I always feel my uncle's presence here, and Temple's."

He had never said as much to anyone else.

She met his remark with thoughtful silence before she surprised him saying, "Your uncle must have loved you."

"What makes you think so?" His tone sounded unintentionally harsh.

She stepped away, eyes dark and full of mystery. "He left you all of this, did he not?" She spread her arms.

As if money—things—added up to love. *How naive.* And yet, was it not money she wanted of him? He was reminded of his purpose in bringing her here alone to talk.

She stopped before a dark lord and his lady. He wore thigh-high boots, the crisp white of the paper outlining a dashing mantle and a stiff Elizabethan collar, sword to the side, his lady in a richly embellished gown, hair bound back in white netting, a white circlet about her brow.

"Miss Rivers . . ." he began.

She pretended not to hear. "Was your uncle's fascination with the dead, or art?"

"Neither."

She turned, as he had hoped, dark head cocked in curiosity, dark eyes full of questions.

"His interest lay in the idea of love everlasting."

"Oh?" She blinked, lips parting, the word in a low gasp.

"He told me once these portraits filled him with a sense of it."

"What of you?" She stepped away, stopping before the rubbing of a Pilgrim couple, cloaks deeply collared, hats wide-brimmed. "Do you believe in love everlasting?"

He eyed her rather than the stoic couple, wondering if it had been budding love first drew him to her, made him defend her so hotly against his cousin's warnings, moved him to ask her to accompany him to the Argyll Rooms. He had experienced in his every encounter with her feelings unlike any he had ever before enjoyed. He was still drawn to her as no other, still felt twinges of his original admiration. But love—eternal love? Could anything withstand the tests of time?

"My uncle never found it," he said bitterly.

"Had he no wife?"

He laughed harshly. "Only other men's."

"Ah," she whispered. "None to rest eternally at his side."

He loved the sadness in her eyes. It echoed his own.

She turned and walked on. He followed, studying the nape of her neck, imagined touching her there.

Who would lie at his side for eternity?

She stopped before another of the rubbings—a doubleted lord, wives at each elbow, They looked identical, the two women. How could one see eternal love in two wives? This rubbing he liked least of them all. It reminded him too much of the vagaries of life, of death, of fortune. He stopped beside Mary Rivers, purposefully close, as close as the figures on the wall, their arms almost touching. Would she step away? Would he, like his father, go lonely to the grave?

"I believe . . ." she said, voice soft. She turned and looked him in the eyes. "I believe in love everlasting."

Her words startled him, for surely what she meant to offer him was anything but eternal.

"Mary . . ." he said, and gently took her hand, for surely now was the time to make his proposal.

She closed her eyes and turned away, hand sliding from his, gaze locked on the silent figures, as if she sought sympathy from the dead. "I have heard the gossip." Her mouth wore a wounded look. "They think me your mistress."

"I know." He stepped closer, protectively, longing to take her into his arms, hesitant to make a move. "What shall we do about such idle gossip?" He captured a lock of hair, held her lightly tethered thus.

She looked first at his hand, the hair, then pinned him with gold-flecked eyes. "Can innocence ever put a stop to mean-spirited prattle?"

He kissed her. It seemed a moment for nothing less. He simply followed the lock of her hair inward, stopping at her mouth, his lips seeking hers.

A glancing kiss. He caught her by surprise. She drew back with a gasp, the lock of hair slipping from his fingers. "My lord!"

"My merry Mary," he said, halting her retreat.

Flustered, she looked him in the eyes, could not help it, so close were they. He read alarm there, anger, too, and veiled desire. Something else. Could it be hope?

He had no hold on her but his gaze, traveling from the softness of her slightly parted lips to the conflicted emotion in her eyes and back again in a taut, breathless circuit.

"How would such a dilemma be resolved in Glastonbury?" he whispered.

She laughed wryly. "Why, nothing for it but the gentlemen in question would have made an offer by now."

Her words alarmed him. He had begun to think her innocent of all his prior suspicions.

"I've a proposal," he said wryly. "An offer."

He clasped her hand, turned it so that it rested, palm up, kissed the cup of it, kissed the beat of her pulse at the wrist. His gaze rose to meet hers.

"I would not have you the object of groundless speculation," he said.

"What would you have?" The words held a throaty challenge, some heat to the question, growing heat in the depths of her eyes, in the hand she allowed to remain cupped in his.

He smiled, enjoying their closeness, enjoying the tension mounting between them.

Slowly, deliberately, he lowered his mouth to hers. She stood stock-still, breath short and ragged, the closing of her eyes the sign of capitulation he awaited.

He did not kiss her, instead, whispered into the delicate shell of her ear. "I would have you, Mary. I have known from the moment I first saw you, that you were what I wanted for Christmas."

The curve of her neck beckoned, the shining tendrils of her hair. Her breath hitched in her throat.

He halted within a breath of her lips to whisper, "A Mary Christmas. A Merry Mary Christmas."

She closed the distance. Head tilting, chin rising, her mouth met his.

He slid his hands about her waist and drew her to him.

Chapter Twenty-four

Mary could not believe what was happening. The world seemed tipped newly askew, a wonderful upsetting of her view of how things must be. He held her, lips warm, arms a safe haven, the most comforting place on earth. He loved her, he wanted her, he meant to make things right again.

She could not begin to grasp the idea that Charles Thornton Baxter, fourth Lord Balfour, the prickly Lord Thorn, wished Mary Rivers of Glastonbury to become his viscountess. She did not even try, simply lost herself in his arms, his lips, his promises—everything for the moment good and hopeful and bright.

The taste of his mouth was the taste of her future. His hands gathered her closer, always closer, when she thought already they were as close as two people could be. His mouth spoke to her of desire, of needs, of his love for her. She knew it was not ladylike in her to allow him such freedom, and yet she wanted his hands exploring the nape of her neck, the length of her spine, the small of her back. She wanted her aching breasts pressed to the hard resistance of his chest, to be clutched close, her belief in love everlasting confirmed.

Desire welled within her, a heat so intense she felt sure it must consume her. She could not get enough of his mouth, his hands, of this wild, overwhelming happiness. So strong was the rise of feeling it frightened her.

She pushed away at last. "You go too fast, sir."

"No. No. Not too fast at all, my dearest Mary. You've

no idea how long I have waited, how many lonely years."

She regretted her own impulse as he released her, smiling with a warmth she had never seen light his face before. Blushing, unable to stop herself from smiling back at him like a fool, she straightened mussed hair and smoothed her bodice, wishing it were as easy to smooth her nerves.

"May I tell Gran?" she asked, suddenly shy.

He cocked his head, the glow in his eyes cooling. "Yes. Of course. If you wish." He turned away from her, as if to examine the rubbings, drifting back down the length of the room as he spoke, his voice echoing hollowly. "I shall begin arrangements for paperwork to be drawn up. Contracts detailing dispensation before we carry on. A solicitor will call. Shall I arrange it for the day after tomorrow?"

How cold he suddenly seemed, how businesslike, to discuss marriage contracts so soon. And yet, he was a wealthy man. Such things were common to this world, a world she must accustom herself to.

"Whatever you wish." She followed in his wake, ardor cooling. Did she make a mistake in accepting? Did she really love this handsome, distant thorn of a man?

He opened the door to the sitting room and held it for her.

"It is settled then," he said with a finality that had nothing to do with his former heat, with the kisses that still left her lips swollen with desire.

"Yes," she said, realizing for the first time he had never said the words, never said, "I love you."

He walked them home, Gran leaning on his arm, she trailing behind. Perhaps it was just the weather. The breeze nipped at her ears, nose, and lips. A nasty draft swept up under her skirt. Leaden clouds promised snow. He seemed colder than ever.

He did not linger in his good-byes, no more than glanced at her in leaving. She had expected more—a word, a look. Anything to salve her guilt in allowing him to kiss her so fervently, to rouse heated desire, to touch her as she had never before been touched.

She could not have missed it in a glance, a smile. She watched him too carefully. There was no sign, no word, no gesture. He left them with a bow and turned to hurry into the wind.

She told Gran over a steaming pot of tea.

Gran almost dropped her cup.

"He has made a proposal? Can it be true? A viscount has asked my granddaughter for her hand! But why did he not say a word of it to me? I am your nearest relative in London. Surely it is unusual that he spoke not a word to me in leaving?"

Mary did not like to reveal her own uneasiness in the matter. She had noticed Lord Balfour's silence. "He sends his solicitor to draw up the marriage contracts the day after tomorrow."

"So soon!" Gran clapped her hands with a gasp. "Before he has so much as met the family? Highly unusual, my dear, but perhaps he wishes the gossip stilled and your future secure before he speaks to your father."

"Yes," she said, unable to suppress a smile at the idea of her mother and father meeting the viscount. *Charles.* She must learn to think of him as Charles. Or would he prefer that she called him Baxter? She could not call him Thornton, never Thornton.

"Surely he would know better than we how such a thing is to be done," she said in all confidence.

It snowed that evening and into the night. Baxter watched it from his bedroom window—a strange, otherworldly sugarspun scene of white blotting out the black, no moon to be seen. Clouded was the sky, snowflakes falling golden in the lamplight, making white the night, the street, the tops of hats and heads.

It slowed the passing carriages, horses hooves slipping—slowed his thoughts as well. The day's race of his mind threatened another headache. One minute he was happy with his situation, body tensed with anticipation, hedonistic heart leaping with desire; the next he felt he had done a great wrong to Miss Rivers, to himself, to the idea of who and what he meant to make of himself.

Would that life were so clearly darkness and light as the view from his window. Would that he might hush gossip as the snow hushed footsteps and horses hooves and wheels on paving stones beneath a pure, untouched blanket of white.

He had asked her to be his lover, and she had said yes. If not for eternity, how long could they make it last? Would his feeling for her melt away like snow in sunshine?

Thoughts like these made him uncomfortable in her company, in her grandmother's company. How did one tuck away guilt? How did one silence the voice of honor and reason within? He heard too often in his mind Temple's snort of disgust, Nanny's tsk, tsk. The idealist within made noise, too. Was this really what he wanted—to shame a virgin, a virgin named Mary, for Christmas?

God help him, this was supposed to be his moment of triumph, and he could not enjoy it.

Given she *was* a virgin.

To think otherwise appalled him. To think she might have had sexual congress with other men—been discarded. No, he could not believe it of her. The very idea disgusted him.

He rang for Temple, and scribbled out a list.

The lad arrived with the bright-eyed attentiveness of youth and servitude. "My lord?"

"I shall require the carriage in the morning."

"Yes, my lord." Temple pulled out his notebook. "What time, my lord?"

"No later than eleven. I wish to take a short jaunt into the country—my uncle's house—to fetch a Yule log. I intend to be back before dark."

"It *is* snowing, my lord."

"Of course, the horses are to be put to harness only if the roads are still passable."

"Anything else, my lord?"

"These items are to be purchased before I leave. Viands will be required for the journey, and you will be so good as to convey this invitation to Miss Rivers? I wish her to accompany me."

Temple nodded as he scanned the list. "Very good, my lord. I understand felicitations are in order?"

Baxter's head rose abruptly in surprise.

Temple was smiling, as if the subject were such that anyone in the household might openly speak to him of it. "Beth said the ladies were very excited . . ."

"I would prefer you and your sister did not repeat any gossip you share amongst yourselves, Temple," he said curtly.

Temple's smile disappeared. "Yes, my lord." He sounded much subdued.

"You may go," Baxter said, unhappy with himself for snapping at the lad.

Temple paused at the door and turned. "Have you set a date, my lord?"

"What?"

"Special days require special planning." Temple's expression was carefully bland—like his father's before him.

Good God! It had never occurred to him that all of his servants must become accessory to his every illicit liaison. There was no real privacy in a house of this size. Did he draw Temple's children into sin, in choosing to sin himself? Just as his mother had made him part and party to her sin?

"I will keep you informed as necessary," he said breathlessly, completely disgusted with himself, and yet, he did not call Temple back. He did not call off his plans for the morrow.

Chapter Twenty-five

She did not know what to make of the gifts the viscount lavished upon her the following morning. Was such an excess of generosity commonplace among the wealthy?

First came Temple with an invitation—an excursion into the countryside.

She gladly accepted. It calmed her fears that Baxter had been in some way put out with her the day before. Seeing him again, like pinching herself, would confirm his offer was real, her future real, the joy that painted her every waking moment—all real.

Next, his lordship's footman, Will, stood at the door, a large box tied with string in his hands, and in the box, a beautiful heavy velvet cape she had seen at Nicholl's tailoring shop. It was the luscious deep red of a fine French burgundy. No sooner did she pull it from the folds of tissue it had been nested in than another knock upon the door brought her Ned, and another box, and in it to warm her hands a beautiful ermine muff with a holly green satin lining and dangling tassels in the same evergreen. A new bonnet arrived last, Temple again, breathing great clouds of steam, his nose red with the cold.

She spread her booty about the sitting room, Gran crowing with delight, declaring it Christmas come early.

"A generous man, your future husband," she chirped.

"He cannot mean for me to wear these things today." Mary fingered the brim of the bonnet. "Can he? Sounds a wet, messy excursion, wading through snow to fetch a log."

"You will be able to afford a dozen such cloaks as Viscountess Balfour," Gran reminded her. "My only concern is whether it is proper for a young woman, whose wedding has not yet been publicly announced by way of public banns, to accept such personal items of clothing from her affianced. It was certainly not done in my day."

"Surely Lord Balfour knows what is acceptable, and what is not? Do you think he will arrange for a special license?"

"Oh!" Gran laughed. "But of course he will."

"You think, then, that I must not wear any of these gifts today?" Mary eyed the bonnet and muff with longing. "You do not think he will find me ungrateful?"

"Far preferable he should find you ungrateful than a forward miss."

Mary, her mind on kisses, a blush firing her cheeks, made no argument. Lord Balfour knew already how forward she could be.

The first thing he asked her when she met him at the door was, "Did you not care for the things I sent, Mary?"

With a blush, her head dipped, revealing more completely the refurbished crown of the old bonnet he had hoped to see replaced.

"If you mean the hat, muff, and cape, my lord," she said quietly with a smile that lit her eyes like stars "they are wonderful! I have never seen anything more beautiful. I do not wish to appear ungrateful, but Gran is old-fashioned, and I did not wish to risk spoiling them in an excursion that promises to be a wet tramp in the woods."

"Is that what you are expecting?" he asked, as he helped her down the steps and into the carriage. Will nipped down from the seat beside the coachman to arrange hot bricks about her feet. "A wet tramp in the woods?"

"We go to fetch a Yule log, do we not, my lord?" she asked, all coy innocence.

"I beg you will call me Charles, dearest. And yes, we have the whole day to carry back with us the Yule log."

"A perfect day for it," she said.

He had to agree. It was a perfect day, the sky a brilliant blue, white clouds scudding the horizon, the horses eager for the road. The sun set the snow's sugary whiteness aglitter, melting the roads clear as they went.

"A perfect day," he agreed, settling beside her in the coach and bidding Woodrow onward.

"Temple does not join us?" she asked.

He smiled. Surely she jested. "He was needed elsewhere."

"And Ned?"

He could not tell her Ned was gone to Glastonbury. "It occurred to me it might be the perfect day for just we two," he said.

She played the shy miss, blushing and dipping her chin. He set the crook of one finger beneath it, raising her gaze to meet his. "I wish to know you better, and find it easier without an entourage."

She nodded, pulling away from his touch. "Where do we go? Gran seemed familiar with the area, but I am not at all acquainted with this part of England."

"Northwest to Hampstead. No more than four miles. My uncle kept a house with a small park there. He was never a very well man. Hampstead offered him relief from the heat of the city in summer, mineral waters, and wonderful walking. It is a pretty place. The groundskeeper has informed Temple that a tree was cut down this summer, the heart of which will make an admirable Yule log. There is mistletoe, too, that we shall carry back with us. And holly and ivy."

"For the ball?"

"Yes, the ball," he said, thinking she would be his by then, an ornament to be decorated for the party as much as the house was to be decorated with greenery. A dress of crimson, perhaps, for his scarlet lady.

"Is it true you hate Christmas?" she asked.

He pursed his lips, startled by the question.

She laughed. "I wish to know you better, too, my lord."

He tried to smile and could not force it fully to his lips. "It is true. I do not like Christmas."

"And yet you throw a ball? And decorate your house?"

"And yet I do."

"Why?"

He listened to the rumbling of the wheels, the steady clop of the horses' hooves, just like that Christmas long ago that had changed everything.

Through a moneyed part of town they went, past beautiful rows of tasteful town houses, rooftops gleaming whitely, fresh as the snow-covered park, where the newly planted saplings, stripped of their leaves, stood shivering in the wind. Their own relationship was just this tender and new.

It was as if this part of the city were designed to remind her of that, of their differences, of the honor he did her in asking for her hand. The women who braved the snowy walkways here on the fashionable outskirts of London plunged their hands in fur tippets, just like the one Balfour had given her. Their bonnets, fur-edged capes, and fine leather boots were of the highest quality and fashion. They went escorted on the arms of great-coated gentlemen, shoulder capes fluttering in the wind, beaver hats gleaming. It occurred to her that he wanted her to look as these women looked, on his arm. As a result, she felt a trifle shabby, a trifle ashamed, even hidden as she was inside the eye-catching protection of the viscount's fashionable coach.

She liked their privacy for many reasons, liked speaking to him thus in the warm, confined comfort of his carriage, just the two of them. He seemed more relaxed than usual, prepared to open himself to her, ready at the least provocation to touch her, to whisper in her ear.

She dared ask him again. "Why dislike Christmas?"

"It is a long story."

"We have miles to go," she reminded him.

He took her hand in his. "And far more pleasant ways to spend them, Mary."

She started to pull away, then thought better of it, saying, "But you would have the relationship deepen."

"Yes." He smiled, lifting her hand to his lips.

"As would I," she said, looking him in the eyes. He

leaned forward to kiss her, but before their lips met, she said, "In all ways, not just this one."

Did he love her, she wondered as the white light of the snowy landscape played across his features. London thinned, empty lots here, new construction on all sides.

Her own father had been slow to tell her mother that he loved her. She had heard some small details of their courtship. What would they think of the viscount who would marry their daughter? She had written to them last night, had sent off the glad tidings this morning. Father's permission had yet to be sought, of course, but how could he refuse?

He sighed and fell back.

She sat, head bowed, hands in her lap. His mistress demure.

"I was loneliest as a boy at Christmas," he said quietly as the carriage carried them out of the noise and ongoing construction of Portland Place toward Regent's Park.

Her bonnet shifted. No longer the ugly brim he stared at, but her eyes—dark, gentle, patient.

"The servants . . ." He smiled, remembering. ". . . bobbed for apples. Played at forfeits. They liked to kiss under the mistletoe. The maids . . ."

"Liked to kiss you?" she said knowingly, as if she were there with him, in the memory, waiting, watching, amused.

He nodded. "Best of all was the dancing. They had nothing more than a mouth organ, a jug, a hornpipe, and a fiddle, but oh, what a noise they made. Laughing and singing and jigging about. Drinking until they dropped. Stuffing their faces with food. Very much like the guests at my balls."

She smiled. Ah, what a smile! The memories fell away. He forgot the past, forgot all but her lips, his desire for her.

She read it in his eyes and grew serious.

"I cannot imagine Christmas without family. This year will be the closest I have ever come to it. Only Gran and I to do the cooking, the decorating, all of my gifts to be sent away by post. I think it must have been very lonely for you as a little boy, watching everyone around you celebrate with loved ones."

"One grows accustomed." He said it brusquely, all too aware of his own defensiveness. "My uncle always sent me particularly special treasures for the holidays. A puppy one year, a pony the next. My first gun. He came when he was feeling well enough. We drank hot chocolate and ate Christmas cakes, and packages arrived by post from whatever exotic place my parents were visiting."

"He was your father's brother?"

"Yes. No love lost between them. An old grudge. He never came round when father returned."

"You have still to tell me the whole. Why were you lonely in the midst of so much good cheer?"

"My father . . ." he began. How to explain? How much? How little? "Lord and Lady Balfour were always away. Trips to the Continent, America, the Jamaican Islands—places far from England."

"Your parents never took you with them?"

"No." He licked his lower lip, could not tell her that was the point, distancing themselves from him.

She shook her head. "But why?

There were skaters in the park, small dots of color in the distance. He chose to look at them rather than at her.

"I remind them of things better forgotten."

"That was long ago. Why do you continue to dislike Christmas?"

It was not what he had expected her to say. The question forced his mind in a direction as new as the houses they passed along the edge of the park.

Did he still dislike Christmas? After all, it was part of the past. He laughed, amused by the notion. "I suppose I got in the habit of it," he admitted. "And no one, nothing, made me question it until Temple died, until you stepped in front of my carriage, into my life, too full of smiles to ignore."

He leaned in to kiss her. This time she let him, her knees bumping his as they took the curve at Park Crescent. His heart sang that she should do so, then sobered as he remembered that it was her intent all along to seduce him.

She turned her head, that he might kiss her cheek, then drew back, eyes sparkling.

"And your mother? Did she get along well with your favored uncle?"

Why should she ask such a thing? Did she know his history already? "She liked him too well, I think."

"Had you no other family? No one else to look in on you?"

A nerve in his jaw ticked. His gaze drifted to the window again. On a hill to their left, boys on sleds gleefully took advantage of the snow. "Mother has a sister, with a son, Gilbert, and three daughters, all younger than I."

"Did she live in London?"

"They went away to the country for Christmas."

"Surely you were asked to go with them?"

Red-faced, the boys stood on the hill, noses cherry red, brightly colored mittens to protect their hands, caps to warm their ears. He had played thus once with his cousins, charged with the same unrestrained energy that sent these boys scrambling up a hillside again and again that they might fly the length of it belly down.

"Once. After that, I remained in London," he said. "My aunt considered me too rambunctious a companion for her daughters."

Expression perplexed, she left it at that. He had hoped she would.

She spoke of her family and told him something of each of her siblings, her childhood, referred to her parents fondly, gave him verbal picture of the house in which she had grown up. Like these dollops of her history, he saw small flashes of their journey through the windows, fields and farms, woods and meadows, the land gently rolling.

Hampstead High Street was as sugar-dusted as her past, abustle with activity, none deterred by the snowfall. Skaters crowded Whitestone Pond at the Vale of Heath as they left the village streets behind to enter a vast whiteness—grass, gorse, and trees draped in the blanket of snow, a fine white mist hanging in low-lying areas.

The wide road narrowed. The horses slowed. The snow-fall had been heavier here. The lane cut through vast expanses of virgin white, only an occasional sledding party cutting tracks to spoil it, and the sunken marks where deer had run.

His own childhood he glossed over as smoothly as the scene before them. He gave her some idea of the shape of things, no harsh outlines, no stark detail. She did not press him with questions.

It was a pleasant passage of time, and all the while he thought of the more spacious privacy they would enjoy at his uncle's house, now his. He would show her the bedchambers on the second floor.

They arrived at The Grove, as the house was called, to the tune of skylarks, pipits, and goldencrest in the oaks along the avenue, feathers puffed against the cold.

"A long time since I have been here," he said, letting down the window, a rush of chill air spilling in.

She half stood, half knelt on her seat, to peer out the lowered window, her shoulder to his. "Plenty of mistle-toe," she said with a smile.

He smiled, too. Abundant clumps of the berries dangled from bared branches, a promise of hundreds of potential kisses.

Dark eyes agleam, cheeks pink with the cold rush of air, smiling lips too lush to ignore, she turned to look at him.

He thought of kissing her again, the warmth of her mouth against his, the eager clutch of her hands at his lapels. He wanted her. She wanted him. He could see it in her eyes. The afternoon promised to be most satisfying in this, the most appropriate setting, this house of trysts. His uncle had brought his lover here. Why should not he?

The horses slowed. He and Mary Rivers sank back into their respective places. Woodrow called a halt to the team.

Will jumped down, and the door flew open. She smiled as Will helped her down, as Baxter stepped down beside her. She smiled in looking about, eyes sparkling.

He hoped to provoke another sort of smile entirely in her before the day was done.

The sun made a fairyland of the park and showed the house to pale advantage—trim, columned, white stucco–fronted—virtually unchanged from the last time he had seen it, Christmas nineteen years ago.

Unfair that a place that had so markedly changed his life went unmarked by the years.

"How pretty!" Mary exclaimed.

"It does present an attractive face to the world," Baxter said noncommitally.

It had worn a Christmas face then, a holly wreath on the door, a kissing ball above. His father had growled at it as he dragged Baxter up the steps, his stride too fast for eight-year-old legs. He had growled again as he pushed past a pasty-faced butler, snapping tersely, "Where is she? Where is my wife?"

The house had smelled of plum cake and peppermint and evergreens.

The butler, frightened as a rabbit, said nothing, but his eyes gave away her direction. Faster now, the clutch of his father's hand too tight, they had charged the stairs, evergreen swags prickly green along the banister, Baxter at a run, the steps a blur, his heart pounding when they reached the first floor.

"Alicia!"

He heard the distant memory of that shout as they stepped inside, the rooms dust-sheeted and rugless, their footsteps echoing on marble.

"I know you are here!" his father had shouted harshly up the stairwell. "Come out. Show yourself."

Beside him, Mary Rivers silently looked about. No lovers' bower he had brought her to after all, just the abandoned shell of his past.

His uncle had stepped into view on the stairs.

"You!" His father had snarled, his rage unparalleled. "My own brother. How could you, Ted?"

"How could I what?" Ted, tall, thin, and always too pale, had offered a pretense of innocence.

"I bring you the what." His father had jerked his arm, pulled him into view, and pushed him toward the upper story, up the first of the steps so that he stood slightly elevated, unsure what was expected of him. Baxter had been sure only that he had in some way displeased his father—as much as his mother did, as much as his Uncle Ted did.

His father's voice, so harsh, seemed that of a stranger. "I know what you do here, the two of you." He swept past, taking the steps two at a time, the muscles in his calves bulging. "Did you think I would not find out?"

He pushed past Ted, left brother and son shocked and silent in his wake, staring at one another, his uncle's gaze unusually penetrating.

"She's not here," he said quietly, futilely.

Shoulder capes flapping like tethered birds, Lord Balfour strode along the upper hallway, opening doors, shouting. "Alicia! Alicia! Come out! I bring your son to see where it all began."

Baxter, wondering what his mother had done to cause such a rage in his hitherto peaceful father, remained on the lowest step, watching, awestruck, ready to believe his uncle's lies because they were calmly voiced. "She is not here, I tell you. Never was!"

A flicker of red caught Baxter's then keen eye, the movement of a windblown cape, outside, behind the house. A woman stepped into a carriage, no more than her back to be seen. Four black horses blowing steam in the cold stood ready to carry her away.

"No one lives here?" Mary Rivers asked quietly, as if she sensed the weight of his memories. "It looks as though it has stood empty for years."

"Nineteen," he said, walking to the window through which one might view, unobstructed, the snow-covered sprawl of the heath. He could not tell her the house might have gone unvisited for another nineteen but for her. He came now, rather than send Temple on this errand, because in taking her as mistress he felt in some small way an unexpected kinship with his true father— his uncle—a man he had hated all of his idealistic young life for the sins he had committed, one of them the sin he stood ready to commit himself.

"What a lovely prospect." Mary, a shadow at his elbow, stared at the view.

Was it? He sighed. Was it a lovely prospect to become all that he had once despised? To understand the weakness of his father's flesh so long after that flesh had turned to dust?

"I do not care for the house, or its situation," he said, a bitter taste in his mouth.

Mary Rivers, in her red cape, turned to look at him, as his mother, red-caped, had turned to see him staring from this very window.

"And yet you do not sell it?" she asked.

"No." He pulled his spectacles from his nose, tucking them away in their case in his coat pocket. The words came, cold as the feelings this place roused in him. "My mother has a fondness for the place."

Chapter Twenty-six

She deemed it a near perfect day, and he the perfect gentleman. They did not linger in the house, pausing only to eat from the bounty of provisions he brought for them, on a table and chairs unveiled from their ghost-like shrouding.

She was glad of it. The place, beautiful as it was, settled a moody cloud upon her host's brow.

He paused at the staircase when they were done, took the first step as if to go up, then turned and said, "Do you care to see the rest of the house?"

She shook her head. "It is such a beautiful day, and such beautiful country to spend it in. I would rather help Ned and Woodrow in gathering the holly and ivy."

He shot one more look up the staircase, as if he regretted her decision. "As you wish."

Outside, Christmas hung like a promised gift on air scrubbed clean by the newly fallen snow, by the sweet rosined odor of the blue-berried junipers that edged the heath. Mary loved the sight of oaks and elms, bare branches stretched toward the bottomless lake of the sky. She loved the clean air, the unbounded view, the rustling business of birds and squirrels.

Ironic that a bird threatened to spoil the afternoon.

They were collecting mistletoe, he up a tree, she gathering the sticky, berried bunches as he cut them down from stunted oaks along the edge of the heath. A flock of buff-cheeked skylarks pecked among the snow-covered acorns, serenading them.

"I like larks above all other birds," she said, face

flushed with exertion, arms full of mistletoe. "Their song is joy made audible."

Another bunch of mistletoe cascaded to the ground, berries exploding in all directions. "They are musical thieves, bent on mimicking every other bird on the heath," he protested with a laugh.

"And cheerfully so," she said.

"Now *there* is a handsome bird." He pointed the curved blade of his knife at a harrier skimming low, shadow in tandem, like a fat gray echo against the snow-covered heath. "He makes flight look effortless."

As if to prove his point, the harrier glided buoyantly in their direction.

Startled, Mary dropped the mistletoe she was holding, raised a gloved hand to shade her eyes, and with a cry of "Oh no!" ran toward her favored larks shouting, "Fly!"

Rare to see a young woman run as Miss Rivers ran, skirt held high, feet plunging with foolhardy haste through a glitter of snow, cloak fluttering in her wake like scarlet wings.

She ran flat out, no thought for anything but the larks, as if with her own speed she might urge their wings to greater effort.

Her shout had the desired effect, sending the birds skyward in an explosive flurry, all but one, which fell prey to the harrier's effortlessly gliding pounce as it flushed—furious wingbeat and liquid song stilled forever in the harrier's decisive grip.

A few feathers drifting lazily, the hunter glided away, the languid sweep of its wings, the smooth power of its flight, even the limpness of spent life clutched in his talons, remarkable to behold.

Defeat slowed Mary's plunging flight at the edge of the heath, skirts lowered, her chest rising and falling in pursuit of lost breath. As if some life were taken from her along with the lark's, she stilled, shoulders slumping, one hand risen to the pulse that beat visibly in her throat.

"Are you all right?" Baxter, down from the tree, fell in beside her as she turned her back to the flight of the harrier.

She tried to nod, bonnet bobbing, tried valiantly to smile, but the upward curve of her mouth broke and fell. The nod reversed itself, her head jerking side to side.

He opened his arms to her. She stepped into them as if it were the most natural of gestures between them, as if there was no place she would rather be.

"I am here," he said. "I am here."

She wept, he knew she wept, a quiet wetting of his lapel. He held her, stroking the velvety back of her cloak, murmuring, "There, there. An ugly sight, that."

He breathed deep the sweet, outdoor smell of her neck, her hair, roses and evergreens, rocking her gently in his arms, the bones of her back fragile. He could feel the beat of her heart quickened by exertion, in the rise and fall of her breast against his.

She sniffed, head rising from the pillow of his shoulder, eyes puffy and pink, features vulnerable as a child's. The humid wetness of her cheek brushed his, a tantalizing lure. He turned to kiss damp, silken skin, to kiss away her sadness, hungry for her lips.

She did not refuse him her mouth.

To the contrary, she met his advances with tender urgency. Witnessing the ending of a life, however small, filled her with an overwhelming desire to appreciate its fragile beauties, and there was an undeniable beauty to the coming together of breath, lips, and tongue.

He tasted of bread and cheese, apple and wine—all that they had enjoyed from the nuncheon basket—and something more—elusive and honeyed, musky and sweet. The flavor of life, she thought, of love. Oh, how she had come to love this man's gaze, his touch, the comfort of his arms and lips.

He had not scoffed at her pity for a bird as her brothers would have. He did not tell her to "Cheer up. The harrier must eat, after all, and it is only one lark among dozens," as her father would have.

He simply held her and stroked the breadth of her shoulders, the small of her back, his ready shoulder a warm comfort, his arms sweet succor. "I am here," he said. "I am here."

She counted herself a most fortunate creature that this man wished her for his wife, that he desired her above all others. Gladly, she gave her mouth to his in a warm cascade of kisses, sweet as the song of the fallen lark.

They loaded the coach with greenery, the top bristling with holly and juniper, the boot full of mistletoe, one seat inside draped in canvas, the canvas covered in long strands of dripping ivy.

Will strapped the Yule log securely behind the coachman's bench.

"So merry does our equipage look, so glad am I to be done clipping and cutting and gathering, that I insist we set off for London singing Christmas carols," Baxter surprised them all in saying.

"Carols, my lord?" Woodrow looked stunned.

"Yes, you know, songs associated with Christmas."

"I know them well enough, my lord," Woodrow said with a chuckle. "It's just I'd no idea *you* knew any."

Mary thought he did such a thing for her sake, to cheer her. She was still subdued by the death of the lark, by the loneliness of house and heath, by the sadness in Baxter's eyes when he looked at the place, when he thought she did not notice.

It was a good idea, the singing. Woodrow had a booming baritone. Will sang tenor remarkably well. Bells jingled on the horses' harnesses, and Baxter knew most of the words. His voice was willing if unschooled, and she had always thrown herself into song whenever the opportunity arose.

They did a creditable job of it. Heads turned and smiles roused wherever they went.

They fell contentedly silent in the last leg of their journey, as they lost the sun, London's streets closing in around them. Baxter reached out to straighten a stray curl at her temple. "This is not at all how I imagined today would pass."

His fingertips were a tantalizing warmth against her skin. Every strand of hair vibrated to his touch. She longed for his arms again, holding her close, making the world safe and warm.

"Have you decided you like Christmas after all?"

He laughed. "I think I might grow rather fond of it . . ." He paused, the smile fading though not the warmth in his eyes. ". . . in your company."

She smiled and settled deeper against the squabs, lulled by the rhythm of the bells, the horses' hooves, by the sway of the carriage. Her body was tired to the bone, her muscles aching after so much physical activity. Odd how content she felt, even though her dress and cloak were a mess, her hands sticky with sap and smelling of juniper, her boots wet through. "Aren't you glad I did not wear the new things you gave me? They would have been ruined."

He leaned forward, laughing. "I intended to have you out of them." He said it dryly, his eyes sparkling with mischief, as if they shared a secret she had forgotten.

"The house . . ." she said.

A shuttered quality closed the depths of his eyes away from her. "Yes? Did you like it?"

"It is sad to see it abandoned."

"You think so?" He sat back, face lost in shadow.

"Does it not strike you as a lonely place, longing to be lived in?"

He smiled, eyelids falling half-mast to further veil his eyes. "It is a place well acquainted with loneliness." He turned to stare out of the window as they turned into Regent Street. Lamplight transformed the window into a flickering frame for the sudden darkness of his profile. "If you like, I could set you up there, you and your Gran."

His suggestion confused her. "Do you mean to live?"

He nodded, the movement of his head stiff. He seemed far more interested in the view than in witnessing her reaction. "Shall I arrange it?"

He caught her off guard with such a question. "I thought . . ."

He turned to regard her. "Yes?"

"I . . . I just supposed we would live here in London."

Did he do this to please her? She saw him as such a city creature. Hard to imagine him happy for any length of time in the country.

"It would be easier," he said, "more discreet, if you were settled away from the city."

Discreet? It seemed an odd word to describe their situation.

"It is a lovely house," she said. "If you think we would be happiest there, I am inclined to agree. Will not your mother mind?"

Her words generated a frown.

"You said she had a fondness for the place."

"Ah." From the darkness issued a dry chuckle. "I think she would understand entirely if I installed you there."

Chapter Twenty-seven

His words came back to haunt her the following morning when his solicitor arrived. Slender, bespectacled, respectably dapper in subdued gray and top hat, Mr. Springer carried with him a leather satchel, which he clutched tight to his chest in skirting the pile of greenery that had been dropped the evening before in the corner of the entranceway.

From the satchel, its belts and buckles ceremoniously undone, he drew forth with some solemnity an intimidating stack of copperplate-covered pages, fanning them out upon the drum table Mary cleared for his use.

"Everything must be signed in triplicate, of course," he said. "A copy for you, one for his lordship, and a copy to remain in my possession." He passed them each a set of the pages.

Gran nodded, pinching her spectacles onto the bridge of her nose. "Of course, of course. But what does it say?"

Springer eyed her rather coldly over the rims of his own spectacles. "Madam, I am sure you will find his lordship most generous."

Gran nodded. "You will, of course, read them to me? My eyes are not so sharp as they once were."

Eyeing the pages down the length of his nose, as if reading were a task beneath him, he began. "The viscount indicates herein—" He stopped, pursed his lips, and asked coolly, "Shall I summarize, madam?"

"Please do," Gran agreed.

"In the first page, then, the names of the parties and their relationship is defined."

Gran nodded, smiling.

Mary bent to the task of reading.

Mr. Springer went on. "In the following pages a list is detailed of Lord Balfour's dispensations for the parties named. For example: for the extent of the relationship, or as long as you deem separate domicile necessary, his lordship promises to cover the costs of this or any other dwelling of similar expense."

"Very kind of him, to be sure," Gran said.

"His lordship herein provides"—he tapped the page as he covered each clause—"an adequate staff for the upkeep of said domicile, a monthly stipend for the payment of said staff, household expenses, wardrobe, and food.

Mary paid neither of them mind. She was too dismayed by the words dancing before her eyes, having got no further than the first page in which the relationship in question was described.

The verbage had nothing to do with marriage. A different relationship entirely was detailed here, far too official in spidery black ink. It took her breath away and for an instant stopped her heart, certainly stopped her ears from hearing a word of what the solicitor was saying, this man who believed she meant to sign away both purity and honor today for a generous list of compensations.

"A carriage is to be at your disposal, along with a coachman and team, all expenses to be covered. And last, but not least, a yearly annuity in the amount you see detailed will be placed at Miss Mary Rivers's disposal, to spend or invest as she will."

Mary's hands and feet went cold, her mouth dry. Her stomach churned. Baxter's remarks rang in her ears, his meaning all too clear now. Small wonder he wished to install her discreetly in his heretofore abandoned country house.

Springer wound down. "Said goods and compensations shall continue as long as this arrangement is mutually agreeable to both parties, said dispensations to continue but not exceed one year following cessation of said relationship."

Humiliated, heart racing, Mary flew up out of her chair, dizzied by her own sudden move.

He glanced up from the last page, expression bland, as if surprised to find her standing.

Just above a whisper, Mary said, "I must ask you to leave, sir, and to take your paperwork with you."

The first trace of alarm colored the solicitor's features. His brows rose. "Madam is not pleased with this offer?"

"Madam is not." Mary could not stifle her rising anger.

"Mary, whatever do you mean?" Gran asked.

Mary ignored her. With every word she felt strengthened. "You will take your papers and go, please."

"But, Mary, surely Lord Balfour has been more than generous." Gran rose, with effort, to clutch her arm.

Springer's brows assumed a more natural altitude, his alarm fading. "Perhaps with some minor adjustments?" he suggested urbanely.

"No," Mary said, moving to the door, which she opened.

Springer took the hint and likewise rose, collecting paperwork, and angular joints about him like a spider sensing unusual movement on its web.

"Shall I leave a copy of the document?" he suggested. "Perhaps upon closer examination . . ."

"I beg you will not." Voice wound tight, she held out the pages she wished to fling in his face. "This arrangement, as you call it, has never, will never, can never be agreeable to me."

He straightened, stashed his ill-met offerings away, and with deliberate efficiency strapped shut the satchel. "I shall so inform Lord Balfour."

"Ahem, my lord." Temple knocked upon the open door to Baxter's study.

Baxter looked up from the directive he was writing— more of Temple Senior's former work— instructions regarding the Christmas goose and bottle of sack to be delivered to each of his tenants for the holidays, a haunch of venison to each of his estate agents, potted pheasant, brandied cherries, fresh livery, and two newly minted shillings to each of his servants.

He pushed back his chair with a contented sigh. "Ah. Temple. I do daily discover how much I depended upon your father. There were certain parts of this Christmas business that I hope he found as gratifying as I now do."

"Your solicitor to see you, my lord."

Anticipation flooded Baxter's chest. Could the paperwork be done so soon? "Yes, yes. Show him in."

Temple turned to obey, pausing to say, "Oh, yes, my lord, I almost forgot. Ned has sent word from Glastonbury. His errand there takes him longer than expected."

Baxter frowned. "How much longer?"

"He did not say, my lord."

"Send Springer in."

"Yes, my lord."

Springer entered Baxter's study with a downcast expression.

"Something wrong?" Baxter asked at once.

"Indeed, my lord. I fear there is."

How could he? she thought. How could he think she would agree to such a proposal? How could he think so ill of her?

His mistress. He wished to lower her so? Wished to officially document the union, and pay her well for her services? The truth wrenched her like a Catherine wheel, flinging sense to the winds, spinning all her preconceptions into oblivion. His feelings, his past conversation with her were in an instant transformed. Too much to comprehend. Too painful. She was, for the moment, benumbed.

Gran demanded answers, of course. "How could you be so rude, Mary? What in the world possessed you to toss the man out on his ear? Do you mean to discard the brightest future likely to come your way, my girl?"

Mary held up her hands, unable to bear further abuse. She felt as if every inch of her had just been thrashed. Speechless, she was unable to answer beyond saying in a hushed, stunned voice, "Oh, Gran, I have been such a fool."

"I should say so," Gran scolded, her color high. "I have never before—" A cough broke her final words, the kind of cough that never failed to alarm Mary.

Gran took a deep breath and fought to spit out "—never witnessed such—" Another hacking cough, and still she tried to say, "Tomfoolery."

Now was not the time to explain, nor to reason why. Mary patted Gran on the back, offered her a handkerchief, and rang for Bethany, realizing even as she did so, she must give the girl back into Lord Balfour's keeping as soon as possible. They must not be beholden to him.

She ordered tea and honey, ran to fetch cordial and spoon, a glassful of water, and a lemon drop for Gran to suck.

And all the while Gran coughed and coughed into her handkerchief, though she did her utmost to stop, her face going first pink, then red, and finally a purplish hue.

"Lie down, Gran. Shall I send for a physician?"

Gran shook her head, sucked the lemon drop, and seemed by sheer strength of will to mute the hacking. "No physician," she said, her voice weak. "We cannot afford the man."

Mary, who knelt beside Gran's chair, sat back on her heels in surprise. "What?"

Gran cut her short with a sharp gesture, irritation strengthening her voice. "Did you think you could keep the thinness of my purse from me forever?"

"When did you realize? How?"

Gran waved her handkerchief in a silencing gesture as Bethany brought in the steaming fragrance of freshly brewed tea, cut lemons swathed in cheesecloth, and a plate full of Christmas cakes.

Mary kindly thanked the girl for her trouble and said nothing until the steaming brew had been poured, the lemon squeezed, and honey dolloped into Gran's cup.

Bethany eyed Gran with genuine concern, saying, "How does a bit of beef broth and some soft white rolls sound to you, Mrs. Rivers? Won't that go down well?"

"Splendid, my dear," Gran said, her voice still gravelly and uneven, handkerchief ready at hand.

Gran waited until they heard the clatter of cooking pots before she picked up the conversation. "I took a look at the books, my dear. Gave me a shock, it did. Your frugal ways began to make sense. And then all seemed settled, problem solved, by way of Lord Balfour's proposal."

Mary sighed, a chill touching the back of her neck, the tea a warm comfort. "I should never have accepted his offer." She gazed at the leaves floating in her cup, wondering if untold answers lay at the bottom.

"I thought you were quite taken with him, Mary. What caused this sudden change of heart?"

A tear salted the tea. "I care for him too much, Gran."

He had said the same about his mother.

Another tear. Mary swiftly wiped it from her cheek. She held the rest at bay, though emotion set her chin to wobbling and her breath felt caged too tightly in her chest. She thought, all too illogically, how much she would like to be held in his arms in that moment, as he had held her in comforting her for the death of something far more important than her illusions.

"I misunderstood," she cooed, mournful as a dove, "the nature of his offer, Gran. Misunderstood it completely."

Chapter Twenty-eight

Mary went to the kitchen to inform Bethany she must return to Lord Balfour's care.

Hard to tell her, but better to get it over with.

She wanted nothing more than to race upstairs for a good cry, to throw herself facedown upon her bed and weep. She could not afford such luxury, could not allow herself to forgo control until he had come and gone. She would not meet him with blotched face and puffy eyes, with all good sense undone.

She was determined he must never know how much he wounded her. She would not make a scene.

The smell of beef broth warming, the yeasty odor of rising bread, the stricken look on Bethany's face as she sank into a kitchen chair, was almost too much to bear.

"Have I done something wrong, miss?" the girl asked. "You do not mean to cast me off without a character, do you?"

"Oh, no, my dear, no." Mary felt as if she had been kicked in the stomach. She forced herself to smile. "You've been wonderful. We are not in the least displeased with you. We would keep you if we could, but we cannot."

"Why, miss? Do you mind me asking? I should so like to stay."

Why, indeed? Mary took a deep breath. "I have had a falling out with Lord Balfour. I fear we shall never be reconciled." She closed her eyes. Hard to imagine a future void of him, void of Bethany and Temple and Will and Ned.

"Oh, miss!" Bethany dashed away a tear. "I am so sorry. Here I am thinking only of myself."

With good reason, Mary thought, knowing she had just taken away Bethany's sense of security, as much as Baxter had taken away hers.

She wanted to hug the girl, but refrained. She was too raw, too ready to come undone. Eyes burning, head, neck, and jaw aching with stifled emotion, she struggled to find the right words. "I do regret this, Beth. I wish above all else this were not happening."

Bethany nodded, then rose to dish up a bowl of broth for Gran, worry etched deep in her young features.

Mary, hands shaking, arranged Gran's tray, her every nerve on edge, unprepared for the banging of the knocker as she picked up the tray. China rattled ominously.

"Is it him, miss?" Bethany asked.

"I think it must be." Mary could not still her shaking hands.

Bethany steadied the tray. "Here. Let me take this."

Mary nodded, wiped trembling hands on her apron, and slipped the tapes that tied it.

Back straight, mouth pinched, she opened the door, unswayed by the cold. There could be nothing colder than her heart in that moment.

He smiled at her.

How dare he smile.

"I would speak to you," he said.

She opened the door wider and motioned him into the downstairs sitting room, the sight of the holly and the ivy, the smell of juniper and yew, nauseating her.

He removed his hat, his coat.

Beth, tray delivered, arrived in time to take his things. With a significant glance at Mary, she left the two of them alone.

Mary made her way to a chair and sank down. Lord Balfour took the chair across from hers, as gentlemanly in appearance as ever, polite and polished in his every move and gesture.

She knew what lay beneath the facade. Anger chased away the tears she had feared spilling.

"Mr. Springer says you will not sign the documents, that they did not meet with your approval."

She could not stifle a bark of laughter. "No, they did not. Nor can they be amended enough to please me."

"I am confused," he said.

Yes, she thought, he was a morally confused sort of fellow to dream he might have her innocence so cheaply.

She refrained from saying so—remarking instead, anger and pain on the edge of her every word, "To the contrary. It is I who have been confused. I thought . . ." She paused, surprised by a sudden rise of feeling, the burn of tears prickling her eyes. She turned to face the portrait of her grandfather, her lips pressed tightly together, regaining control. She would not lose her composure. She took a deep breath and began again, her voice stronger, "I misunderstood your proposal, my lord."

"Ah! In what way misunderstood?"

"I thought . . ." She bit down on her lip, blinking furiously, determined to hold onto anger, not to succumb to tears. She drew a ragged breath. "I thought your offer honorable, sir."

Her words pierced him like a knife, shaming him.

He had no response ready. He had come wholly prepared to dicker over settlements, ready to offer her more money, different lodgings, a larger annuity. But marriage! She had thought to marry him! Good God, what had he done or said to mislead her so completely?

He opened his mouth to say something, anything.

She turned her back on him and walked to the window, as if she could not bear to look at him. Her voice, when she spoke, sounded shaken.

"I believed you wished me to be your wife." She bowed her head and spoke in a voice cold and lifeless. "As that is not your intention, as your offer, in fact, is . . . offensive to me, I must ask you to leave. You will, of course, take Bethany Temple with you?"

Her reflection's chin wavered when she said the girl's name. Her voice almost failed her. She blinked at the view furiously, on the brink of tears, then whirled, eyes bright, glaring at him, as she strode past to hold the door open.

Speechless, humiliated, dizzied by the turn of events, he studied features grown dear to him with the feeling that they belonged to a stranger. This woman of endless smiles had no smiles for him today. Would she ever again?

Blood heating his cheeks, he stepped past the pile of greenery they had happily gathered, into the entryway, the smell of Christmas strong.

Her grandmother sat sphinxlike, waiting in her Merlin chair, Bethany at her side, pink-cheeked, eyes swollen from crying, clad in her outdoor things, a small carpetbag at her feet, his coat and hat held ready for donning.

Oh, God, he thought. What had he done? How many lives had he adversely affected with this dreadful misunderstanding?

Mrs. Rivers regarded him with the kind of disappointment old Mr. Temple had on occasion shamed him with. "It is true, then, my lord? You thought to make a fallen woman of my granddaughter?"

She slapped him in the face with her calmly voiced accusation. How did one respond to such a question? He could not agree with her. Neither could he deny that in society's eyes, in the eyes of her family, his proposed actions would have toppled this woman he thought to love.

That he destroyed Mary Rivers had never entered his thinking. He had wanted only to make her his, to make her comfortable, to make her happy. He had never quantified the effect his actions would have on her family, on her future. He could not deny what the old lady accused him of.

"You will understand, my lord," she said in her gentle old voice, "when I say you are no longer welcome."

There was no polite or proper way to walk away from such a confrontation, no elegant turn of phrase, no amount of bowing or scraping to free him of this humiliation.

A man without honor, no longer welcome.

He said nothing, simply caught up his hat and coat

from Bethany's forlorn arms and strode from the house as fast as his dishonorable feet might carry him, then kept striding when he got to the street, in need of air, of space, of physical exertion.

Bethany Temple followed. He heard the bang of her carpetbag against the door, heard her plaintive cry of "My lord. Please! Wait! I cannot walk so fast."

He turned, fuming, grabbed up her bag, and strode to the door of his town house with it, then waved her inside.

She scuttled past like a frightened rabbit. He did not care to be feared by women any more than he liked to be reviled by them. And yet, no word of comfort could he find within himself.

He was a monster. Women ought to run from him, to cast him from their presence. He turned on his heel as soon as the door closed in her wake, striding along Regent Street, deaf to the sounds of wheels on cobblestone, of bells on harness, of voices lifted to carol the season, blind to the sight of parcel-laden shoppers, to the glitter of goods in carefully arranged shop windows, to the clouded horizon that promised more snow.

Christmas again, tearing his heart out, like so many Christmases before. He had thought this year different. He had thought the curse lifted.

Past Hill's Military Warehouse he strode, where together he and Miss Rivers had bought wool breeches and coats for the poor, a moment of honor for this dishonorable man. Across the street, Carpenter and Westley's, where she had helped him to see as never before. Not clearly enough it would seem.

Stride lengthening, he passed Ponsonby's Gliders, where all might be made golden but the dreadful thing he had asked of her. Travel agencies then, and the coaching office to tempt him farther afield. But where might a dishonorable man go to outrun the crushing sense of his own guilt?

Heels rapping on pavement, hands jammed in his pockets that they might do no more damage, that they might touch no one, he looked inward and liked not what he saw.

Others who braved the cold bumped into him, as if
he were hard to see, as if a dishonorable man filled the
space upon the walkway insufficiently.

What had he brought to pass? What damage done?
What pain inflicted? What ugly, unworthy part of himself
had risen to the fore, to consider disgracing a woman a
logical course of action, a desirable one?

He passed a gunmaker, a furrier, then paused in front
of the marble angel in the window of Gaffin's Carrara
Marblework. Could she ever forgive him?

The angel stared back blankly, no answers for him.
He fled the storefront, fled the memory of merry Miss
Mary standing winged in front of the window. He
crossed Air Street, and narrowly missed being run down
by a coach-and-four, his brush with death inconsequen-
tial, his mind elsewhere, on far more important and life-
changing matters. Here she had stood beneath the columned arcade, a sheaf of windblown invitations clasped
in mitted hand—cheeks, nose, and lips rosy with the
cold, the goodness in her self-evident.

He walked faster, the row of columns counting off his
sins, past a hatmaker's, a billiard hall, a window full of
stuffed birds, winged beauty stilled. He thought of
skylarks.

Had he thought to cage love—to capture a woman's
smiles? Would her plumage have dimmed, her song
stilled?

Why in God's name had he listened to his cousin, the
fool? He ought to have trusted in his own initial impression of her. How stupid to believe she plotted against
him.

The corsetmaker's sign brought fresh heat to his
cheeks. He had wanted her—still wanted her.

What in God's name was he to do? Reinvent feeling?
His future? He could not go on living in the same street
as her grandmother, forever reviled.

How did one reorganize the emotions of the heart?
He still wanted her, loved her. His sensibilities did not
change simply because she found him contemptible.

He walked on, the cold a tonic, the smell of snow
upon the air in keeping with the chill of her rejection.

He did not stop for breath until he stood outside Newmann's Livery, where he crossed the street to stand upon the very spot where he had watched her weeping outside the post office—it seemed so long ago.

Troubled by the memory, by memory of the gift Will had been sent to bring back from Glastonbury, he walked on, head bent, no interest in the plate glass window displays: wine and tobacco, lamps and chandeliers, umbrellas and canes. He crossed Beak Street, to which he considered adding an *l,* then trudged on, the columned arcade ending, a thin wash of sunlight breaking through the clouds, trying ineffectually to brighten his outlook.

Another block and he passed a coach builder's, the sweet smell of a perfumerie, the sweeter smell of a confectioners, ahead his haberdasher's. The Argyll Rooms—more memories of her. He crossed the street, frustrated. Outside the unfinished Hanover Chapel he was accosted by an Italian image boy, plaster statues grasped in dirty mittens.

"A Wellington, *signor*? You give to someone for Christmas, *sí*?"

Baxter frowned and shook his head impatiently. "No heroes for me, lad. Not today."

"No?" the boy persisted, running along beside him, thrusting a shapely, scantily clad form into his hands. "A Venus then? A *bella donna* for a *bella donna*."

The plaster casting was rather pretty—the Venus de Milo. Baxter had read of the find, seen etchings. A peasant had dug up an armless statue on the island of Melos more than six months ago. Some considered her the most beautiful depiction of woman in antiquity.

The grace, the shape of her, reminded him of Mary. He turned the helpless beauty in his hands, armless, powerless, completely enchanting. "I'll take her," he said, seeing something singularly apt in the purchase, for what had he tried to make of beautiful Mary Rivers but a pocket Venus? And who was he, but a fool on the street who would buy her with a house and a handful of silver?

*   *   *

He made his way back home, Venus in his pocket. He must make this right somehow, must go to her, offer to marry her, beg her forgiveness. Would she have him if he asked her now?

He had no opportunity to find out. When he arrived at her doorstep and stood considering what he must say, a coach, it's topside heavy with trunks, the team that pulled it sweated and blowing, stopped behind him with a great deal of noise.

A voice called out, "Baxter! Is that you?"

He turned, convinced the voice was his mother's. Indeed it was she who stepped down when the footman opened the mud-spattered door.

"Mother! What in the world are you doing here?"

"I am come home for Christmas, my dear. Are you not glad to see me?"

Chapter Twenty-nine

℃

Restless in slumber, Mary woke more than once that night to the rattle of rain above or the rattle of Gran's coughing below. The rain washed away the last vestiges of snow, erasing what little sense of Christmas was left in her.

Every time a coughing fit began, she swung her feet out from under the covers, rising to light a candle that she carried with her downstairs. On Gran's bedside table she kept Dr. James's Fever Powder, Godfrey's bottled cordial, and a spoon, along with a pitcher of filtered water, a glass, and a dish of hard-boiled candy.

Gran apologized each time for waking her, and opened her mouth obligingly to accept the spoon, the sip of water, a hard drop of peppermint.

"How could he, Mary? How could he?" she asked. "I shall have no peace living next door to him now."

How could he indeed? Mary had no answer.

The rain on the windowpane, in candlelight, made it look as if the world wept. Not Mary. She would not give in to her own despair, not with the more important matter of Gran's health to focus on.

"I am sorry, Gran," she said thinly, no desire to so much as touch upon the topic.

Gran would seem to think of little else.

"I liked him, Mary. Really liked him. He seemed the perfect match for you, my dear."

Her heartache intensified with words meant to be a comfort. Mary inhaled deeply, a hand pressed to her chest, unwilling to speak of the raw pain of discovering otherwise.

The third time she woke, Gran said, "How could we be so taken in? He seemed such a nice young man. A gentleman. He asked us to his ball."

Mary shivered, vulnerable and exposed in her nightshift, her feet blocks of ice. Drawing her shawl closer, she said wearily, "We must forgive and go on." Kissing Gran's cheek, she whispered, "And you must get some sleep."

These words were more easily said than done. Once wakened, Mary could not slide easily into sleep again, her mind too ready to entwine the same troubled thoughts.

How had she dared to believe herself worthy of a viscount? How had she so misunderstood their relationship? How could she ever face him again? Dear God, she must write to her mother, recanting all that she had written in the last. How was she to explain why she had turned down the offer of a viscount without revealing the whole ugly truth?

Her shame, she knew, was a public thing, a quiet scandal, not to be hidden, not to be mourned in private. All of London would soon know some part of it.

Rather than lie sleepless, fretting, Mary lit a second candle, and framing herself in the light, sat down with pen and paper to scrawl out a message to her mother.

The empty page taunted her. What to say? She stared at it, uncertain. In fact, she fell asleep, candles guttering, facedown on the still unblemished page.

He did not sleep. How to sleep when one had always believed oneself honorable only to discover it a lie? He could not be comfortable, could not allow mind to fade into nothingness, as if naught had happened, as if he had not deceived and disappointed both himself and the young woman he admired above all others.

He knew she did not sleep either when he saw candlelight throw dim flickers on the rain-washed street below more than once. He longed to go to her, to creep out of his house, to creep into hers, to declare himself a fool, a fool in love. Would she not have him, thorns and all? Could she forgive him enough to accept the delinquent offer of his hand? He would give it to her, if only she would take it.

An urgent pounding on the door found Mary staring at the ceiling the following morning, eyes aching with sleeplessness, the spill of her worries incessant. Her first thought was Bethany would get it. But then she remembered with a sinking feeling that they no longer had the luxury of Bethany to answer such a summons.

She threw on a wrapper, tucked her feet into hand-knitted slippers, and flew to the window.

Could it be him? she wondered. Had he slept as ill as she? Did he mean to make this right somehow?

Mary lifted the window sash and stuck her head out, rain dripping in her hair and down her neck.

A mobcap below the window, not a beaver. Not Balfour but Bethany, nose bright as a holly berry, standing on the rain-drenched step, wringing black-mittened hands.

"Bethany? Is that you? Is anything wrong? Have you forgotten something?"

Pink-cheeked, her breath puffing upward in little clouds, Bethany Temple cried out, "Oh, miss, I beg you will help us! An emergency of sorts. We require your assistance most desperately."

"I have business to attend to," he said over the rim of his coffee cup when his mother insisted he accompany her, that they leave at once.

Lady Balfour pushed her plate away, food untouched, her manner far more serious than was her custom. Baxter had been surprised to find her haunting the breakfast room before him, fully dressed, obviously prepared for an outing. "Can it not wait but an hour? The carriage stands ready at the door, and I would greatly appreciate your opinion in choosing a gemstone for my sister."

He shook his head, set aside his half-emptied cup, and waved away the plate Holloway stood ready to set at his place. He shrugged on his coat and stood hand on the doorknob, resolve firm. He would ask on bended knee.

"I am sorry, Mother, but the matter is too important to delay."

"More important than what I have come half a continent to tell you?" Her voice was brittle, shrill, her rise from the table abrupt. Silver clinked china. She knocked over her glass with a carelessly dropped napkin.

He turned, amazed. "What?"

"Your father . . ."

His eyes narrowed. Not his father. Only the man who pretended to be.

". . . has abandoned me for another woman."

Baxter closed his eyes in pained disbelief.

Christmas, he thought. Always at Christmas!

Mary threw wide the drapes to the pewter gray of the sky and set breakfast before her Gran. "How are you feeling this morning?"

"Ready for Christmas!" Gran said cheerfully, no trace of the night's cough to be heard. "Ready for a new day, for a quiet Christmas Eve, just the two of us together. And you, my pet?"

Gran slid a worried look her way as she bit into her toast.

"I've an errand," Mary began, wondering how to make Gran understand. "A favor I would do, must do, for Bethany Temple."

Gran's smile faded. "You cannot mean to set foot in that dreadful man's house again."

Mary shrugged. "How can I say no, Gran? It is Christmas Eve. I cannot let Ben Temple lose his job for no more reason than my pride."

Gran shoved aside the tray, no longer interested in breakfast.

"You will regret it mightily should Viscount Balfour ever hear you were there," she warned.

Mary hoped he never would. She did what she did for Ben, for Bethany—to prove to herself she could hold onto the best within herself despite a painful pricking from Lord Thorn.

"Bethany swears he will be gone all day," she said. "My only worry is will you be all right?" Mary helped Gran from the bed. "Left alone for most of the day?"

"And why should I not be?" Gran retorted.

"Your cough seemed worse than usual last night."

"I am fine," Gran insisted. "Right as rain. You go, now, and save Temple his position."

"I shall return every hour upon the hour." Mary bent and kissed the softness of her cheek.

Gran caught her chin between her palms, cupping it close to her own. "He does not deserve you, you know, my sweet."

In the carriage, his mother told him of Spain, and how the earl had become smitten with a younger female there. Voice low, almost inaudible above the clopping of the horses' hooves, her demeanor was that of a woman defeated.

Baxter listened with a growing sense of sadness—with the feeling he had heard it all, seen it all before.

At last, he thought, the earl takes his revenge.

He did not want to hear it, did not want to listen to his parents betrayal of one another for a second time. His own betrayal of Mary Rivers was too fresh, his need to speak to her too strong, to make all right between them.

The carriage came to a halt, as requested, in front of J. Leonard's Glover and Hosier.

"He is undeserving of my steadfast affections," Lady Balfour was saying.

Baxter, who judged his mother's steadfastness as faulty as his own, said, "What do you mean to do?"

"Do? What can I do?" she asked with heat as she thrust herself from the carriage. "I shall wait for him to come to his senses." She looked back over her shoulder. "I wonder . . . have you taken leave of yours?"

"Me?"

"I hear the most disturbing accounts of your behavior of late, Baxter. Of the company you keep."

*   *   *

Mary hesitated on the steps leading to the basement-level servants' entrance to Balfour's town house.

Bethany, waiting, popped her head out of the door with a grateful smile before she could change her mind. "Thank you for coming, Miss Rivers. Do hurry in out of the cold."

"He is not here?" Mary confirmed.

Bethany opened the door wide to the blissful warmth of the kitchen, to the heavenly smell of cinnamon and cloves. "Gone all day, Ben says. I know you've no wish to see him. I would never have asked you if I thought your paths might cross. I was shocked to learn he did not mean to . . ." she stopped, blushing.

"Yes," Mary said, no doubt as to what she had heard.

"Marry!" His mother counseled as she fingered satin, silks, and lace, thrusting her hands into the latest leathers in lavender, lemon, and buff. "Marry a nice girl who will never disgrace you—a girl who will always be true."

Baxter opened his mouth to tell her, but she was not yet finished.

"A young woman of similar station and wealth, whose impeccable reputation stirs no gossip, my dear. For it is gossip I hear of you of late in connection with a female most ineligible."

Baxter waited until the glove salesman had taken away the last of several dozen trays of his wares before he said, "I had no idea you kept tabs on me, Mother. What gossip do you hear? And from whom?"

She waggled freshly clad fingers at him, smiled as if pleased with her hand and the meddling it did. "I have my sources," she said.

He tested a sample swatch of butter-soft kid, tender as the feeling that his mother cared to know something of his life.

"Which of my good relatives would that be, pray tell? I have not laid eyes on any of them but Gilbert for a twelvemonth, so I am at a loss to see how they may be any more informed than you."

"Gossip, Baxter! Sylvia tells me you are the talk of the town."

Sylvia. That meant Gilbert had been loose-tongued.

"She tells me you have appeared in public with a country girl on your arm—a young woman better suited to the kitchen than the drawing room."

Mary tied on an apron as she followed Bethany through a flurry of unusual heat, steam, and activity in the kitchen. The cook looked frazzled. His assistants quailed whenever he opened his mouth to voice short-tempered demands.

Bethany said nothing until they reached the quiet oasis of the servants' staircase. "Ben and I spoke of leaving," she said then, low-voiced, her expression serious. She paused on the landing. "But, you will understand, our family is in need of money."

"I do understand," Mary said, "better than you may imagine."

"Penniless is she?" his mother said harshly as their parcels were loaded into the boot.

Wordless, Baxter opened the door, helped her up, got in, and tapped the trap, signaling the coach into motion.

His mother required no answer.

"I suppose this dairyman's daughter hopes to winkle a marriage proposal out of you. I told my sister you would never be so taken in."

Baxter stared at the passing shop fronts. Too many of them reminded him of Mary, of his unintentional humiliation of her.

"I am touched, Mother, that you would so heatedly defend me," he said wryly.

"You will admit, then, there is a fortune-hunting dairymaid?"

"A young woman," Baxter said calmly. "My neighbor."

The carriage halted. Will jumped down to throw the door open.

As Will helped his mother alight, she asked, "And does she pursue you, as I am told?"

Will stoically pretended himself deaf to the words, but Baxter knew his mother's whisper carried.

"No." He bent his head to the wind as he stepped

out, considering his every word, grip tightening on his hat brim. "Quite the reverse, Mother. I have pursued her."

Mary's nose wrinkled at the smells—the tangy bite of juniper, the clean scent of pine. The ballroom was stacked with bundles—prickly piles of red-berried holly, white-berried mistletoe in clumps the size of coach wheels, great trailing wads of ivy, so many one could not easily make passage from the hidden doorway to the center of the room. Stacks of juniper branches, too.

The Yule log alone was orderly, positioned in the fireplace, ready for lighting.

"Please understand, miss," Ben Temple called to her from the heights of a stepladder that allowed him to garland the top of a window on the far side of the room. "I had half of the greenery arranged, the stairway decked, the windows wreathed."

"What happened?" She plucked up some ivy and set to work assisting him.

"I made the mistake of asking his lordship what he thought of my handiwork."

"What did he say?"

"Why, that he wished it all gone."

"And so you took it all down again?"

"Yes, only to meet with his displeasure this morning, for of course the halls must be decked for the ball."

Lady Balfour eyed a ruby-studded bracelet, her glance enough to induce the jeweler to remove it from its case, to offer to clasp it about the countess's wrist.

Lady Balfour indulged him, admiring the chased gold into which the stones were set. "She will not be there, will she?" she asked. "This girl? Tell me you did not make the mistake of asking her to attend."

"To the contrary," Baxter said. "I asked both Miss Rivers and her grandmother to come." Her name came softly to his lips as he bent over a tray full of rings— sapphires and diamonds. He wondered which one would look best on Mary's finger.

"Do they smell of milk and manure?" she asked contemptuously.

"Roses," he said. "She is kind. Helpful. She holds her family in high esteem."

"Will your guests rate them so highly?"

"You need not worry yourself. She will not come to the ball unless I can convince her otherwise."

His mother nodded to the clerk, who took the bracelet away for boxing. "And why should you attempt to convince her?"

"Are you not interested in hearing why she chooses not to come, Mother?"

Temple hopped down from his ladder, shoved it sideways, and climbed up again to finish off the top of the doorway. "I do appreciate your help, Miss Rivers. It will take a miracle to finish before the ball. I have little hope we can accomplish the deed. As a result, I shall get the sack, but we three shall do the best we can. Right?"

"Only three of us?"

"Yes. I warn you, the staff refuses to help. Most of them would not be at all disappointed to see me disgraced and dismissed."

His mother stood, mouth agape, on the street.

"This dairymaid dares to think you dishonorable?"

"Yes, and rightly so."

Mr. Holloway, Lord Balfour's thin butler, appeared, evidencing no signs at all of surprise in being required to circumnavigate so much of the outdoors in the ballroom. "Yes, miss, you rang?" he asked with the deceptively bored air of a man who had all the time in the world to attend to Mary's needs. "May I ask what you require?"

"A minor miracle," she suggested quietly.

Lady Balfour's voice rose over the noise of the carriage as it pulled up to fetch them once again. "No matter, Baxter. An unschooled country girl will have no idea how to run a household, a staff."

She ignored the coachman's tip of the hat.

"It takes experience, a firm hand and knowing ways to run a household with any success."

She accepted Will's assistance in mounting the step without a word of thanks.

Holloway shook his balding head as if with the greatest disappointment.

"I'm sure you will understand, Miss Rivers, the staff is very busy today, preparing for this evening's ball."

Mary nodded. "Of course, Mr. Holloway. A great pity, though. I think it will reflect badly on all of the staff, most especially on the head staff, should the guests be required to step over great piles of greenery to get to the dining room and the dance floor."

The weight of the little box felt good cupped in Baxter's hand.

The ring had been purchased without fanfare—a quiet aside to the clerk and one more small satin-lined box was added to the growing pile Lady Balfour accumulated. Baxter had made no remark of his purchase—of his intentions.

Mother would only stand in his way—meddling in something he may have ruined all chance of already. The weight of the box in his hand pleased him. It felt right. It felt like the future.

Chapter Thirty

Mary sat on the stairs, two of the chambermaids on the steps above, two below. They had set up a sort of relay, as she and Lord Balfour had on the night they had addressed invitations to his ball. The maid at the top of the steps was snipping wire and forming hoops. Below her, another bound two of the hoops together with string and handed the airy sphere to Mary, who added greenery—holly sprigs at the top, and ivy wound below, to soften the look.

The maid below Mary tied mistletoe bundles in the middle of the hoops, and the young woman at the foot of the stairs tied on ribbons and lace. Ben hung them as soon as they were readied.

Mary recognized the irony of it—building kissing balls for a man whose kisses she had denied herself forever. She wanted to laugh aloud. She even wanted to shed a few tears. She did neither, simply kept fingers busy and mind diverted with Christmas carols. Music, even their poor, uneven singing, made the work go faster, cheering her despite the realization that she would not be here this evening to see the final results of their miraculous efforts.

Bethany, cheeks pink with the cold, joined them in singing the end of "On Christmas Day" before she leaned close to Mary to say, "Your Gran does well. She enjoyed the hen Cook sent her and the boiled cabbage and potato."

Mary smiled. "And did she try to convince you to

leave Lord Balfour's employ the entire time you were there?"

Bethany blushed, smiled, and nodded. "Only half the time." She took up one of the hoops to help wind greenery.

"Miss Rivers." The maid at the head of the stairs handed down another hoop.

"Thank you, Millie. I am having trouble keeping up, so fast do you work."

Millie ducked her head, bashful of the praise, not too bashful to ask, "Do you mind telling us a Christmas story, miss?"

"Glastonbury?" his mother muttered as the coach carried them onward. "I do not know a soul in Glastonbury. I ask you—who of any importance has ever come of Glastonbury?"

"Joseph of Arimathea once lived in Glastonbury," Mary began her favorite Christmas story.

"From the Bible, miss? That same Joseph?" Millie asked.

"Not Mary's Joseph!" the girl at the bottom of the steps exclaimed.

"Do you not know your Gospel, Amy?" Millie threw a mistletoe berry at her. "This is the Joseph who helped to carry Jesus' body from the cross."

Mary nodded. "That's right, and it is from him we get the legend of the Thorn."

"Thorn?" Millie's eyes widened with interest.

"Like the master?" Amy whispered.

The others shushed her, exchanging surreptitious glances, quieting to hear what Mary had to say, hands busy.

Mary smiled. "It is said Joseph was a merchant in tin and lead, who came to England to teach the Gospel to the Druids in the West Country."

"The Druids!" the maid above her asked in disbelief. "I have never heard of this."

Mary nodded and held up her half-finished work.

"The very Druids who used mistletoe in their religious rituals—who gave us the Christmas kissing ball."

The horses set off. His mother took his hand, an unexpected gesture of affection.

How many times as a child had he yearned for her touch? Now that she gave it, he felt awkward, his fingers out of place. He gave her urgent grasp an uncertain squeeze.

Her manner was gentle and coaxing.

"You will marry wisely, Baxter, will you not? You will honor the family name, won't you?"

"Honor?" His lips twisted wryly. "What of love?"

"Joseph was not well loved by the English." Mary's voice echoed in the stairwell.

"Too busy believing in elves and forest gods to see the truth, were they? Our ancestors?" Millie asked with a laugh.

"Too set in their ways," Amy said. "You know how it is, you believe something for so long you can't recognize it for the lie that it is when the truth hits you in the face."

"Wise words, Amy. It was certainly true for poor Joseph. The Welsh thought him mad for his beliefs. King Aviragus refused to be converted, offering Joseph land instead, to build a church in a little village called Ynyswitrin."

"Where's that?" Bethany asked.

Mary's smile broadened. "Why, Glastonbury of course."

"Why should you think yourself in love with this dairyman's daughter, Baxter?" Lady Balfour muttered in disgust. "Why should you so lower yourself?"

"In truth, I cannot hold myself higher than Mary Rivers, now can I, Mother?"

"Whatever do you mean?" She laughed, her voice rising in disbelief. "You are titled, wealthy, well connected in society, and the son of a titled gentleman."

"Illegitimately so," he said flatly, unwilling to give further credence to the family lie, angry that she expected it of him.

Her mouth dropped open. "What?"

"How would society receive me, I wonder," he said dryly, unable to look at her, "if it were widely known I am nothing but a bastard."

"In Glastonbury," Mary said, wiping mistletoe-stickied hands on her apron, "Joseph's message was met with as much scorn and disbelief as anywhere else. Will you be so good as to hand me another bunch of mistletoe, Mr. Holloway?"

The butler hovered in the nearest doorway, busy with candelabra and polishing rag.

Stiffly, he put down the branched silver. Looking around the hallway as he bent to comply, at doorways wreathed in garlands, mistletoe everywhere, he said, "You are to be commended, Miss Rivers, in accomplishing so much in so little time."

The maids exchanged sly glances.

"We have done splendidly," Mary said as carefully as she wound ivy to the wire. "Thanks to the help of so many hands."

Dignity intact, Holloway bowed and went back to his polishing.

"Where were we?" Mary murmured.

Temple spoke up as he rearranged his ladder. "No one believed in the poor fellow."

Mary smiled. "Oh, yes. Joseph, who was, as you may well imagine, disappointed, discouraged, and down-hearted, went for a walk up Wearyall Hill."

"A singularly appropriate name for a hill," Bethany said.

"Good Lord!" His mother's face was a picture of disbelief. Her hand flew to her throat, as if to stop the words. "Whatever are you saying, Baxter?"

Jaw working, Baxter stopped himself from answering for a breathless moment. The truth had too long been held captive for it to easily slip his mouth now.

*   *   *

"Joseph required his pilgrim's staff to help him up the steep incline," Mary said. "He went, head bowed, leaning upon his staff, praying all the while for a miracle to convince the English of the truths he told them."

Baxter drew a deep, fortifying breath leaned toward his mother, and began, "I saw you leave that Christmas Day."

"Christmas Day?" She shook her head, confused. "Whatever do you mean?"

"You wore a red cloak," he interrupted quietly. "Your carriage stood waiting."

Recognition dawned in her eyes.

"But, Baxter . . ." She shook her head, trying to hold onto the lie. "Surely you don't believe . . ."

He was loathe to hear more, loathe to succumb to the anger that welled within. He kept his voice tightly reined.

"Did you think you kept it secret? Did you think I would not notice the way he looked at you? The way he stole caresses when he thought the man I believed my father was not looking. Did you think to fool him, too?"

"Baxter! Not another word! How dare you say such things to me. I am your mother!"

"He knows. He's known all along." His voice grew quieter as hers grew more shrill.

"No," she cried out, lips thinned. "I will not believe it. He has never said anything to that effect."

"Said anything!" Baxter laughed contemptuously. "You had only to observe his actions and the truth be known. Did you never wonder why your husband despised his own son?"

"How dare you say such a thing? You know that to be the greatest and most ungrateful of falsehoods." Her voice escalated, turning heads in the carriages they passed, attracting the attention of those who walked along Regent Street. "Balfour loves you," she railed, color high. "He has been a good father, provided you every luxury."

Baxter refused to allow the anger that burned within to take over. Fists clenched, voice well schooled, he kept his gaze focused on the street, on the dark shadow of the carriage as it ran tandem with them.

"For years I thought it my fault, something I had done, or wasn't doing. I questioned why he could not bear the sight of me. Why my uncle doted upon me."

He looked at her then, witnessing the tragic cloudlike drift of rage, sorrow, and disbelief that painted the landscape of her features.

"No more, Baxter." Her hand flew to cover the horrified O of her mouth. "You must not say these things."

He was not to be stopped.

"I questioned why the two of you left me so often in the care of others, why I was packed off to school when Nanny fell ill, why my father absented himself from every holiday, whisking you off to Europe at every opportunity."

"Oh, God, Baxter, stop!" she cried, hand pressed to her breast. "You break my heart."

He could not stop, could no longer contain the years of pain. He threw words like stones. "As you broke mine again and again when I was but a boy, madam, and craved the affection of my parents? Why did you abandon me, Mother? Why?"

"Why? You dare ask me why?" Tears sprang to eyes that blazed with a fire of emotion as her voice rose to an impassioned crescendo. "I loved him! Betrayed him! Don't you see?"

He did not see. He had never seen her face so distorted with passion, with grief.

"You claim to crave my affections . . ."

"Yes."

"I warn you!" She shook a gloved finger at him. "Love is a dangerous thing. I loved him! Don't you understand? I loved one Balfour and betrayed the other, only to discover I loved him even more."

"My father?"

"Therein lies the tragedy. I love my own husband— who should have been your father. I cuckolded him, gave him his brother's baby as heir. Don't you see how terrible my love is, Baxter? I could not risk you to it."

"But . . ." His thoughts whirled.

"Do not speak to me of love, as if you have the slightest idea what it may mean. I would only ask that you do a better job of it than I have. My dear"—she leaned close—"you ruin her. Surely you see that. As surely as I ruined your childhood in believing I had married the wrong Balfour."

"I love her, Mother. None other," Baxter said, his hand on the box with the ring in it, his voice tense with a growing excitement. "I mean to marry her."

From the foot of the stairs, as he took up two more of the kissing balls, Ben asked, "Did Joseph get his miracle?"

Mary's fingers never paused as she wove ivy in and out, in and out. "Joseph," she said, "stopped to catch his breath, sitting down to pray upon the very spot where an abbey was later built. He planted his staff in the ground, that he might lean upon it, and as he prayed, the staff took root."

"It didn't!" Millie gasped.

Mary's smile grew. "It broke into bud."

"It never did."

Smile never wavering, Mary shrugged, hands busy with the last of the greenery. "Believe what you will, but the thorn tree grows still, in Glastonbury, near the abbey ruins. It blooms white flowers flecked with a pink that the locals call the blood of Christ."

"Do you believe the story, miss?" Bethany asked.

"Sounds awfully far-fetched to me," Holloway muttered.

Mary ignored him. "You would ask if I believe in miracles. And I do. I am not the only one. Every Christmas sprigs of the thorn are cut and sent to the royal family."

"Are they really?" Millie asked.

Ben bore in an armload of garlands meant for the stairs. "Yes, but it cannot be true—about the tree, about Joseph."

Mary rose to help with the garlands, the maids rising with her. "The horticulturist who came from London last year to look at the tree was inclined to agree with you."

"Just as I thought," Ben said.

"Until he saw the thorn."

"Changed his mind, did he?" Millie winked.

"He claimed it was not a native of England."

"No? Where does it come from, then?" Bethany asked.

The answer came, unexpectedly, from the bottom of the stairwell. "Palestine. It comes from Palestine."

Lord Balfour stepped from the shadows.

Chapter Thirty-one

℘

Baxter's entrance shocked them, none more than Mary. She had been so sure she would not see him, that her participation in today's decorating would remain a secret, that she felt caught in something illicit by the sound of his voice, by the click of his heels on the marbled floor. She was caught unaware, by the power of his appearance and the pull of his presence.

The sight of his face, of his familiar buff coat, of the top of his shiny new beaver top hat, quickly swept off to reveal the gleaming order of fair hair, left her knees suddenly weak, her hands fumbling, her heart in her throat. A wave of heat swept upward from her chest, flushing throat and cheeks. As if hands and brain were no longer correctly connected, she dropped the garland she was tying, so that a twisted swag of holly and ivy drifted down on top of him.

He caught it single-handedly, looking directly up at her, eyes agleam. With smooth, loose-limbed purpose, he strode up the steps.

"I commend your decorating efforts," he said to Temple on his ladder as he passed, though his gaze strayed not from Mary's face. Something in his manner, in the look he cast upon her, reminded her of the first time she had seen him, the lion on the prowl.

She wanted nothing more than to flee down the stairs and away. What could be more humiliating than for him to find her here, decorating for a ball she would not attend?

She studied his shoes, unwilling to meet his eyes as he came to a halt before her.

He held out the bit of greenery. "Miss Rivers," he said, "if this is yours, I hope it may be an olive branch?"

She squinted against the light of the chandelier behind his head, feeling stupid, humiliated, and trapped.

New humiliation—a woman's cultured voice rose from the base of the stairs. "Is this your milkmaid from Glastonbury, Baxter?"

Lady Balfour! She could be no other—followed Lord Balfour up the stairs. At her heels came Will and Holloway, laden with Christmas parcels.

Hemmed in, outnumbered, without a word, Mary plunged down the stairs, away from this man, away from potentially greater humiliation.

"Wait! Mary, Don't go!" he called, footsteps clattering on the risers behind her.

"I would prefer that you call me Miss Rivers, my lord," she called over her shoulder, breezing past Lady Balfour with no more than a polite inclination of the head.

Blindly intent, she slipped past a wide-eyed Will, a gape-mouthed Holloway, her goal the door.

"Please, Miss Rivers. Do not be so hasty."

He was right on her heels.

She flung wide the door, reminded of her missing cloak only when a blast of cold air hit her in the face.

My cloak, she thought, *is downstairs.*

She turned, jaw set, heart ready to race into the wind, head too practical to risk it.

"Mary." Baxter stood in her way.

She skirted him, head down, unable to meet his eyes, heart thumping as if she ran a race.

"Please wait. There is something I would say to you."

She did not wait. Could not. She must get out of the house, away from him, as soon as possible. She could not walk fast enough to please herself, could not trot down the stairs to the kitchen with enough speed.

Never fast enough to outrun him, regrettably.

He caught hold of her elbow on the stairs. "Mary, please. Don't run away."

She wrenched free, continuing on her way, her words breathless and heated. "You must understand, my lord. I would never have set foot in this house again had I thought there any possibility I might encounter you here."

"But I am glad you are here. There is something . . ."

"I came for Ben and Bethany's sake. Do you understand? No one else's. I owed it to them. You, sir, I owe nothing."

"But . . ."

"There is nothing you can say to me I would wish to hear," she said coldly. "Nothing."

"Not even that I love you?" The words echoed in the stairwell.

She paused in the corridor that led to the kitchen and turned to face him, anger rising. "That least of all, my lord. I do not believe in a love that would keep a woman mistress, that arrives on the doorstep in the form of a solicitor who would pay me for that love, who would have me sign away my future for it."

"Neither do I."

She thought that was what he said as she stepped into the heat, steam, and clatter of the kitchen, into the smell of roasting capons and baking bread. The staff, intent on their work, gave her little notice as she headed for the cloakroom. They did not so much as slow their chopping, stirring, and spit-turning until Lord Baxter followed her, shouting, "Did you hear me? Neither do I."

His words, his appearance, silenced the clatter of whisk and knife blade, stilling every movement, turning every head.

"I was wrong, Miss Rivers," he said into that awful stillness. "I did not mean to insult you. Can you not find it within yourself to forgive me?"

They stood motionless, none of them daring to look at her. She could not believe he would so publicly apologize, but he seemed oblivious to all but her.

"I am sure I will, my lord. Someday." She plucked her cloak from the rack by the door.

He was faster than she, sliding to his knees, blocking

the door, cutting off her exit. "I beg you, Mary. Do not let us end like this."

He tried to take her hand.

She did not give it to him easily. Her hands, pitiful specimens indeed, stickied with pine rosin and mistletoe sap, scratched and reddened by the day's work, were not fit for grasping. In fact, she braced herself against his words, his touch, sure he would wound her again if she was not vigilant.

"Let me go, my lord," she begged him quietly, unwilling to provide further entertainment for his kitchen staff.

She hid one hand beneath her borrowed apron, fumbling in her pocket with the other for her mittens.

He did not give up easily, grasping her wrist as she extracted the mittens, crying out in hushed dismay, "Good Lord! What's this!"

She stiffened and tried to pull away, but he had fast hold of her wrist, all of his attention focused on the angry scratches marring the paleness of her skin.

"Hot water! Soap! Clean linen! At once if you please!" he insisted, rising, the size and force of him surging up from the floor with such inexorable will and strength of purpose that the kitchen staff burst at once into frantic activity to answer his wishes. Mary allowed herself to be rushed along in his grip as he swept a clear spot on a table two steps from the door with one hand, his other still firmly clasping her wrist.

"The other hand," he said. "Is it scratched as well?"

"It is nothing," Mary protested, struggling to regain possession of her limbs.

He shook his head as he gently pushed open her clenched fingers, taking from her the mitten, that he might more closely examine her captive palm. "Why ever did you not wear gloves?"

The chief's assistant saved her from responding, bearing in the steaming kettle, a scullery maid at his heels, carrying a basin, soap, and fresh linen.

Mary made a noise of protest, attempting one last time to pull away.

"Come," Baxter insisted. "Do not fight me. You shall not leave until I have seen to them. Tincture of iodine," he instructed the maid. "And salve. Thank you, Gaston."

"*Oui, monsieur*. Anything else?"

"Close the door behind you," Baxter said.

Mary's heart raced faster as the young man complied. The door shut them away from the curious in the kitchen.

He released her to pour the water into the basin, to test the heat of it with his fingertips.

Mary made no attempt to run away, simply stood, hands clasped, despising herself for the weakness of her heart. His attentions should have been in every way hateful to her, and yet they were not.

She found herself fascinated by the movements of his hands, these preparations made all for her. A part of her did not want to leave, to put him behind her forever.

"Come, let me see," he said.

This time she complied, giving in to the danger of his hands against hers, daring to look him in the eye, her flesh fully aware of his every touch, her insides quaking as he frowned at her careless disregard.

He plunged her hands in the hot, soapy water, held onto her when she cried out against the sting and would have jerked them out again.

He let go to fish for the lozenge of soap, drawing her fingers out of the water briefly to run the soap over them, massaging her fingers.

This union of wet flesh, hot and sliding, alarmed her. The union of their gazes above the steaming water disturbed her even more.

Her head insisted she jerk her hand away, but heart and body would not obey.

She closed her eyes, fingers spasming, unprepared for this sudden slide into capitulation. She opened her eyes to find him studying her, his breath and hers coming faster, his hands sliding, clasping her fingers between his with unmasked desire. His eyes spoke of a hunger, a loneliness, that echoed her own. She lost herself in them, surprised the water between them did not rise to a boil.

The door opened.

"Miss Rivers?" They both looked up to see his mother

in the doorway. Mary jerked her hands from his, away from the bowl, her reaction so abrupt, water splashed.

Lady Balfour's brows rose. "I see I interrupt," she said coolly. "But perhaps you will think it important. Bethany Temple tells me your Gran is having a coughing fit."

Gooseflesh rose on Mary's damp arms. "Oh, dear. Thank you for telling me." She whirled, headed for the door, drying her dripping hands on the apron she stripped from her waist as she went.

"Shall I send for a physician?" Baxter's voice followed her.

She shook her head, breathless, panicked, ready to bolt. "I don't know."

Chapter Thirty-two

The coughing spell was worse than usual. It would not be stilled with water or hard candy, honeyed tea or camphored handkerchiefs. A spoonful of Godfrey's cordial finally did the trick. Weak with exhaustion, Gran lay back, voice and hand trembling as she thanked Mary.

"I shall just rest now, my dear," she said, eyelids fluttering, her lips and cheeks too pale, the silence in her room after such a barrage of hacking startling.

"Yes, Gran." Mary tucked her in, smoothed the wispy hair away from Gran's cheek, and quietly shut the door in her wake.

She stood in the hallway, her back to the door, the bottle of medicine and wet spoon in her scratched hands, legs gone wobbly, her stomach quaking with subsiding terror replaced by guilt.

She should have been here to stop the coughing as soon as it started. What stupid, stupid games did she play with her future, with Gran's, in spending the whole afternoon at Lord Balfour's, stringing kissing balls? What a fool she was—a selfish, thoughtless fool.

Mary sank to the floor beside the door, weak-kneed and ashamed, listening to the clocks ticking, listening to Gran's breathing, slowing the mad race of her heartbeat, wishing she were not alone.

Before she could fall too deep into melancholy, Gran started to cough again, and Mary was onto her feet and into her room, cordial in the spoon.

He came when Gran had stilled a second time, tapping

softly at the door, hat in hand, eyes big with concern. "Is she all right?" he asked.

The air smelled of snow. The cold bit at her nose, sweeping up under her skirt as she stood in the doorway, nodding, afraid to speak to him, afraid to invite him in, afraid to lose what little backbone she had left in her.

"I have sent for my physician," he said. "His name is Crowley—a good man."

She opened her mouth to object—could not—said only, "Thank you."

"Is there anything else I can do?"

His voice was too kind, his eyes too caring. She shook her head, afraid she might burst into tears should he ask her anything else. With some relief, she pointed at the coach that came to a halt before his door. "Your guests arrive, my lord."

He frowned and nodded, then stepped back. "Send for me," he said, donning his hat, "should you need anything."

Gran woke bleary-eyed to sip some water, refusing to eat, her cough revived. She subsided given another spoonful of Godfrey's, and Mary went to the kitchen to reheat the broth she had made, supping on yesterday's bread and a bit of leftover capon. She longed for her mother, her sisters, as she worked in the quiet kitchen, for her brothers as she shoveled fresh coal into the fire-places. Her father, she thought, as she twitched back the curtains for the twentieth time, would have made sure a physician arrived in a timely fashion.

The sun went down, and still he had not arrived.

Frost laced the windows, as cold and misted as the idea Gran might not live till morning. Mary stared past paper snowflakes at a clouded, starless night, her hands folded in prayer, listening with trepidation to Gran's un-even breathing.

Outside, cheerful voices called to one another in the street. The sound of arriving carriages at the Balfour town house seemed ceaseless.

She had once wondered how any man might despise Christmas. Now she knew. Now she understood. She could not fathom the idea of Christmas without Gran, a day of mourning. She could not bear the idea of another hour alone.

Bells jangled cheerfully in the street. Her thoughts jangled, too, no cheer to them.

Would Gran die? Was this her punishment for weakness? For allowing Lord Balfour undue freedom? For enjoying it?

"Mary," came a hoarse whisper.

"Yes, Gran. Are you thirsty? Here, take some water." Gran's forehead was hot, her cheeks and hands, too. Gran drank thirstily.

More voices from the street, the sound of coach doors slamming.

"How nice of so many to come," Gran said.

Mary refilled the glass and glanced out of the window. "Lord Baxter's ball would appear to be a success of the highest order."

She turned back to find Gran sitting up in the bed, ghostlike in her nightrail, wisps of hair curling about her head, hand raised as if to welcome someone. She smiled, eyes fever bright, scanning not the window, but the darkest corner of the room.

"So nice of you to come," she said, shaking an imaginary hand.

Thin, her voice sounded, so very thin.

Mary clutched the glass, speechless, eyes fixed on the darkness, skin crawling with nameless dread.

He did not come. He did not come. He did not come. The evening ticked past, the door opened on the cold, bleak night again and again as his guests were announced, and still Crowley did not come.

Baxter suffered in his absence, heart in constant expectation, nerves on edge, the box in his pocket. Ready. Waiting. Untimely.

He plastered a smile on his lips, played the good host, listened halfheartedly to niceties, responding in kind, steering his guests toward the food, toward one another. He shook hands and smiled smiles. He accepted kisses beneath the mistletoe, meaningless kisses—no fire in them.

He was ready to throttle the man.

He stepped outside to stare at the lit windows next door. The upstairs was dark.

We economize, she had said.

Shivering, oblivious to the first few fine flakes of a new snow, he drifted closer.

The downstairs sitting window glowed. Her Gran's room shone dimly. A shadow passed the window. It must be she. Why did the damn fellow not come?

He had to go to her, if only to apologize for the delay. Coatless, Baxter kept walking.

She opened the door before he could knock, splendid in his evening clothes, no overcoat to warm him. Steam plumed, a thin white feather, from his lips as the hand he had lifted to ply the knocker found only air. Upon that hand, a white dancing glove. He wore, too, a worried look.

"I saw you from the window," she explained. She could not tell him how ridiculously happy she was to see him. She should not be happy with him at all. And yet, she was—happy to see anyone, happy for the moment not to have to face the dark corner in Gran's room alone.

"I stole away to apologize for the doctor's late arrival. I do not know what detains him," he said, nose and cheeks pinked with the cold.

"On Christmas Eve?" She had to laugh, the sound brittle on the night air. "Any one of a dozen things, I would imagine. Perhaps he entertains guests." Her gaze drifted to the line of carriages that waited in the street, coachmen hunched against the cold.

"Of course." he stepped back from the door, as if to leave. "I shall send him over straightaway, as soon as he arrives."

She stopped him with hand raised, her voice breaking, "Please do, my lord. I am afraid . . ."

"What?" He was beside her in an instant. "Afraid of what?"

"She sees things. In the room. Speaks when no one is there. I fear the worst."

"Good God!" All the joy drained from his features.

Another coach pulled through the line of waiting coaches, turning his head.

"I do apologize," she said, feeling stupid to have burdened him with such a remark. "I ought not to have told you such a thing while you are in the midst of entertaining."

"At last," he murmured, and waved and called to the disembarking passenger. "Here, man, here!"

Dr. Crowley bent over Gran's bed, rawboned, gaunt-cheeked, his long, thin fingers on Gran's wrist. Dark brown eyes serious, he asked, "Baxter tells me she is seeing things?"

"Yes. People, in the corners of the room."

"Talks to them, does she?"

Mary nodded. "How bad is it?" she whispered, fearing the worst.

He took a moment to answer, increasing her dread, as he laid a hand upon Gran's forehead, leaned down to listen to her chest, and sniffed her breath.

"She is feverish," he said. "Which can lead to delusion, but . . ." He frowned.

"Not dying?" She asked breathlessly.

His brows rose. "Not dying," he said calmly. "But tell me, what have you given her?"

"Vinegar compresses, lemon-barley water, a dose of Doctor James's Fever Powder, and three doses of Godfrey's cordial over the past four hours to stop her cough and help her sleep."

"Godfrey's? So much?" He chuckled. "No wonder she sees things, my dear. It is an opiate. Not to be used lightly."

Mary felt compelled to defend herself. "Nothing else would stop her coughing."

"Ah." He scratched something in a notebook, then tore out the page. "Have this decoction of hyssop prepared by an apothecary. Two spoonfuls mixed with honey every time she has trouble with the cough. Until then, fever powders every three hours until her forehead cools, and to help still the cough and soothe her throat, horehound drops, raspberry leaf tea, and eucalyptus steam bowls. No more Godfrey's." He waggled a warning finger.

She nodded, feeling like a scolded child, then thanked him and saw him to the door. In closing it on the cold night, she felt an almost hysterical relief coupled with self-recrimination that knocked the wind out of her.

She did not allow herself to weep. Gran might hear, might assume the worst. She sat, instead, in the sitting room, candles guttering, two gone out. She made no move to replace them. Gran was not dying! She had, with all the best intentions, made her condition worse instead of better!

A knock upon the door.

Baxter stood shivering and coatless on the step. "What did Crowley say?" he asked.

Mute, she held the door wide.

He stepped in, bringing with him the breath of the night, a swirl of cold air, the blessed presence of another.

He followed her to the ill-lit sitting room and took a chair opposite the settee she sank into. "Is she going to be all right?" he asked in the gentlest of voices.

The coals in the fireplace readjusted themselves with a spray of sparks. Wind whistled thinly at the window. A horse whickered in the street.

She laughed, the sound brittle, on the edge of tears. "I am to blame. Gave her too much medicine—an opiate. I feel the perfect fool." Shaking hands covering her mouth, she said, "I feel as if I have ruined your ball, involving you in my stupid error."

"Too late." He shook his head. "It was already ruined."

"Why? What went wrong?" Her voice skated perilously close to the breaking point. "Temple tried so hard to make everything perfect."

He leaned across the space separating them and crooked a finger beneath her chin, raising it that he might look her in the eyes. He smoothed a tear from her cheek.

"You were not there, Mary."

Her breath caught in her throat. His touch, the words,

broke down her defenses. She choked on a sob, pulling away, turning her head.

"Care for a shoulder to lean on?" he asked softly, his voice so kind, warm, and gentle it provoked a greater flood of tears. She could not see him for the blur as she nodded and allowed him to enfold her in the smell of cedar and bay leaf as he sank down on the settee beside her.

Her cheek nestled against the rough comfort of damp wool. His shoulder solidly braced her cheekbone. He tucked his handkerchief into her hand.

"I was so worried about her," she said, voice muffled. "I felt so powerless, so alone."

"I am here," he whispered.

"Yes, you have been so kind, so generous in calling in your own personal physician. I understand, at last, why you so despise Christmas."

"Miss your family, do you?" His voice was as soothing as honeyed tea, vibrating from the depths of his chest. The warmth of his hand cupped the crown of her head, stroking her hair lightly.

She nodded, thinking of the times her father had held her thus as a child. "I begged them to come." Her voice caught, the final words breathy. "They would not."

"I know," he said. "I know."

He pressed his cheek to her temple and stroked the loose tendrils of hair at the nape of her neck. A tear dampened her freshly dried cheek.

His tear—it startled her.

"I understand," he said, his breath warm in her hair. "I am here. I will stay with you."

Overcome by the power of that single tear, utterly useless and but for him abandoned, she wept into his coat front, muting the sobs, the sound of her own despair startling.

He soothed, "There, there, my dear. You are not alone."

At last she quit her sobbing, raised her head from the comforting cradle of his shoulder, and, averting her tear-swollen face, dabbed at wet cheeks and puffy eyes.

"Your guests," she said. "Surely you are missed."

"Would you not miss me more?"

She was going to weep again, and she did not want to weep, not with him staring at her. "But you have a houseful of friends," she protested. "Your mother has come all the way from Europe. You cannot abandon your own ball."

"Do you wish me to go?" he asked quietly.

She sighed, turned into the comfort of his arms again, and said into the lapel of his coat a muted, "No."

"Good." He rested his cheek against the top of her head. "Do you forgive me?" he whispered into her hair.

She pushed away from the comfort of his chest, that she might see his expression in the candlelight's dim flicker. "It is loneliness I see, is it not?" she asked him, voice subdued. "It has been loneliness you kept hidden from the very beginning."

He said nothing, the depth of feeling in his eyes enough, the heat, the longing. He pulled her close again and held her fiercely, her cheek pressed to his chest.

"I cannot be your mistress," she said sadly, fingering the edge of his lapel.

Laughter rumbled deep in his chest. "Then you shall have to marry me."

She sighed, knowing it would never happen. "But we are of different worlds."

He pushed her from him, eyes bright. "That cannot keep us apart."

She shrugged, shivered. She must be logcial, realistic. She must avoid falling into his embrace again. She crossed her arms, shielding herself. "It *has* kept us apart. It does."

He rose abruptly to pace the room, then stopped in front of the window, hair limned golden by the lamplight from the street, his face in shadow.

"That is the past. I am more interested in the future." He crossed the darkness that separated them, his movements fluid, self-assured. Kneeling before her, he brought her hands together, pressed a box into her palms, and whispered, "My future rests in your hands."

"Does it?" she asked quietly, marveling at the incredible comfort she took in his just being near, her hands in his.

A sound came from the street outside, the slam of coach doors, a lilt of voices—guests come late to the ball.

"What if I told you that I am not what you think? That the truth, were it known, would tumble me from the very society you consider a boundary?"

She clutched the box, wanting to clutch at him instead. "Whatever do you mean?"

Candlelight gilded his cheek, his lashes. It made a halo of his hair. "I am a bastard," he said.

The words hung in the air between them like ice crystals.

What did one say in the face of such an admission?

No time for a reply. The door to the street flew wide, admitting a gust of cold air and a flurry of skirts and voices.

"Happy Christmas, Mary, my dear. We are come at last!"

Her mother. Silhouettes loomed in the doorway to the sitting room.

"Mary! Gran? Where are you?"

"Why is the house so dark?"

Her sisters, Ellen and Evie.

Baxter stepped into the shadows.

Mary rose with a cry of "Mother? Is that you?"

"Mary, my dear." They walked right past him, her mother and sisters, arms laden with parcels. The room smelled suddenly of snow and wet wool, of lavender-and-roses perfume.

"Why do you sit here, alone, in the dark?"

"How is dear old Gran?" Evie tossed her packages onto the nearest chair and held her arms wide for a hug.

Mary ran gladly to meet them, gaze fixed on the shadow that was Baxter as he passed in front of the window on his way to the door, which he held wide for her father, who came in blindly, laden with a ham hock in one hand, a wheel of cheese in the other, calling out heartily, "Happy Christmas, my dear. I hear you have been missing us."

"Light some candles, Evie," her mother instructed. "Ellen, a kettle for some tea. Amy, give the fire a stir."

Mary still clutched the box he had given her. The edges bit into her palm as she was engulfed in hugs, first from each of her sisters, and then her father. Her brother, Joseph, blocked her exit at the door as he entered, bearing a trunk.

"So, it's him, is it?" he asked, nodding at Baxter's receding form, snow cascading from his cap, his grin cheeky. "Sent for us, he did."

Openmouthed, she retreated before him, before the onslaught of trunks, Edward and David bearing in more baggage. She owed Baxter this, too.

She almost ran after him, but Gran's health must be explained—the cough, doctor's orders, fever powders, steam, and tea.

She got caught up in the warm, bright welcome noise of them, all the while wondering what was in the box in her pocket, wondering why Baxter had left without a word.

He stepped into the street by the coach and almost ran into Ned as he rounded the vehicle, a plump valise in each hand.

"My lord!" Ned's breath fogged the darkness white. "I do apologize for taking so long. Wondered if we would make it in time for Christmas. The roads were more difficult than expected."

Baxter clapped him on the shoulder. "I am pleased you convinced them to come. I got your packet by post."

"It survived, then?"

Baxter nodded.

Ned cocked his head toward the window where the entire family might be seen, candlelight casting them in a golden light as they gathered at the old lady's bedside. "Your coach convinced them to come. They would never have braved the roads otherwise. A nice lot, they are. I quite enjoyed their company."

With a sigh, Baxter looked heavenward, voicing a silent word of thanks at the bleak, clouded sky.

She did not need him now, he thought.
He went back to his ball.

Mary slipped away at last, no thought for her appearance, no time for the dressing of her hair or the donning of ball dress. She simply dashed next door to thank him, never mind the stares her plain appearance garnered, never mind that she must push her way through a glittering mass of strangers.

He stood with his mother, framed by the two beautiful young women from the night of Christmas carols at the Argyll Rooms. All were impeccably dressed for the evening, gloves to the elbow, gilded fans fluttering, shawls artfully draped in case bared shoulders should chill. They viewed her breathless arrival with shocked expressions.

It did not matter.

His eyes shone at sight of her, and his mouth broke into a smile that set her pulse to racing. As swiftly, the smile turned into a frown of concern.

"Your Gran?" he asked.

She smiled. "Much revived. I must return, but I came to thank you, my lord. I know my family's arrival is your doing, and you could not have given me greater gift this Christmas."

She drew the box he had given her from her pocket.

"For that reason, I cannot accept this." She did not notice the hushed attentiveness of the room as she pressed it into his hand.

"But you have not opened it," he protested, his expression troubled, his hand unwilling to accept the burden of the box.

"It would not be right of me to be further indebted to your kindness. I would ask instead if you would do us the honor of dining with us tomorrow, that we might in some small way repay you for the Christmas joy you have delivered."

"I would be honored." He sighed, his frown deepening. He turned the box between agitated fingers, removing the string binding. "There is something else you can do for me."

"Yes, my lord?" At last she became conscious the waiting crowd watched with openly intrigued expressions. His mother eyed them both keenly. What favor would he ask of her in front of these people?

"Your hand, Mary?" He held out his.

"My hand?" Blood heated her cheeks.

"I am given to understand it is a fair one," he said, echoing the very words he had uttered that first day he stood upon Gran's doorstep.

A muffled ripple of exclamations from his guests, a sigh from his mother as he opened the box, revealing not the ring everyone expected, but a sprig of greenery.

"The Thorn," she said, voice breaking, tears springing to her eyes. "You have brought me a sprig of the Thorn!"

Gently, she pulled it from the box.

Smile widening, he watched, awaiting her reaction.

She was completely unprepared for what had been slid about the base of the greenery—like a crown, a winking glitter of sapphire and diamonds.

Her mouth dropped open. Her knees weakened at sight of such a ring.

"Will you help this Thorn take root, Mary? Bloom?" he asked it softly, that no one but she might hear. There was, as he spoke, a trace of loneliness in his eyes, the loneliness that had drawn them together, a loneliness she longed to erase.

"Are you sure it is my hand you want, my lord?" She felt she had to ask.

He took the Thorn from her, slid the ring from its stem, and spoke loudly enough that his mother reacted with a start, that the young ladies at her side went wide-eyed. "Will you marry me, Mary Rivers? Will you make merry my every Christmas?"

She could not help smiling as she put her hand in his and he slid the magnificent ring on her finger in front of all assembled.

On Christmas day Charles Thornton Baxter stepped from the warmth of his town house into a still, snow bedecked street, the heat of his breath misting ghostlike,

his glasses fogging with the sudden change in temperature, the wine bottles in the box in his arms clinking
faintly as he rubbed the lenses clear again. Today Regent Street was quiet, all the shops closed, locked doors
beribboned or wreathed, no vendors hawking wares at
the street corners.

The windows across the street glittered. Nash was entertaining again. A coach pulled slowly to the doorstep
to deposit warmly dressed guests amidst laughter and
slippery progress to an icicle-draped doorstep. There was
little other traffic to muddy the glittering spun sugar
snow in the street.

The air smelled of wood smoke and coal fire, roasting
duck and evergreens.

It smelled of Christmas.

He turned his face to a pale gray sky. Snow starred
the lenses of his glasses and gave him cold kisses on his
cheeks. Far prettier than any snowflakes ever cut, the
flakes drifted thick and white as cotton wool from above,
muffling sound, painting pretty the city, settling briefly
in glittering, star-shaped snowflakes upon the bright,
holly berry red muffler at his throat.

His matching red leather gloves, also starred with
white against the dark wine box, brought a childish thrill
of pleasure.

He smiled and wiped his glasses.

Not understated, such a red. Perhaps not the proper
attire for a proper gentleman, but he was not really a
proper gentleman, was he? Never had been. And the muffler was a gift from Bethany Temple, who had knit it herself, the gloves from Ben. Surely even dear old Temple
could not object to such cheerful gifts from his own
children.

The bell rang from St. Phillip's as Baxter's mother
joined him on the step, resplendent in fox-fur tippit and
matching hat. "A lonely sound, the bell." She sighed.

"Ah, but wait," Baxter said. "Listen. There is another
to join it." He pointed east, toward All Soul's. Bells
sounded faintly in the distance.

She tucked a gloved hand in the crook of his elbow,
saying, "Ah, yes. I had forgotten."

"Come!" He patted her arm. "They will be waiting."

The windows next door were fogged with the warmth within. Candlelight glowed cheerfully around the stark, white, paper-cut snowflakes pasted to the panes.

In the bow window, as if on a stage, one could see the family gathered in the sitting room, making final touches in the preparation of a table glittering with china, crystal, silver, and pale napery. He could hear the muted noise of laughter through the window. They were a merry sight, dressed in their finest, cheerful and busy as more candles were lit, bowls of food brought in, and Gran pushed into the room by one of her grandsons.

She looked well, he thought. She cried out in delight at sight of the room, as she made an effort to rise, the better to see the table.

Mary's beloved family, he thought. Soon to be his.

Anticipation gripped him, heart and stomach.

"Do you know, I do not much like Christmas?" his mother murmured as they mounted snow-dusted steps, as heads turned to the sound of their knocking. "Never have."

The Riverses responded at once with waves and smiles and a final flurry of activity, an enthusiastic welcome even before the door opened in a warm gust that perfumed the air with cinnamon and cloves, roast duck, and fresh baked bread.

Mary Rivers's father bid them enter, open-armed, with a cheerful "Happy Christmas, my lord! My lady. Come in. Come in. Very pleased you could come."

Baxter stepped back to allow his mother to go first, removing his hat as he entered, shaking and stomping off snow, taking hankie to freshly fogged glasses. Mr. Rivers found a spot on the crowded hall tree for the perching of hats and cloaks, and made satisfyingly appreciative noises at sight of the wine Baxter had brought.

Baxter helped his mother from her furs to a cheerful chorus of "Happy Christmas!" and "Do come in!" from the sitting room.

In the doorway, beneath a spray of mistletoe, Mary Rivers waited, dressed in her plum-colored finery, anticipation and expectation bright in her eyes, cheeks rosy, his ring upon her finger.

"Merry Christmas, my Lord Thorn," she said, a twinkle in her eyes.

"Baxter," he said. "You really must get in the habit of calling me Baxter, my dear, now that we are to be married." He pulled the bright scarf from his neck, tucked it carefully into the pocket of his overcoat, and taking her hand, murmured with a growing smile, "Do you know, I begin to think Christmas the finest day of the year. My favorite of all the seasons."

And then, taking full advantage of the mistletoe, he kissed her, and she, twining hands about his neck, soft as ivy and just as clinging, kissed him back with all of her heart.